What readei
The Glendale Novels

MW00511863

"Just finished The Glendale Series and loved it! I have never read a story that described the salvation experience so completely and beautifully! As a Christian and avid reader, I sometimes get nervous about starting a new book because I don't know if the content will line up with my faith and beliefs, but this was never an issue in these books. Thank you for writing books that Christians can enjoy! God Bless!!!"

– Julie B.

"I have read lots of Christian novels by top authors...but I find this series the best I have read. So well authored and covers situations that people are facing in today's world."

– Elaine P.

"So glad I found the Glendale series. ...Your books have a bit of Kingsbury flavor and I haven't enjoyed a series like this since the Baxter Family books."

– Terri B.

"I discovered Ann Goering about a month ago. I have read every one of the books I could find on Amazon. I am 70 years old and wish I could have read Christian books like these when I was a teen. So many lessons in her books that take so long to learn."

– Linda S.

"Your books have been a blessing to me. So much examples and teaching, that we can get from your books for today's living. As for me, being God's minister will like to use your books in youth groups, women, family, etc... I pray that your books may be translated into other languages. I will like to have them in Spanish. Dios te bendiga Ann."

– Alida R.

"This was a beautiful story of the transformation of one young girl, a love story, and two young hearts. This is a refreshing book that is enjoyable as it does not have all the bad language and other things that many romance novels have. Give this a try, you'll be glad you did!"

– Mark Y.

"For one so young, Ms. Goering displays remarkable Christian maturity. She has crafted a story which speaks to the problems faced by the many children of divorce. ...THIS BOOK SHOULD BE REQUIRED READING FOR YOUTH GROUPS EVERYWHERE!!!"

–Patricia M.

"I just finished this series. I thoroughly enjoyed it. The characters were realistic and feel like friends. The author has a gift with storytelling. I appreciated the faith theme and that the stories were all clean. I definitely recommend The Glendale Series!"

– Abigail

"God has reached in and healed my heart through this series and I am deeply blessed by it."

– T. Heintz

"Found it very hard to put these books down. Cried a lot at the tender and not so tender moments. Love the way she brings The Lord into the everyday lives. She reaches into everyday lives, struggles, triumphs, and such that we deal with every day we breathe. Thank you that we have authors who write books like this to give people who don't know Jesus to see Him in fiction, but realize that the message He has is for everyone. I pray that these books will touch lives!"

– Margaret P.

"I just finished the third book in the Glendale series. I have spent the better part of the last week totally engrossed in the lives of Joe and Jessica. Their story truly touched my heart. I'm in youth ministry at my church and watch so many of my teens go though the hurt and loneliness that Jessica did. I cried when she found salvation (in the middle of the lunch room at work I might add). Truly wonderful books that I will be recommending to some of my teen girls. Thank you so much-I am officially a huge fan!"

– Billie Jean E.

"I just finished the final book in the Glendale Series. ...I've never cried, laughed, or giggled so much!"

– Kayla M.

"This author is becoming one of my favorites. I enjoy her plots, and hate to stop reading to do everything else I need to do.

– Paul H.

THE GLENDALE NOVELS

The Glendale Series

Glendale

A New Day

Promising Forever

Mothers of Glendale

One Desire

Gray Area

Silver Lining

Ann GOERING

A NEW DAY

A Glendale Novel

COVERED PORCH PUBLISHING

A New Day

Edited by Eileen Fronterhouse

ISBN-10: 0989086615
ISBN-13: 978-0-9890866-1-5

Library of Congress Control Number: 2013934564

www.coveredporchpublishing.com

www.anngoering.com

Requests for information should be addressed to:
Covered Porch Publishing, Ann Goering, PO Box 1827, Hollister, MO 65673

This book is a work of fiction. Names, characters, places, and incidents are fictitious and a product of the author's imagination. Any resemblances to actual people or events are coincidental.

Printed in the United States of America

17 16 15 14 13 A 7 6 5 4 3 2 1

This book is dedicated to my Savior, the only One who gives freedom and an eternal future;

My husband, who gave me the gift of being waited for;

And my mom, who is a beautiful and strong woman who taught me to trust in the goodness and timing of the LORD, even (or especially!) when things look hopeless.

One

Jessica Cordel stood facing her bedroom door, feeling as if it was the only thing that separated her from that which wanted to consume her, overtake her and pull her back down into the pit she had lived in for the first fifteen years of her life. In reality, the only thing on the other side of her door was her dad and step-mom.

When she had awakened that morning, it took a few moments to realize where she was and what was real. At first, she thought she was fifteen again, her mom and dad were at work, and she would have the house to herself. Then she remembered.

Her father, a senator who was always too consumed with work to have time for his family, had an affair with Jari, a young girl in his office. He had thrown Jessi and her mother out and married his new girlfriend. Jessi and her mom, Carla, had moved back to Carla's hometown and lived there a year – a year that had turned out to be a life changing, magical and remarkable year for Jessica.

After a lifetime of being lonely and consumed with an unfulfilling quest for pleasure, she had found family, belonging and depth. And she had found love. When she moved to Glendale, Joe Colby had been a challenge – the golden boy who didn't date. As the months wore on, though, he became her lifeline, her best friend and eventually, her lover.

Which, she reminded herself, was the reason she was back in her old room in D.C. When Joe had abandoned all he held dear, when he had laid aside all of his convictions, morals and dreams in a flawed plan to keep her in Glendale after her father demanded her return, she had realized just how deeply she loved him. And she realized that really loving him meant leaving Glendale and leaving him. If she had stayed, he would have given up everything he had ever wanted, and she couldn't live with that. More than anything else, she wanted him to be happy.

The knock came again, drawing her back to the present, and she warily walked over and opened the door.

"Good morning, Jessica," her dad said tightly.

"Bill," she answered, her tone dull. His eyes snapped as he looked at her, but he took a deep breath before speaking.

"Call me Dad, as you used to – and as you should."

"You don't deserve that title," she told him.

She may have returned to D.C., but that decision had nothing to do with her father's threatening demands. Her heart had softened during her year in Glendale, but now, as she looked at him, she felt the hardness coming back.

Desperate to stop it, but unsure of how to curb her wrath, she stood absolutely still, unflinching under his intense gaze. She let the indifferent facade come across her face and the numbness overtake her. She hated feeling like this, but didn't know how to be the girl she had become in Glendale back in D.C., in her father's house. Everything was different here. Those who were soft got trampled on and hurt; allowing the hardness to return was the only way to survive.

"Deserving has nothing to do with it," he answered, his voice sickeningly pleasant. "You won't call me Bill again, is that understood? Now come have breakfast with Jari and me. I have to leave for work soon."

She shook her head in disbelief. "Do you think I'm happy to see you? Do you think I want to be here? Do you realize that I had a life in Glendale – that I had friends and I *liked* it there? Why do you think I would want to come back here and live with you and your girlfriend?"

She could see that her last comment burned him.

"She's my wife, Jessica!"

"Oh, that's right. Just like mom was. For how long, Bill? Are you going to wait until she gives you her youth, the best years of her life, and then trade her in on a newer model? Is that how it's going to work again?"

His face reddened. "You are grounded, young lady."

She threw up her hands. "What would I do if I wasn't? Grounding me is no punishment, Dad! My life is back in Glendale, not here in D.C."

He spun around and marched out of her room, slamming her door so hard the house shook. She crossed the room and locked the door quickly, not wanting to give him the opportunity to think up a response and come back in to spew his venom at her. She sank to the floor in front of her door and started to cry. Since she had cried herself to sleep after arriving the night before, she wouldn't think she would have any more tears, but they still came.

"I chose this," she reminded herself. "I made the decision to come back here." She wished it wasn't true, but it was. She could have been lying in her bed in Glendale, her mom puttering around getting ready to leave for work down the hall. She could have gone swimming with Joe's sister Kara and gone down to the river with Joe like she had the night before last.

She remembered the look of passion in his pale green eyes – passion for her – and the shame. As she remembered the deep shame and grief in his eyes, she felt sure that her decision had been right.

No matter how horrible her dad made life for her, no matter how much her heart ached, no matter how deeply she longed for her life in Glendale, she had made the right decision. Of that she was sure.

Joe had forsaken his God for her and sacrificed his everything on an altar built in her name. She shook her head. She couldn't let that continue. She wasn't enough for Joe Colby.

Although she didn't know or understand his God, she knew that somehow his God was big, limitless and fulfilling. She felt small and shallow. Joe wasn't like other boys. He was different. He was more intriguing, handsome, confident, and full of purpose than anyone she had ever known. No, she would never be enough for him if she was his everything, and she couldn't bear that. She wanted him to be happy, fulfilled and content, even if that meant she had to be out of his life.

One thing was certain, though. If she was going to live back under her father's roof, she had to get rid of any softness that had crept into her heart during her time in Glendale and replace it with steel. Otherwise, she knew she would never survive.

~~~~

Jessica stayed in her room for two days without coming out once. She didn't eat or talk to anyone. She knew she was right to leave Glendale, but she didn't know how to resume living in D.C. She was a different person than she had been before and didn't know how to fit into her old life. Everything she had once done seemed so distant and meaningless now. More than once she asked herself how she had ever wanted to come back.

Finally, in the afternoon of the second day, she heard a quiet knock on her bedroom door. She opened it cautiously. She wasn't trying to avoid people as much as she was struggling to balance who she was with who she needed to be.

Jari stood outside her door with a delicious looking Panini and a glass of lemonade. Jessica offered her a shy smile and held the door open wider. Jari smiled back and walked in, handing the food and drink to Jessica.

"Thank you. I didn't think I was hungry, but maybe I am."

"I thought you might be," Jari answered, sitting down in Jessica's egg-shaped chair. Jessi took a seat on her bed and began to devour the sandwich.

Jari sat and watched her for quite some time, not saying anything. When she spoke, she surprised Jessica.

"I know it must have been hard for you to come here. Why would you want to come? Your entire life was in Glendale – everyone you loved. But," Jari paused, her entire face gentle, "I'm proud of you for coming. Even when you didn't want to and didn't agree, you honored your father by respecting his wishes."

Jessica wasn't as irritated by the comment as she would have thought. Maybe it was the way Jari said it. She seemed so gentle, so caring, so aware of how Jessi was feeling.

"I didn't come for him," Jessi told her, finishing her last bite of sandwich.

"Then why did you come?" Jari asked.

"For Joe," Jessi found herself saying before she thought better of it. Jari looked confused, but didn't pry. Finally, Jessi continued. "I love him, Jari," she said simply.

"And he loved you; I could see it when we met you two for lunch a few months ago." Jari's words stirred up a longing in Jessi's heart.

"Which is why I had to leave," she explained as much for her sake as Jari's. "If I had stayed, his life would have been nothing like what he wanted it to be. He wants to play football in college, go to seminary and be a pastor. I can't fit into that picture. He needs to be focused to achieve his dreams, and I would just distract him."

Understanding spread across Jari's face. "What if that's not what he wants anymore? What if he—" Jari shut her mouth and didn't finish her sentence. Instead, she took a deep breath.

Jessi shook her head and answered as if Jari had finished her question. "It has to be like this. This is best."

Jari nodded slowly. "I bet you miss him."

Jessi found herself near tears again. "More than I know how to handle." She bit her lip. "It hurts."

Jari winced at the raw pain in the young girl's voice. "I wish I could make it better."

"Me too."

When Jari stood and left a few minutes later, taking Jessi's empty plate and glass with her, Jessi kicked herself for being so open.

What was Jari going to do with the information she had just shared? Would she tell her dad? Would she use it against her? Would it become ammunition in a future battle? She had to remember that she wasn't in Glendale anymore. People here were different. Jari was different. She had to be. After all, she had stolen Bill Cordel away from his family without batting an eye. Nice people didn't do things like that. Jessi groaned, regretting everything she had said.

Jari had been such an object of Jessi's anger and hatred for the last two years, but now, in her presence, Jessi found herself spilling everything. She didn't understand it, but she no longer felt angry toward her.

Jari seemed so different than she had before Jessi and her mom moved to Glendale. Jessi had never spoken to her then, in the early days of the affair, but Jari had always seemed arrogant and smug, rebellious and uncaring.

Today, Jari seemed to genuinely care and want to help – she felt like a friend, not an enemy. But, Jessi reflected, maybe that was how she worked. Maybe that was how she sank her claws into people, like her dad. Maybe she pretended to care, to genuinely want to help and then, when people trusted her, she made her move. Well, Jessi would not be fooled again.

Still, the thought of fighting Jari and keeping her at arm's length all the time seemed exhausting. She didn't want to fight anymore. During her year in Glendale she had learned how wonderful peace was – how nice it was to feel safe. It had been such a relief not to constantly have to fight someone simply to stay alive, to keep her heart from being broken time after time. She longed to feel like that again.

She wanted to feel loved, secure and enjoyed. She had felt it with Joe, but now she wanted even more, perhaps even more than Joe could offer.

She turned to stare out of her window. The only thing about feeling that peace and not fighting all the time, was that you had to be able to trust the other person. And in this household, a trustworthy person would be hard to find. Despite their brief encounter, she wasn't convinced she could trust Jari, and she was certain she couldn't trust her dad. After all, he was the one who had taught her to fight to survive.

Two

"Jessica," Bill said before taking a drink of wine. She looked up warily and waited for whatever he was about to say. Jessica had been back in D.C. for two weeks, and this was the first time Bill had made it home for dinner. Despite her lack of enthusiasm, he insisted she be present at the meal.

"I've instructed Jari to complete the necessary enrollment paperwork for your old school," Bill continued.

Jessi slowly shook her head. "I don't want to go back there."

"Why not? It's the best school in town. It's where you've always gone. It's where all the sons and daughters of congress go."

"Exactly! Dad, nothing is normal there. Everyone is rich and spoiled and egocentric."

"Oh, Jessica, see, this is why I had to bring you back from the woods. You're content with normal when you could have the extraordinary," he told her, speaking to her in a tone normally reserved for a small child. "You're going. The academics are much better, and you'll have an appropriate circle of friends...and appropriate young men to choose from, should you decide to date."

Jessica seethed. "Is he what all this is really about? Did you move me from Glendale to get me away from Joe? Was he not an *appropriate* suitor for the daughter of Senator Bill Cordel? Were you worried that I would marry someone who wouldn't give you some kind of a political advantage? Or were you just jealous because I love and respect him more than I've ever loved and respected you?"

"Who said anything about marriage? You're sixteen,

Dear," Bill responded calmly, smiling at her as if they were in the middle of a pleasant conversation.

Bill dismissed any further conversation on the topic of Joe with a wave of his hand. He turned to Jari and smiled. "Darling, I was also wondering if you would take Jessica shopping tomorrow and buy her more appropriate clothing for her station in life here in D.C. It seems she's been in the country a bit too long. We have the Ganter Project banquet coming up, and she'll need something nice."

"I have clothes, Dad!" Jessi erupted, her blue eyes snapping.

He gave her a condescending smile. "Jeans and cowboy boots don't cut it in D.C., Jessica."

"Jessi looks lovely in whatever she wears, Bill, but yes, we can go shopping. It might be fun to both get a new outfit. It's always nice to have an occasion to shop!" Jari interrupted, halting the full-blown fight that was about to ensue.

Jessi went back to her dinner, putting a lid on her simmering rage. But Bill would not let it be.

"Jessica, my friend Allen Buchanan has a son around your age. He invited us over for dinner the beginning of September. We would like you two to meet."

"Isn't it a little early to be thinking of arranged marriages?" Jessi asked sarcastically.

"He's a young man with a lot of potential. And he's older than you – he just turned twenty-one. But here you go talking about marriage again; I just said we would like you to meet. What do they teach you down there in Glendale?" Bill asked, his condescending smile in place, his voice as smooth and controlled as ever.

"That what we do now echoes in eternity," Jessica whispered under her breath, quoting something Joe had told her. Jari heard and sent her a warm smile.

"What do you stand to gain from this?" Jessi asked suspiciously after a few seconds, knowing her dad always had a motive. Bill Cordel only smiled and continued eating.

Jessi watched him in disbelief. He was even worse than she remembered. Once enchanted with her handsome and powerful father, she had always scrambled for his attention. Now, seeing him for the selfish, hurtful and critical man that he was, she wanted nothing to do with him.

"I'm not interested in Allen Buchanan's son, and I won't go to dinner."

"You will," Bill said easily, continuing to enjoy his prime rib.

"I won't. And I've lost my appetite – you'll have to finish without me." Jessi pushed her chair back and stood, throwing her linen napkin down in her plate. She saw Jari start to say something then stop as Jessi turned to leave the room.

"When you're shopping tomorrow, get something for dinner at the Buchanans' too, Sweetheart," Bill called after her. She slammed her bedroom door in reply.

~~~~~

Jessi was lying on her bed flipping through a magazine when she heard a quiet knock on her door. Knowing that her dad had left for work, and the house staff would never disturb her, there was only one person it could be.

She hadn't seen Jari since dinner the night before and expected her to come in demanding they go shopping to fulfill Bill's wishes. She sighed before calling out for the blonde woman to come in. Jari entered looking hesitant, yet calm. She was biting her bottom lip, even as she smiled.

"I have something to say to you," Jari said, kneeling on the floor beside Jessi's bed.

Jessi continued flipping through her magazine. "I'm all ears," she answered, sounding completely uninterested. Jari took a deep breath, and Jessi rolled her eyes. Whatever Jari had to say, she would rather not hear it.

"I'm sorry, Jessica."

"For what?" Jessi asked, slightly caught off-guard by

the heartfelt declaration.

"I'm sorry for ruining your family, for stealing your dad. I'm sorry that I dishonored you, your mother and even your father." Jessi didn't know how to respond, but shifted her eyes to look at her young step-mom. She recognized the red paths down Jari's cheeks where tears had recently traveled.

"You didn't have an affair all by yourself," Jessica finally pointed out, feeling the need to respond to Jari's pleading eyes. The blonde looked so ashamed. Jari didn't deny Bill's part in the scandal. For that, Jessi was glad.

"If I knew then what I do now, I wouldn't have done it," Jari said, and Jessi could see that she meant it.

"Why not? Because this side of the fence isn't as green as you thought it would be?" Jessi could understand if Jari's infatuation with Bill had quickly worn off. Jari hesitated.

"Because of what I did to your family – to your mother, to you." Tears sprung to the older woman's eyes, and she wiped them away with her slender finger tips. "I committed adultery and sinned in the sight of God. Yet the destruction that came from my sin was not mine, but yours. You paid for my sin, while I profited."

Jessi turned her eyes away, unable to deal with the intensity of Jari's expression. Jessica realized that as badly as she had hurt, as angry as she had been, Jari was equally as remorseful.

"I know I hurt you, and I'm sorry," Jari continued. "If I could put your world back together like it was before I came, I would." Jessi knew in an instant that Jari spoke the truth.

"I don't want my old world. I don't like who I was then," Jessi offered.

Jari looked down at the ground, her hands palms-up on her knees. Jessi knew there was nothing else the woman could say. It was up to her now. Jessi studied Jari's face, her pretty features, her downcast gaze, her teary eyes – and finally spoke.

"Jari, I forgive you. You did hurt me and my mom, but," Jessi paused and thought of the man who had taught her this very lesson. She echoed his words. "Everyone makes mistakes. You are free from all shame or condemnation on my part."

Jari looked up at her quickly, openly surprised at Jessica's statement. Jessi took a deep breath and held her gaze. Slowly, Jari nodded and smiled.

"I fought the LORD on having to apologize. I've fought Him for days. Not that I didn't mean it or didn't want to speak the words," she assured before going on, "I just... they felt so shameful, and I thought you would throw my apology back in my face," Jari admitted. Jessi nodded in understanding. She knew what it felt like to be ashamed.

"So, you're a Christian?" Jessi asked, watching her step-mom for her reaction. Jari nodded slowly.

"I have been for about six months. I've spent my life justifying my actions, but realized how wicked I was when I realized how every sin I had committed pierced the skin – and the heart – of the One who died that I might live."

As soon as Jari's words registered, Jessi sat up quickly, her magazine falling to the floor. "Will I never get away from him?" she cried out in desperation, the familiar ache filling her chest again.

"Jesus?" Jari asked, confused and thoroughly startled.

"Joe. You sound just like him. He was a Christian. Always talking about Jesus. Now, talking about Him just makes me think of Joe – reminds me of him. It's like he calls out to me, always trying to keep my attention on him."

Jessi stood and went to the window, staring out of it. Her thoughts of forgiveness were completely forgotten, and all she could think about was her boyfriend. She wondered where he was and what he was doing. She could feel Jari watching her for a moment, then heard her walk quietly to the door.

"Maybe Joe isn't the one calling to you, Jessi. Maybe it's not him who keeps trying to get your attention."

Jessi's heart gave a wild flutter that she couldn't describe. She turned to ask Jari what she meant, but the older lady had already left the room. Jessi turned back to the window and impulsively glanced up at the sky.

Was there really a God up there? One who kept putting people in her path who knew Him, and would tell her about Him? If there was a God, did He really care that much about her? Would He put effort into planning who would cross her path? Did He really care if He had her attention? Would He really call out to her?

"I leave the ninety-nine to go after my one who is lost, Dear One."

The breath of a whisper fluttered across the surface of her heart, just below the surface of her hearing, yet above her cognitive reasoning. She crossed her arms, protecting herself from whatever unseen source had spoken the words. Feeling strange and decidedly not alone in her room, she crossed it to turn on some music.

She grabbed her magazine and resumed flipping through it. Even as she turned the pages, though, she could not deny that the whispered statement sounded exactly like the voice she had heard the morning she left Glendale. It was the one that had convinced her to lay down all her selfish desires to put the good of another before herself – the small voice that had taught her the true meaning of love.

~~~~~

Jessi threw the book she was trying to read onto the floor and pulled the blankets of her bed up over her head, trying to escape from the reality of her life. She had been trying to read for the better part of two hours, but had only turned the page a few times. What was worse was that she couldn't remember any of what she had read. All she could think about was Joe.

She missed him. She missed him so much. Missing him made her insides ache and she felt as if she was being ripped to pieces. She wanted to talk to him, to hear his voice. She wanted to be with him, to hold his hand. She wanted to run all the way back to Glendale, throw her arms around him and beg him to love her again. She wanted him to love her as he had the night before she left, to love her as he did every day, to love her for the rest of her life.

And she knew he would. He would welcome her back with open arms. He would buy her a ring, they would get married, and he would work with his dad. He would be a faithful and loving husband until the day one of them died. That was why she couldn't go back. Not now, not ever.

Her throat began to burn as if she had strep throat. "Why can't I be with him? Why do we have to be apart? Why do I have to make this decision?" she whispered to herself. A few tears turned into sobs. She knew the answer to every one of her questions – because she loved Joe Colby enough to want him to be happy more than she wanted to be happy herself.

She sobbed in her bed until her tears dried. Then she just lay there, hugging her pillow. She had never felt so alone or so resigned to the fact that she would always be alone. Her loneliness was self-afflicted, but knowing that didn't make it any easier.

Despite her misery, she never truly considered going back or answering one of Joe's numerous phone calls. She couldn't answer even one of his calls, couldn't talk to him or see him. If she did, he would never move on and accomplish everything he wanted to accomplish. No, it had to be a clean break.

But oh, how she missed him. She missed his sister, Kara, who had become her best friend. She missed her mom. She missed her grandma. She missed her friend, Tacy. She missed Joe's parents, Chris and Hannah.

She had felt like a part of the Colby family. They had

enveloped her. If she couldn't be with Joe, she wanted to go to his house, lay her head on Hannah's lap to cry, and let the motherly lady comfort her. She mothered Jessi in a way no one ever had. She baked her cookies, included her in all the family get-togethers and spent time really listening to her. While she knew her mom loved her, the successful and beautiful Carla Cordel often seemed more like a friend. Hannah Colby was a mother.

Jessi had considered calling Hannah or Kara several times, but always decided against it in the end. If she called them, they would surely tell Joe, and his determination would be renewed.

Additionally, she wasn't sure either of them would want to talk to her. She had pulled Joe away, caused him to stumble, and then left him broken-hearted. No, if she called Kara or Hannah they would surely reject her and turn her away. She couldn't bear that. She'd rather not call.

"Why? Why does it have to be like this?" she moaned into her sheet.

"I know the better way. My ways are higher, Dear One."

This time the quiet whisper brought with it a comforting peace, as if someone had settled a warm blanket over her. The pain subsiding for the time being, she drifted off to sleep.

~~~~~

Jessica walked aimlessly around the house. It was four in the afternoon and she was bored. She didn't know what to do with her time anymore. When she was younger, she would have run next door to Anna's, but she didn't feel like seeing Anna or Kayly. She had seen them once since returning and was frustrated by their time together.

All they wanted to do was talk about boys, clothes and parties. Neither of them were the least bit interested in which college they would attend in a year, what they wanted to do with their lives or anything else of any significance.

While she was with them, she couldn't stop thinking of Morgan and Montana, the little girls she had met a few months earlier at a homeless shelter she visited with Joe.

Cold, hungry and parentless, the little girls had pulled strongly on the strings of her heart. As she sat in Anna's lavish bedroom, she wished she could find Morgan and Montana and show them to Anna and Kayly. She would show her friends that there was more to life than boys, makeup and hair.

Although she hated to admit it, Jessi had been bored by their immature conversation. She had no desire to go back.

She sat down on the couch and grabbed a magazine. It held her attention for a few minutes, but then she found her mind drifting again. Was there more to life? What was it? What could she do to understand the significance she felt whenever she thought of the two orphans? She felt as if she had some part to play, some purpose in life that she could sense but not comprehend.

Her insides felt all stirred up by a new, relentless longing that she couldn't describe. Truth be told, it wasn't new. She had been feeling it for a long time. She had thought she could fulfill it with the very things Anna and Kayly sought out day after day. But more and more she realized she had a closet full of clothes that were the latest fashion, she lived in a beautiful house that was the size of some hotels, she had fought for and won the love of the most handsome and intriguing man she had ever known, and yet the longing continued to go unfulfilled. In fact, it was growing.

She longed for something of significance, something worthwhile, something true, something real, something deep. She ached for something that was deeper and bigger than herself. She wanted to accomplish something of real importance.

The day before, she had taken a risk and told Jari about the longing she was only now beginning to acknowledge. It was too consuming, too overwhelming to keep to herself any longer. She didn't know what it was or what would satisfy it. She needed help.

Although Jessi didn't understand why, Jari had looked pleased when Jessi shared her feelings. Jari listened to Jessi, seeming as if she was trying to refrain from breaking into a grin. After a few moments, she recovered her composure and listened attentively. When Jessi was done, Jari was quiet for several moments before asking, "Have you ever thought about the fact that it may not be *what* but *who* can fulfill that longing?" Jessi hadn't understood what she meant and was about to ask her, when her dad walked in the door. The conversation ended abruptly.

He had immediately been upset that the sprinklers weren't on in the front yard. "There's a watering restriction, Bill," Jari tried to explain, but he didn't want to listen. He had to keep up appearances, after all. The lawn of a senator should not be brown.

As soon as he said that, Jessi retreated to her room, annoyed. All he ever cared about were appearances.

Later that night, after thinking about her conversation with Jari, she had reluctantly admitted that the woman had quickly turned into an unexpected friend. She had wished her dad would go back to work so they could keep talking.

Realizing that another conversation with Jari was possible now, Jessi went searching for her, finding her lounging on a floating chair in the pool, a book in her hand. Jari saw her come out onto the patio and smiled. "Get your suit on and come suntan with me. I'm ready for some company."

Jessi didn't want to appear as if she had been purposefully looking for Jari, so she shrugged. "I noticed I was losing my tan this morning, so I came out to see how hot it is. I don't like to tan if it's too hot."

Jari shielded her eyes with her hand and looked at the thermometer on the side of the house. It was positioned between the elaborate patio table and built-in outdoor entertainment center. "I think it says around eighty-eight degrees, doesn't it? It's a beautiful day for sun tanning. If you get too hot, you can always jump in."

Jessi shrugged again. "I guess you're right. I'll go change."

"Good! Make sure you hurry. Your dad will be home soon, and we'll need to get ready to go. We have that banquet tonight."

Jessi stopped in her tracks. "I'm not going." Jari shielded her eyes with her hand again and looked at Jessi.

"Your dad told you last night he expected you to accompany us," Jari told her with careful, measured words.

Jessica felt stress and frustration build inside of her. She was tired of the games her dad played, tired of being controlled, tired of her life being orchestrated for the sake of his selfish ambitions.

Since arriving back in D.C., her frustration and despair had been steadily growing. She couldn't stomach the thought of spending one more night going through the motions, pretending in front of his supporters, friends and acquaintances whom he was so determined to impress. All for the sake of how it made him look. The idea made her sick to her stomach.

"So, just because he says he expects something from me, I have to do it?" Jessi asked, hooking her dark hair behind her ear. So this was it. After pretending to be an ally, Jari was assuming the role of Bill's drill sergeant in his stead. Jessi had known it would come eventually.

"Well, you probably should," Jari said slowly.

"Why? What has he done because I expected something from him? Is he a loving father just because I expect him to be? Did he put our family first, just because I wanted him to? Did he ever attend even one of my birthday parties because I expected he would be there? I think there are a lot of unmet expectations here on his part, Jari, and I think I should be allowed one every now and then."

As if knowing he was being talked about, Bill walked through the patio doors and out into the sunshine. He grabbed Jessica and kissed the side of her head, then walked to the edge of the pool. "Jari, great news – my approval rating is up by two percent. The numbers came in right before I left the office."

Jari smiled. "That's great, Bill!"

Jessi was starting to wonder if maybe Jari was a saint instead of just a Christian. She felt like vomiting at Bill's smug declaration, while Jari was obviously rejoicing with him. Jessi wondered again how her step-mom could even stand her husband.

"We should all head inside and get ready for dinner," he continued. "We have to leave in two hours, and neither of you look close to being ready." Bill turned to go into the house.

Jessi cleared her throat. "I'm not going to the banquet tonight."

Bill turned slowly. "Yes, you are. You bought a new outfit for it, and I want to be accompanied by my wife and daughter."

There were a hundred things that came to Jessi's mind to fling back at the man standing in front of her, comments about how his wife and daughter should include Carla, Jessi's *mom*. Out of respect for the lady now swimming to the side of the pool, Jessi didn't say any of them.

"I'll say it again. I'm not going. I don't want to go. I don't know what the Ganter Project is, and I don't care to. I'm not the politician, Dad, you are. I want to stay home tonight. I don't feel well," she said, trying to keep her tone even. It was true – her stomach was feeling a little queasy.

"That's out of the question. You're going. I'll brief you both on the project in the limousine on the way." He turned to go in the house as if the matter was settled.

"No, I don't think you heard me. I'm not going. This isn't up for discussion. I didn't ask if you wanted me to go, I said I'm not," Jessica answered, her tone firm. She pushed her dark hair behind her shoulder and waited for his reply.

Bill's eyebrows drew down hard over his blue eyes. "Since when do you think you can make a decision like that?"

"Since when do you think you have the right to summon me and send me away as you please?" she shot back. "You sent me to Glendale because you were tired of having a daughter, then you summoned me back because you decided you wanted me again. You boss me around as if I were your servant and flaunt me to the masses to display your fatherly side. I am nothing to you but a tool to portray the image your supporters want to see – doting husband, loving father. I am no more than a pawn in the game you play and I'm tired of it! I won't play your game anymore! Your only desire for my presence is how it makes you look!" Jessi accused.

For the first time in her life, she thought she saw hurt in her dad's eyes. "That's not true," he said quietly.

"Isn't it, Dad? Isn't it? I exist for the purpose of boosting your approval ratings, just like everything else in your carefully strategized life." She took a deep, calming breath, pressing her hand to her stomach. "I'm not going tonight. Let your approval ratings rise or fall as they will. You cannot make me."

Her dad responded with fiery anger, just as she had expected, any trace of hurt or remorse long gone. "You're going or I'll—"

"Or you'll what?" Jessi taunted, interrupting. "You have my phone, I'm already grounded, my boyfriend is as good as a million miles away, I'm not hungry, you can have my car keys, my room is my favorite place...what are you possibly going to take away from me that either doesn't matter, or hasn't already been taken?"

"You're going," Bill ground out, looking as if he was about to blow a gasket. Still, Jessi knew it was an empty threat. There was nothing else he could do to her, nothing else he could take.

"Make me," she challenged, and pushed by him on her way to the house. He yelled her name as she went through the patio doors, but she continued to her room, slamming and locking the door.

The worst part was, what she said outside was true. And if she had nothing left that could be taken away in order to hurt her, if she had nothing left that really mattered, than what did she have to live for?

Three

Jessica stared at the white stick in her hand in disbelief and intense fear. Memories were fighting for possession of her mind. She was instantly back beside the river. Joe was kissing her, holding her, whispering his love for her. Suddenly, she was seeing the burning in his eyes and the determination in the set of his jaw. She was feeling his hands on her skin and the heat of his body against hers. She heard him laying out his plan to keep them together.

She opened the bathroom door, walked through her bedroom, down the hall and into the kitchen. She stopped in the middle of the floor and waited until Jari finished pouring her glass of orange juice and turned toward her with a bright smile. "Good morning!"

Jessica held up the pregnancy test and swallowed hard. Her knees were shaking. "Jari, I think it's time to tell you, I'm not a virgin anymore." Jari took a few steps forward, a frown on her face, not understanding what the white stick was. Jessi could tell the moment it dawned on her.

"Oh my word. Jess, are you serious?" Jari's voice was soft. She took the test from Jessi's hand and stared at it. "Maybe it's wrong."

Jessi shook her head and pressed her lips together, the corners of her eyes moist. "It's the third one I've taken." It was quiet for a long time.

"Joe?" Jari finally asked, looking up, her hands falling to her sides. Jessica bit her lip and nodded.

"It was just one night!" She let out something between a laugh and a sob. "The night before I left, actually. I never thought I could actually get pregnant in one night!"

"Oh Sweetie, that's all it takes!" Jari said, reaching out

and wrapping her arms around Jessica as the teenager started to cry. Within seconds, sobs shook Jessi's young body.

"What am I going to do?"

Jari pressed Jessi's head against her own shoulder. "Don't worry. We'll get through this."

"I have to tell Dad."

"We'll tell him together," Jari promised.

Jessi put her arms around Jari, clinging to her only source of help. "Are you sure?"

Jari nodded firmly. "Yes. You do not have to do this alone." Jessi clung to her. "What about Joe? How are you going to tell him?" Jari asked softly. Jessi took a step back and drug her slender fingertips under her eyes, shaking her head. Jari looked surprised. "You're not going to tell him?" Another head shake from Jessica. "Don't you think he should know?"

Jessica stared out the kitchen window for several moments before looking back at Jari. "No," she finally said. "He has things he wants to do, and he won't ever get the chance to do them if he has a wife and a baby. It's even worse than before. No," she said again, more firmly this time. "I won't tell him. I'll give him the chance to have the life he deserves."

Jari took a step forward imploringly. "What if the life he wants is with you, Jess? He wants you, and he would want your baby! He is a good man. He would *want* to be a father to his child. He would *want* to know and take care of you."

Jessica's blue eyes grew teary again. "Sometimes you don't want what's best for you."

Jari studied her. "What if part of Joe's plan for his life is to achieve those things that you talk about with you at his side?"

"God wants Joe for his own purposes," Jessi said bluntly. "All I do is mess things up."

"Maybe He can use you two together."

Jessica shook her head. "I don't believe in God."

"Don't you?" Jari questioned. "Because if you don't believe there's a God, then you left the man you love for no reason at all. There's a difference between believing and serving, Jessi. I think you believe there is a God all right – you believe enough to surrender your own happiness for the sake of His greater plan."

"I did it for Joe, not God."

"Did you?" Jari pressed. "Because Joe wants you. It's God who you think has all these other plans for him."

"Jari, I'm not telling him."

"It's your decision, Jess," Jari conceded after studying her for several moments. Jessica nodded. "We should see if we can get you a doctor's appointment this afternoon. You've been here almost two months – you need prenatal care. And we'll need to get prenatal vitamins," Jari told her, moving on to the practical needs associated with Jessica's pregnancy. Jessi nodded, thankful that Jari knew what to do.

Jari took the number for her doctor out of her clutch and dialed the phone. "How have you been feeling?" she asked as the phone rang.

"I've thrown up several times during the last month. I thought at first it was just Dad, but when it continued, well…that's why I took the test."

Jari nodded. "Are you tired a lot? I hear that's common."

"I have been able to take naps in the middle of the day, but then again, I normally can. I've felt extra emotional maybe. I thought at first I was just depressed about coming here, but I guess this explains it."

The receptionist picked up, and Jari convinced her to squeeze them in before lunch. "Thanks, Jari," Jessi said softly when Jari hung up. She had been afraid to tell anyone, afraid to admit the truth, even to herself, but Jari had been so gracious, so sympathetic. Jessi appreciated it more than she knew how to express. Jari smiled.

"You're welcome. Now let's both get showered so we can make your appointment. The office is on the other side of town."

Once they were both ready, Jari drove Jessica to her appointment. Jessi felt self-conscious as they walked into the doctor's office. She wondered if everyone knew why they were there.

Jessi cringed inwardly at the thought of being an unwed teenage mother. Would people look down on her? Would she live the rest of her life in shame? What about her friends? She had always been the one to remind them to use birth control, and here she was pregnant. What an ironic twist. She shook her head. How had this happened? It had only been one night.

She thought about the reality of telling her dad, mom, and grandma the news. She cringed. She pictured what the next several months would be like, about giving birth, about what it would feel like to be seventeen with a baby. She felt herself shudder.

Jari reached over and took her hand as if she could read her mind. "It's going to be okay, Jessi. This little one, despite the circumstances, was planned for and designed. Life is beautiful, Jessica, even if it wasn't created on purpose. Not one baby is conceived without the hand of God. He is forming this little one within you even now – knitting together its innermost parts, lining things up just right to give it the perfect combination of attributes to accomplish the purpose He has for it. God is giving this baby a certain eye color, skin color, hair color. He's putting great care and attention into every little detail of its little being."

Jessica shook her head. "You don't understand. What we did was wrong – by God's standards, by Joe's standards, it was wrong."

Jari nodded, but didn't miss a beat responding. "Whether or not what you did the night before you left was wrong, this baby did not surprise God. This life growing within you is not wrong. God has a plan and a purpose for this little one."

"Is this my punishment? My punishment for taking Joe from Him?" Jessi asked, her voice little more than a whimper.

"Honey, I think it's more like your blessing – the beauty amidst the ashes," Jari told her gently. "You died to your own selfish ambition, and now you see that out of death comes life." Jari could see the beautiful young girl in front of her didn't understand and continued.

"You say Joe has things he needs to do, things he's supposed to achieve. Well, this little one is now one of the things you need to do. You will have the honor of raising this little one, teaching it, and loving it. What a great and beautiful gift you've been given. And," Jari shot Jessi a smile, "it's a piece of you and a piece of Joe. No matter how long you're separated, you'll be joined together in this little baby." Jessi nodded slowly, liking the thought of that.

Maybe, if God did exist, maybe He had given her something extraordinarily special to remember Joe by, a way to continue loving him, even though she had given him back to God. If that was the case, maybe He was as merciful as everyone said He was. Even on the night that Joe actively declared his love and commitment to her, and she unknowingly stole him away, God had given her a gift. The thought was too much for her to bear. How did Someone, at the very moment they were being stolen from, give a gift to the thief?

The thought made her uneasy, and yet something deep inside her knew it was true. She listened for that little whisper, to see if it would share anything, but all was quiet. Yet, she felt peace wash over her, and the fear and anxiety that had gripped her heart just moments before, dissipated.

This baby was a gift. Her gift. And she would accept it as such. It was growing within her now – a little piece of her and a little piece of Joe. She hoped the baby had chocolate brown hair and pale green eyes like its father.

When the nurse called her name, Jari followed Jessi out of the waiting room to the back part of the clinic. Jessica hadn't been bold enough to ask, but was grateful when Jari came with her. She didn't want to do this alone. The nurse weighed and measured her, then took her blood pressure and pulse. Then, she sent her into a room where she said the doctor would come to see her shortly.

When the doctor came in, Jari smiled and greeted her, then sent Jessi from the room. Jari and the doctor talked, and when Jari opened the door to bring Jessi back in, both were welcoming and kind. Jessi wasn't sure what Jari had said, but the doctor seemed to know about the situation. Doctor Holly Corvich was neither condescending nor judgmental.

Dr. Corvich was a sweet, middle-aged woman and as understanding as Jari. She asked Jessi questions about how she had been feeling. They spent a long time discussing nutrition, care, and what Jessica needed to be doing and staying clear of during the next several months. Dr. Corvich then calculated her due date, based on the date of conception, and told her she was due April fifth. She was nine weeks pregnant.

Finally, she asked Jessi to lie down on her cushioned table and used a Doppler to listen to the baby's heartbeat. Dr. Corvich found it almost instantly, and Jessi's eyes grew wide as the fast swishing rhythm filled the room.

"It sounds good and strong," Dr. Corvich said with a smile. The doctor's eyebrows drew together as she moved the Doppler and found the little heartbeat again. She moved it back to where it had been before and counted something using her watch, then moved it back to the other location counting once more.

"Is something wrong?" Jessi asked, growing concerned as Dr. Corvich shot a look up at Jessi, then back at

Jari.

Dr. Corvich shook her head. "No, but I'm getting two heartbeats."

"What does that mean, Holly?" Jari asked, getting up from her chair to come stand beside Jessi. She took Jessica's hand and held it tightly in her own.

Dr. Corvich gave a weak smile and turned the Doppler back on. She found the first location and as the heartbeat filled the air, she said, "This is baby number one," she moved the Doppler to the other side of Jessi's abdomen, "and this is baby number two."

~~~~~

Bill had to be told. As much as she didn't want to have that conversation with her father, Jessi knew it needed to happen. Jari called his favorite restaurant on their way home and made dinner reservations for three. The hope was that if they were in public, the conversation wouldn't get as ugly. It had been Jari's idea, and Jessica hoped it would work.

Later that day, Jessica appreciated that Jari wore Bill's favorite dress, hoping to distract some of his attention. Jessica wore a modest pink dress shirt and a pair of gray slacks. She left her hair down, long and loose – there was no need to antagonize him more than necessary. She might as well look the part he wanted her to play. Maybe it would soften the blow.

Bill looked pleased as they met him in the parking lot of Les Champignons and walked in together. He escorted Jari with one arm and Jessi with the other. The host held Jari's chair for her and then Jessica's, as he seated them at a table in the back where it would be more private, just as Jari had requested.

Bill ordered a bottle of champagne. Once he had poured his first glass and they had ordered their food, Jessica cleared her throat. She looked at Jari for support, and the blonde smiled reassuringly and nodded.

"Daddy, I need to talk to you about something." He

took a sip of champagne and smiled at her.

"Okay, what is it, Sweetheart?" She took a deep breath, her stomach feeling queasy. The last thing in the world she wanted to do was to tell her father what she was about to tell him.

"What I'm about to say may come as a bit of a shock, but I want you to promise to be understanding," she started, hoping to ease him into it. Bill looked at Jessica suspiciously, then glanced around to see who was sitting nearby.

He took another sip of champagne and quietly said, "You're not going back to Glendale, Jessica. Put it out of your mind – it's not up for discussion."

"It's not that, Bill. Hear her out," Jari interrupted, softly hitting his arm, revealing that she too was on pins and needles.

He turned and raised an eyebrow at her. "You know what this is about I presume?" Jari nodded firmly, meeting his stony gaze. He turned back to Jessica. "Fine. Go on."

Looking at him, Jessi failed to find any of the words she had rehearsed in the mirror as she got ready for dinner. Still, she had started. Now she had no choice but to finish. "Daddy," she finally said, her voice faint. "I'm pregnant… with twins."

Bill's face went as white as a sheet, and for a moment Jessi wondered if he was actually having a heart attack. His fists clenched, he went stiff, and he stared up at the ceiling. He took three long, deep breaths through his nose, his head tipped back, his eyes shut. With each one, Jessi felt a little smaller, a little more intimidated. Suddenly, he shot a glance around as if wondering if anyone had heard what his daughter had just said.

"Don't be a fool, Dear. Talk about this rationally," Jari said calmly, her tone even and firm. Infuriated, he glared first at Jari, then at Jessica.

"Tell me that was a joke," he ground out between clenched teeth, his attention settling on Jessica.

"I'm pregnant," she told him again. It wasn't any easier to say the second time.

He gave a dry, humorless laugh. "Well, isn't that lovely? You're pregnant. My sixteen-year-old daughter is *pregnant*! And you tell me not to act like a fool, Jari? Obviously someone was fooling around," he paused for effect. "But it wasn't me!"

Jessica and Jari were quiet, and their silence only served to increase his anger. He let out a huff, then hit the table with his hand. His face flushed red, chasing away the pallor. "Jessica Nicole Cordel, I can't believe you did this. I just can't believe it. The haircut, I forgave. The tattoo, I forgave. Even you dating that no-account boy, I forgave, but this? I cannot and will not forgive this. This is beyond forgiveness, young lady," he told her, his voice strained with indignation. "I knew you were disrespectful, rude, and disobedient, Jessica, but I never dreamt that you would stoop to this level. We are in politics – we are supposed to be an example to the people of America, and the only example you're setting is telling unwed teenage girls to go out and get pregnant!"

"No, Dad, you're in politics. I'm not," Jessica said, choosing not to respond to any of his barbs.

"Just in case you don't remember how this works, you reflect on me. You being a little slut and getting pregnant before you're married makes me look bad to the American people."

Jessica shrank back against her chair. She was too stunned by his name-calling to respond. Jari wasn't so slow, though.

Bill had no more than finished his sentence when Jari reached out and slapped him across his cheek. He jumped back in shock, nearly knocking his chair over. He pressed his hand to his face and looked around, horrified to see people at the surrounding tables looking their way after the loud smack of the slap. Jari, however, was in no way deterred by the watching eyes. She leaned forward in her chair, her eyes burning into his.

"Bill, I don't care what she's done or what she does, you will *never* call your daughter a slut again! Ever. Is that clear? If you ever speak to her like that again, I will leave before nightfall and take Jessica with me," Jari told him. Her voice was calm and quiet, yet there was no mistaking the sincerity of her words. "If you continue to think that your public appearance and your approval ratings are more important than your family, one day you're going to wake up and realize that you don't have a family left. You cannot treat people, especially your daughter, like you just did."

Bill sat still, shocked by his usually calm and mild-mannered wife's speech. "You know as well as I do that while I worked in your office," Jari continued, "we had an affair for months, and *you were married*! Not to mention, we were both old enough to know better. So, if you want to lay blame for this, then you had better lay it at your own doorstep, because you set this example for her. We both did."

Jessica was silent, just as shocked as her father by Jari's quiet outburst. All three of them sat still and quiet for several long, tense moments. Jessica was barely able to offer a thank-you as the waiter set her food in front of her.

"How far along are you?" Bill asked hesitantly, his tone clipped.

"Nine weeks."

"Excellent. You can still resolve the issue."

"Resolve the issue? Have an abortion? Is that what you mean?" Jari cried. "These are your grandchildren, Bill!" Bill held up his hands in surrender.

"It's Jessica's body, her life. I simply think she should know there are options." Jari started to argue, then turned to look at Jessica.

"What do you think, Jess?" Jari asked, her expression strained. Jessi didn't hesitate.

"It's not an option. I can't. When Joe's sister Kimberly was pregnant, I felt her baby move, I saw him after he was born…it's a real person." Jari looked relieved, Bill disappointed. He wisely kept his reply to a curt nod and counted on his fingers.

"You're due in April?"

"April fifth."

He shook his head in what looked to be a mix of disgust and disappointment. "You won't even be able to finish school."

Jessica's head hung. "I know." She had thought of that, too. She wanted her high school diploma.

Jari shook her head. "I've already thought that through. I'll homeschool you. We'll start after Labor Day, just as you were planning. We'll go through Christmas break so we can get ahead, and maybe you can have your diploma by the time the babies come."

"You would do that?" Jessi asked, her voice hopeful.

"Of course," Jari told her, patting her hand.

Jessi smiled, feeling hopeful again. "Thank you."

"Is it…um…." Bill paused and cleared his throat. "Is the father that Colby boy?"

"Yes."

"Are you going to get married after you graduate?"

"No."

"Why not? You would think someone who is supposedly such a 'good man' would have the decency to marry the girl he impregnated! Do you both presume that I'll support you for the rest of your—"

"She's not going to tell him, Dear," Jari said calmly, interrupting him.

Bill turned to look at Jessica sharply. "What does she mean you're not going to tell him?"

"I'm not telling him," Jessi said firmly.

"But—"

"Joe is not going to know," she reiterated. The issue

was closed.

He threw up his hands. "Fine. Have it your way."

The rest of dinner was tense and quiet. Bill threw in a few small digs, but stayed mostly quiet due to the warning looks he was receiving from his wife. When Jari and Jessi were back in Jari's car, Jessi let out a deep breath and put her head in her hands.

"Just remember that it's over, Jess," Jari said softly, pulling out onto the crowded street. Jessi nodded, knowing that as much as she wanted it to be, it was far from over. She had survived telling her dad, but she knew he would continue to throw it back in her face for the rest of her life.

Four

Jessi helped herself to more eggs and bacon, then put jelly on another piece of toast. "Are you getting enough to eat, Jessica? Remember you're eating for two now." Bill's snotty tone grated on Jessi's nerves.

She chewed her toast slowly, then took a long drink of apple juice. "Three, actually."

"Remember to *drink* for three, Jessi. Let me get you another glass of juice. I bought the one hundred percent apple juice this time. The clerk said it was better since it doesn't have all the added sugar in it," Jari said, rising from her chair.

"I'm okay, Jari, but thanks. I don't think I can drink anymore right now."

"Sure, my drink is empty and you're offering to fill hers while it's still half-full," Bill pouted.

"Why would she get you more apple juice when you're already drowning in hate?" Jessi asked, her head beginning to throb. She was tired of his snide remarks and sarcasm. She was tired of the constant battering. She was tired of having to defend herself all the time. She was tired of him only showing interest in her when he could throw in a dig or bring up the option of abortion.

And the worst part was that he was getting to her. Sometimes she would lie in bed in the middle of the night and wonder if an abortion wasn't a good option after all. In fact, she began to wonder if it was her only option.

She was bringing two children into the world with a father they would never know, a hateful grandfather, a grandmother who was addicted to her work, and a very young and selfish mother. What kind of a life was that going to be for her children?

Was it selfish to give birth? Would it be better to have an abortion as her dad wanted and avoid putting the babies through the misery she was sure was coming? Was an abortion the kindest option?

Oftentimes, she ended up putting her hands on her abdomen and crying herself to sleep. She would wake up more resolved than ever to be a good mother, to put her childish ways behind her, and to give her children the life she had always wanted. Then, after another day of loneliness and her father's remarks, she would go to bed and worry, sure that she wasn't fit to be a parent. She just wanted the vicious cycle to end.

"Oh, but you, my dear, are bubbling over with sweetness," Bill replied after setting down his cup of coffee. Jari put her hand to her head as she quickly grabbed Bill's glass and stood. "Jessi, you're straining my wife," Bill quickly pointed out, motioning to Jari.

Jessi held her tongue. She wanted to bite back at her dad, but didn't want to say anything that might hurt Jari. Jari had shown her nothing but love, understanding and companionship. In a time when she felt so alone, Jessi was holding on to her with both hands.

"I'm sorry," she said, turning her face away as she pushed back from the table. She wasn't hungry anymore. In fact, she felt sick.

"No, Jessi," Jari protested, coming back to the table with a full glass of apple juice for Bill. "Finish your breakfast."

"Let her go. You don't have to coddle her anymore," Bill said, waving his hand in the air.

Jari turned on him, then bit her tongue to keep hateful things from spilling out of her mouth. She sat down in her chair in submission, but her look said it all.

Bill's chair scraped the floor loudly as he scooted it back, infuriated by the look Jari had given him. "Jessica, look at this! Look at how you are coming between us. You have my own wife mad at me."

"It's not my doing," Jessi said, scraping the food off her plate into the trash.

"I knew I shouldn't have brought you here. I knew you would come between us," Bill continued, pointing his long finger at Jessica.

"I didn't ask to come."

"Oh, give me a break! You were itching to come – probably because you and that Colby boy were falling apart! You gave yourself to him in a last ditch effort to keep him, and it didn't work, did it? Not even that was enough to convince him to stay! Your very nature repulsed him, didn't it?"

"Bill, stop it!" Jari cried standing up between them, her face pale. He side-stepped her and kept going.

"That sniveling part of you came between the two of you just as it's coming between me and my wife. You did the same thing to your mother and me! We were happy before you came along. You drove us apart!"

Jessi turned and ran out of the kitchen, her stomach beginning to heave, her vision blurred with tears. She caught her dark hair in her slender hand as she leaned over the toilet, her stomach churning until it was empty. She could hear her dad and Jari yelling in the kitchen. She peeked out the bathroom door, then crept to her room to get her keys. Jari was quietly sobbing by the time Jessi had retrieved her car keys and purse and made a break for the door. She hesitated with her hand on the doorknob, feeling guilty about leaving Jari alone with him.

"What do you expect, Jari? That I'm going to be *happy* my daughter is pregnant? How do you think that reflects on me? How do you think that makes me look to voters? How do you think that's going to look when you stand on one side of me, and she stands on the other, seventeen-years-old and nine months pregnant?"

"This isn't about you, Bill! It's not! For once, think about someone else. Think about Jessi," Jessica heard Jari plead.

"When I brought her here, I was hoping for my sweet and beautiful daughter to accompany me on the campaign trail this year. Instead, she's soiled, pregnant and compromised – and everyone will know it."

Jessica couldn't listen to any more. She slammed the door behind her, cutting off her dad's vicious words. She got in her car, pulled out of the garage and sped out of the drive.

She thought about going to Anna's or Kayly's, but immediately decided against it. When they realized she was pregnant, their teasing had been more than she could stand. Although they said their teasing was in fun, they made it clear that her life was basically over. How was she going to have any fun when she had *kids*?

She wiped at her tears and went to the mall. It was a place that had always brought comfort before, but as she walked around, it just made her feel empty. There was more to life than clothes, shopping and money. There was love, family, joy and purpose. And she had lost it all.

She left the mall and went to the only place that made any sense. She pulled into a parking place and stared at the abortion clinic. Her hands tightened on the steering wheel of her car until her knuckles turned white. If she climbed the stairs and went in the door, in an hour she could come back and everything would be as it had been. She could tell her dad, and for the first time in her life, he might actually be pleased with her. The thought tugged at her heart.

She told herself it was the best thing for the babies. It had to be. She was too young to raise them. Her dad had made it perfectly clear that he would not offer any financial support once the babies were born. If she chose to have them, she was out of his house and cut off from any financial provision. She couldn't go back to Glendale to her mom's – not with Joe's twins. He would know in a matter of hours. Realistically speaking, a seventeen-year-old with two children didn't have many options. Even if she could get a job, what would she do about childcare? Medical expenses? A place to live? Diapers?

If she had them, they could all three end up on the streets. What kind of a life was that? She thought of Morgan and Montana again, the little girls she had rescued from the homeless shelter mere months ago. What if those dirty, hungry, sad little faces belonged to her own children a few years down the road?

Besides, they weren't truly babies yet – just fetuses. It wasn't as if she would be killing a baby. Isn't that what her dad had told her over and over? She shuddered, yet she opened her car door and put one foot out. If they felt any pain, surely it would pale in comparison to anything they would feel if they were born. Especially being born into her family.

"Don't take the life of your children. Trust in My plan." The words were quick and sure. She wasn't sure if they had resounded in her car or simply in her head. They were so loud they made her jump. *"They are alive. You know it to be true. Even now I am forming them. Flee this place and do not return. This is a place of death and destruction. Choose life."*

As the last words echoed in the stillness, she felt a small flutter in her belly. Then another. She had never felt anything like it, yet she instantly knew what it was. Her unborn children were giving testimony that they were alive – they were moving, and she could feel them.

Without giving thought to the speaker of such bold words or if she even believed, she shut her car door and quickly left the parking lot. As she pulled out onto the street, a dark fog seemed to lift, and she found herself appalled at what she had considered doing.

She suddenly felt cold and shaky. She laid her hand

protectively against the small bulge of her abdomen. She may feel empty and broken, her future may appear dismal and bleak, but she carried life. Of that, she was now sure.

She drove back to the mall, not knowing where else to go, but stayed in her car. She sat very still, willing the little ones inside to make themselves known again, but they didn't. Still, she did not doubt that they had. She had felt them, and they were very much alive.

She closed her eyes and remembered a park nearby where she had played as a child. She found it and pulled into the first available parking place. It was a warm day for early November, but still chilly enough that the playing kids were dressed in coats. Pulling her hair up into a ponytail and shrugging into her own jacket, she headed to the playground. She settled on a bench and crossed her legs, leaning back to watch the children.

There were kids running everywhere, laughing and shrieking. Two girls of about eight were on the swings, pushing themselves with their toes, talking more than swinging. There was a group of little boys making a train on a twisty slide. They hooted and hollered as they finally let themselves slide down. A small blonde-haired girl who looked to be around the age of two, was in one of the baby swings, and her mother was pushing her gently. Her small legs stuck straight out and her innocent smile was full of joy.

Jessi let out a deep breath and folded her hands across her tummy, vowing that she would never think of babies as fetuses again. They would grow into living, breathing children like those playing in front of her. She looked at the little boys on the slide again, then back at the little girl in the baby swing and found herself wondering what her own babies would be. Maybe she would have two boys or two girls, or maybe one of each. Whatever the case, it didn't matter to her. What mattered is that they would be a part of Joe that she would have forever.

The sky was blue, the late fall sun shone down on her, and the wind played with her hair. She sat and watched the kids for a long time. When her cell phone rang in the early afternoon, she was relieved to see Jari's number. Jari sounded worried as she asked where she was. When the older woman gently prompted, Jessi agreed to go back to the mall to meet her.

Jessi got back in her car, revived. The sun and children's laughter had refreshed her heart and given her new hope.

This time, she parked her car at the mall and climbed out. She met Jari inside the front door, and Jari gave her a long, tight hug. "I wish I could take back what he said today," Jari said, her expression sad.

"It's okay. I'm used to it," Jessi responded, her voice dull. Jari shook her head emphatically.

"It is *not* okay," she responded fiercely.

Jessi thought of telling her what she had considered doing, but decided against it. Instead, she opted for the better news. "I felt the babies move earlier."

Jari's sorrowful expression transformed into one of sheer excitement. "You did? When? How did it feel?"

"A couple of hours ago. It just felt like a little flutter, but I knew it was them. It happened twice."

Jari's pretty face spread into a grin. "They were both saying hello."

"Maybe so."

Jari looped her arm through Jessica's and started pulling her deeper into the mall. "We have some shopping to do today. I want to look for ideas for the nursery."

Jessi shook her head in confusion. "The nursery? I'm not allowed to stay, and I don't know where I'll go yet... there may not be a nursery for awhile."

Jari leveled her gaze at Jessica, and her intensity conveyed the finality of her words. "You're staying. Bill has agreed. You and the babies will have the east hall."

Jessi didn't know what to say as she felt fear and despair fall away. Even if she had to endure her father, she would have a home to raise her children in. She nodded and managed a tight, "Thank you." She wasn't sure how to express her overwhelming gratitude to this lady who had so thoroughly surprised her, coming to her defense time and time again. Since arriving in D.C., and especially since finding out about her pregnancy, Jari had given her the greatest gift Jessi could ask for – she had given her hope.

~~~~~

"Two girls!" Dr. Corvich said, moving the ultrasound transducer to double-check the gender of Jessi's babies. Jessi caught her bottom lip between her teeth and smiled, looking at the images on the screen. Two little backbones, both perfectly formed, four little hands, four little feet, two precious little heads. Two girls.

Jari released a delighted squeal and clapped her hands. "Girls! Jess, you're having girls! I told you they were girls! I just knew it!"

The swishing sounds of their little heartbeats filled the room, sounding as if two people were playing jump rope. Jessi could not stop smiling.

Five

"Are you really going out in that?" Jessi turned from slipping her sunglasses into her hair and raised an eyebrow at her dad.

"I was planning to. What's wrong with it?" She looked down at her black turtleneck sweater and maternity jeans. The shirt had a high neckline, and she could find nothing inappropriate about it.

He shook his head. "No, it's a lovely top, I'm just not sure that it's…well, flattering in your condition," Bill said.

Jessi's eyebrows shot up as his arrow struck its mark. "Are you saying I look fat in this?"

One side of his mouth tipped up. "I didn't say that, Sweetheart, you did."

She threw the contents of her water glass at him. The water soaked his face and splattered the front of his dress shirt. "Don't call me Sweetheart!" she yelled, and ran into her room, slamming the door.

She threw herself onto her bed and buried her face in her pillow. Her cell phone jangled on the bedside table, and she grabbed it. She was so weak at the moment that she hoped it was Joe. She would answer it and tell him she would meet him wherever he wanted if he would just promise that she could be with him forever.

But it wasn't Joe, it was her mom. She clicked the on button and sniffed a hello. She hadn't talked to her mom in ages.

"Jess, how are you, Baby Girl?"

Jessi took a deep breath to steady herself. "I'm doing good. How are you?"

"I'm on my way to a client's office. I'll be there in

just a minute, but wanted to call and say hello."

"It's Saturday, Mom."

"It's really busy at the office right now," Carla said, making excuses as she always did.

"It seems like you're working twenty-four seven," Jessica told her, not able to keep the concern from her voice. There was a slight pause.

"There's no reason to be home anymore," Carla finally answered, her voice full of sorrow.

Jessi wanted to respond, but nothing she could say would help – she knew exactly what her mother meant. She tried to think of something to change the conversation to, but came up blank. She hadn't told her mother she was pregnant, that she was homeschooling, or that life with Bill had become unbearable. She wanted to shelter her mom from everything unpleasant, but now found herself without safe subjects on which to fall back. Her life currently wasn't very interesting. It ended up not mattering, though.

"I saw Joe yesterday. He's home for Christmas break," Carla said casually.

Joe. Jessi's heart stopped beating for a moment, then came back to life with a heavy thud that made her chest ache. "Where?"

"He came over. He brought me some Christmas goodies from Hannah and Kara," Carla paused. "He asked about you again, Hon."

"What did you say?" Jessi questioned instantly. Carla sighed.

"I told him you were doing fine. He didn't ask anything else, but I could tell he wanted to." Jessi swallowed a painful lump in her throat.

Was he forgetting about her? Not that she would blame him; she had left him without an explanation and, for all he knew, she never looked back. He took a risk, and she must have confirmed all of his fears.

"How is he?"

"He looks good. Fit. He looked peaceful...he just looked like he always looks – confident, purposeful...you know." Jessi's heart ached. Yes, she knew.

The desire to see him again, to reside in his confidence, his peace, his purpose, his joy, his love, was almost a physical pain. She knew just what her mom was saying, even though the words hardly did justice. There was no way to describe the green-eyed man. He was indescribable, unfathomable. She wished she could see him with her own eyes. She wanted to see for herself that he was okay.

She saw him every week on television when he rallied his teammates to take wins on the football field, and in the interviews with the college sports broadcasters after the games. But to see him in person, to ask how he was doing, sounded too good to be true. She found herself suddenly jealous that her mom had the opportunity.

"I just pulled up to the office. I need to get inside. Love you," Carla was saying.

"Love you too," was all Jessi had time to answer, then Carla was gone.

"Tell her I can find her an Alcoholics Anonymous group that meets in Glendale," Bill said, a smirk on his face as he meandered into Jessi's room.

"She was working," she explained, instantly defensive.

"Right. Is that what she told you?"

Jessi felt the longing that had filled her just moments earlier, turn to rage. Why wouldn't Bill Cordel let anything go? Why would he forever insinuate that Carla was an alcoholic simply because she had too much to drink during the weeks he was taking her only daughter away by force?

Jessi wanted to scream at him that her mom was doing better now and that her wine intake had ended after having time to adjust to the losses of the spring and summer; yet she knew it wouldn't do any good. He enjoyed focusing on the negative so much that he wouldn't believe her even if she told him. It would do nothing to stop the hurtful way he talked about her mother. Just as no amount of explaining could ever change the way he talked about her.

No, every mistake they had ever made would be ammunition for him for life. And he would never miss an opportunity to cash in. Jessi's mind screamed at her, asking the same question it asked so frequently. *Why did he enjoy hurting people so much?*

Jessi shut her cell phone, then unfolded herself and stood. She closed the distance between them with measured steps. She stopped so close to him that he took a step back, feeling uncomfortable. She followed him.

"You may sneer at her moment of weakness, but she cries because of yours. She works too much when she hurts, but you hurt those who love you. Well, you can't hurt me anymore, Dad. Do you know why?"

"Why, Jessica?" he asked dryly.

"Because I don't love you anymore. How's that feel?" she asked, taking a step back and folding her arms. "How does it feel to have an entire state buffaloed and have the one who knows you best, your daughter, hate your guts? If anyone should be mocked and pitied, it's you. At least she has people who love her. The only people that can even pretend to like you are those on your payroll or who have something to gain by using you. If you were to die today, not one sincere tear would be shed at your funeral. Certainly not by me."

His hand was so quick that she had no time to step back from the slap. It stung her cheek and turned her face violently. "Don't you ever speak to me like that again, Jessica Nicole Cordel."

She pressed her cool hand against her burning cheek, then raised clear, icy blue eyes to his. "Maybe I won't, but you can't keep me from thinking it," she told him. She shoved past him and grabbed her keys.

"Don't you dare leave this house!" he threatened.

"What are you going to do about it?" she taunted.

"I'm serious, Jessica Nicole! If you walk out that door—" Undeterred by his empty threats, she walked out the front door and slammed it, cutting off his words. She was backing out of the drive by the time he flung the front door open. She sped down the street. She didn't have her purse or her cell phone, but there was no way she was going back for either. She had finally had enough.

She'd had enough of his cruel, cutting remarks, his snide innuendos and his general affection for hurting those in his household. It was bad enough when his words inflicted pain on her, but she couldn't stand by as he shot his poisonous arrows at her mother and Jari any longer. She had to get away. Something had to change.

She drove around town for awhile and ended up back at the park just south of the mall. She climbed out of her car, her body stiff, and shrugged on her winter coat to ward off the December chill. She sat on a bench and watched kids play. She closed her eyes and listened to their laughter, pretending that she was young and one of them.

Surely her mother was watching, preparing to push her on the swings. She was only eight, and didn't have a care in the world. The sun would bring freckles to her young cheeks, and she would erupt into giggles as her mom caught her to tickle her.

"Why are you crying?" The small voice rocked her out of her daydream, and Jessi quickly opened her eyes. A little girl with brown hair and eyes was looking at her, concerned. Jessi quickly checked and found that hot tears were rolling off her chin. She hadn't even realized it. She attempted to offer the girl a shaky smile.

"I'm just sad."

"Why?" the little girl questioned. Jessi bit her lip.

"I'm not sure why I'm alive," Jessi answered honestly. The girl giggled.

"I know why you're alive!"

"Why?" Jessi asked with a gentle smile, wiping at her tears with her coat sleeve.

"To help those who are hurting, just like Jesus is helping you." Jessi's mouth fell open and her heart skipped a beat.

"Olivia, time's up! We have to go!" a lady called from a bench not far away. Olivia started toward her mother. Then she turned and impulsively threw her arms around Jessi's neck.

"Don't cry. It will be okay," she whispered to Jessi as she squeezed her neck tightly, then turned to run as her mother called to her again. "Goodbye!" she called over her shoulder with a pretty little wave. Jessi waved back. After watching Olivia take her mom's hand and leave, Jessica doubled over her knees and began to weep.

What she wouldn't give to have that kind of peace and joy, that confidence and assurance – and it resided in just a child! Why couldn't she, at seventeen, figure out something that a child, barely more than a toddler, could?

Jessi felt frustrated and full of sorrow. The longing she had felt so often lately, returned with even greater force. What was she missing? This longing to be loved, to belong, to know someone cared, to work toward something meaningful, to know that there was more to life than what she saw, was overtaking her. While she floundered to understand, a little girl had it all figured out – Jessi had seen it in her face.

Why didn't she understand? Why couldn't she feel the same way? What was it going to take?

She thought of Joe, the Colby's, and Jari. They were like peaceful water in the middle of a storm. They all possessed what she wanted, but she didn't know how to get what they had. And the one thing she had learned over the last year and a half was that she couldn't live off theirs. It wasn't enough to extend to her. She felt better in their presence, but when she was by herself, she was just as lonely, desolate, and empty. Lately, even when she was with Jari, the difference between what they inwardly had was obvious to Jessica.

She had learned enough to know that even as much as she yearned for Joe, he wasn't enough to satisfy the deep longing in her soul. As crazy as the thought was to her, even if she were still with him, he wouldn't be enough.

What had little Olivia meant, saying she was alive to help people who were hurting? And how was Jesus helping her? Were the little girl's words some clue to what she was to do with her life? To what her long-term plan should center around? The idea of helping hurting people appealed to her. Others were hurting like her, like her mom, like the people at the homeless shelter, like the people she saw around her every day. They needed help. Still, she didn't know how. How was a broken person supposed to help broken people? She had nothing to offer.

Her tears having dried, she sighed and watched the children play. It was all so confusing to her. It felt as if the answer was right in front of her, inviting her to understand, but she couldn't. It was like a puzzle that was missing the final piece, and she couldn't tell what the picture was without it.

Jessi stayed at the park all day and into the night. One by one the children left with their parents, and the park emptied. Still, Jessi didn't move from the bench. At that moment, an empty park felt better than her father's house.

It was a little past ten when a tall blonde sat down beside her. Jessi jumped at the lady's sudden appearance, but Jari didn't say anything. She just picked up Jessi's cold hand and held it for a long time. Jessi had cried herself out and had no more tears, so she just sat and looked at the empty playground.

"You're a beautiful girl, Jessica Nicole Cordel. Even

more beautiful because you carry life." Jari must have heard the comments her dad had made about her appearance. Jessi shook her head.

"I used to think I was," Jessi responded, her voice dull.

"Jessi, Sweetie, you are beautiful, smart, wonderful and loved!"

"And loved?" Jessi cried. "By who? My father?"

"By me!" Jari answered emphatically, and Jessi turned and wrapped her arms around her, sobs once again shaking her slender back. Jari smoothed her hair and pressed her own cheek against Jessi's head.

"Go ahead and cry, Dear. Cry out all that hurt."

"Does he enjoy hurting people?" Jessi whimpered. Jari sighed.

"Sometimes, I think he really does."

"I can't take it anymore," Jessi admitted.

"I know."

Jessi took a shuddering breath. "So, Jari, what now?" She almost wished Jari would make good on her threat to leave Bill and take Jessica with her. Jari gave a sad smile.

"Let's go get a bite to eat. I'm starving."

"And then home," Jessi said, her voice dull. Jari nodded slowly.

"Give him another chance, Honey."

"How many? How many chances?" Jessi demanded.

"Seventy times seven," Jari responded softly. Jessi frowned in confusion. "Jesus said seventy times seven," the older lady explained.

"I'm not Jesus," Jessi scoffed.

"No, neither am I." Jessi's heart constricted at the sorrow in Jari's voice.

"Where do you want to eat?" Jessi asked, pushing herself to her feet, changing the subject. Her back ached from sitting, and her legs were numb from the cold. It took a moment to find her balance after sitting for so long.

Jessi saw Jari's eyes move to her cheek as she turned to face her, where she was sure there was now a bruise in the shape of Bill Cordel's hand. Jari pursed her lips, but didn't mention it. Instead, she looped her arm through Jessi's.

"There's a cute little café down the street that stays open until midnight."

Six

Jessi slid into the back pew quietly, glad that no one except the greeter at the front door had seen her come in. She slid her dark sunglasses up into her hair and wrapped her arms protectively around her growing abdomen. All the people around her were standing, singing words to a familiar song. Jessi closed her eyes and took a deep breath. It was familiar because it was a song Joe used to sing. It was wonderful that these people were singing it now.

She had woken up at six in the morning with a desire for Joe that was so intense it made her stomach upset. The babies felt it and started to move and kick. She had no choice but to get up then, so she chose to take a shower and get ready. She went to eat breakfast and found Jari already at the kitchen table, ready for the day. She wondered about Jari's early rising, but didn't ask. The woman hadn't commented on Jessi's quietness, but when Jessi grabbed her car keys, Jari was only one step behind with her own purse.

Once she was out of the house, Jessi climbed behind the wheel of her car, Jari taking the passenger's seat, and drove around town for awhile, not knowing where she was going or what she was looking for. They drove for almost an hour before Jessi spotted a small, peaceful-looking church whose full parking lot implied that a service was taking place. She turned in without thinking twice.

All morning she had felt empty, lonely and scared. Something had to change. She couldn't live like she was living any longer. She couldn't continue with the pointless and hurtful fights with her father, the deep ache of missing Joe, the immanent responsibility of being a single mother of two, the uncertain future, or the meaningless direction of her life. Her future was spiraling wildly out of control, and she was desperate.

She had seen Kara, sweet, innocent Kara, so steady and sure as she relied on her God. She had seen Joe, rock-solid and peaceful because of his God. She had seen Chris and Hannah, calm, loving, and content, living by the name of their God. She had seen Jari live like a lovely, peaceful river in a house full of rapids, because of her God.

Jessi had a revelation that morning when she woke up – the final puzzle piece was Jesus. It had to be. All of the people in her life that had what she wanted – what she really, truly wanted on a soul level – they served this one same God. There was no conclusion to come to other than, if she wanted what they had, that is what she was missing.

But how did it work? She didn't know. How could she have the same God? Would He want her? How did she qualify to serve Him? How did she get Him? What would He require of her? Was there any initiation? How did He really make such a difference in people's lives? How would that look in her own? Was their God the one who had uttered the quiet whispers across her heart? She was afraid of what lied ahead – afraid and confused – but she was determined to find out.

The sign in the front of the church had read, 'Want peace? Find Jesus.' That was enough for her. She had turned in and was out of the car before the engine had completely shut down. Now, she stood very still beside Jari and felt a gentle wave of calm wash over her heart. The tension in her shoulders eased, and her muscles relaxed. She took a deep breath and closed her eyes, listening to the song.

As if Joe was standing beside her, she could hear him singing the melody in his rich, low voice. She sighed in relief. In the entire city of Washington, D.C., this was as close as she could be to him. She smiled at his memory.

"What are you living for? *Who* are you living for?" the pastor's voice was soft and inquiring. Jessi looked up, surprised. The pastor stood in front of the pulpit, looking out at his congregation. "Is what you're living for able to give you what you need? Will it be there for you always; until the end of time and beyond that into eternity?" The pastor squeezed his eyes shut for just a moment, then looked out into the crowd, right at Jessi. His eyes locked with hers. "He only comforts, but Jesus saves. Don't mistake the messenger as the sender anymore, Dear One."

Jessi's face went white. The pastor was talking to her. In front of everyone in the church, he was talking to her. About Joe. She had worshipped him, relied on him as he had worshipped and relied on his God. She could see it now. But how could the pastor know? She dropped her eyes in shame. He nodded to the pianist and another song started.

Jessi's heart beat wildly as she listened to the words. They penetrated her heart. A shiver ran through her. The song spoke of forgiveness, mercy, and unconditional love – the love of Jesus. Her mind was suddenly filled with words Joe's father had read the Christmas of her junior year – words about a heavenly God born on earth, words of a perfect King dying for the sins of the world and rising again on the third day. The memory left just as quickly as it came, and she shivered again as she felt a gentle pull on her heart.

Countless words spoken by Joe ran through her mind, one sentence after another, until she felt as if she might explode. *'Jesus loves you, Jessi.' 'Jesus is waiting for you, Jessi.' 'Turn to Jesus.' 'God is real! He is living, breathing, seeing, real!' 'He waits for us to come home, no matter how long it takes, Jessi.' 'He takes us back, no matter how many mistakes we make.' 'He loves you, Jessi. Open your eyes and see how He loves you.'*

Kara's quiet words spoken throughout their friendship flooded Jessi's mind. *'He'll take care of it.' 'I've prayed about that history test and turned it over to Him. He's in control now.' 'Don't worry about it, Jessi, God has a plan for your mom.' 'Jessi, I know I'm loved and beautiful whether Justin tells me or not. I can't find my identity in him – it's in Jesus.'*

The tugging at her insides became stronger with each remembered phrase. She had felt it at the time, but now it was intense. Broken by the sweet memories, Jessi raised watery eyes to the front of the church. On the back wall was a wooden cross with a white cloth dipped in red hanging across it. As her eyes fell upon it, the children inside her moved violently. She wrapped her arms tightly around her belly and closed her eyes in sorrowful pain as a vision of a broken man on a cross flashed across her mind.

Her mind filled with the picture, as if a movie was playing on a theater screen inside her head. Thunder boomed as His head dropped, and suddenly a curtain ripped in two, the moment undoubtedly of great importance, although she didn't understand why. She felt the heaviness of the moment. She saw the skies grow dark in the middle of day and saw the blood dripping from His hands and feet to the rocky ground beneath Him. She cried out and sank to her knees, her forehead resting against the pew as she felt a crushing sorrow come upon her as she realized that the man was dead.

Then He was there, beside her in her mind, and He reached His bloody hand out to her. She realized that this broken, wounded, sad man was reaching out and offering to take her brokenness, her wounds, her sadness, upon Himself. He had been standing there all along, waiting for her to take His hand, and she simply had not seen it.

How could she not have seen it? It wasn't hard, it wasn't complex, it was just about taking His hand, about saying yes. How could she have missed it, missed *Him* – this glorious Man who radiated goodness and holiness – for so long?

She felt a warm, steady arm reach around her.

"He loves you, Sweetheart, and He's waiting for you. Say yes to Him, Jessi," Jari offered in guidance, and Jessi could feel the woman's warm tears soaking through the sleeve of her sweater.

The reality of Jari's words hit her like a rock. He was waiting for her. He always had been. "Yes, Jesus. I want to stop running from You," Jessi whispered, and Jari held her close, rocking her as she cried.

Jesus Christ, Son of man, Son of God, had been perfect and blameless, yet had come to earth to show *her* the way and died on a cross for *her* – to pay the price required for her to be with Him forever. He had paid the ransom for *her* life. He hadn't come only for the world – it was also personal – He had come for *her*!

A long shiver ran through her. How could she have ignored that? All the things that she had done wrong, all the terrible attitudes she had, all the wrong intentions, and still He was waiting for her. Even after she had ignored His sacrifice, shunned His painful and selfless act that allowed her to come to Him. It was incomprehensible. After all the time she had wasted trying to understand how she could get what Joe, Jari and Kara had, she finally knew the truth. It had nothing to do with what she could do, and everything to do with what He had done. It was His free gift to her, there for the taking.

"Pray with me," Jari offered. The words resounded through Jessi's mind and she heard Joe say them, just as he had a hundred times.

"I'll pray with you," Jessi agreed brokenly.

"Jesus, Prince of Peace, Mighty God," Jessi said the words after Jari. "I invite You into my heart, and I confess with my mouth that You are Lord and Savior!"

Jessi crumbled over her stomach as she prayed, tears starting to run from her eyes. Suddenly, she felt another hand on her back, then another and another, and without opening her eyes, she knew that the people of this church, the other believers in Christ, people who didn't even know her, were surrounding her and praying with her.

"I know You died on the cross for me because You

love me, and I ask that You forgive my sins. I had a debt that I couldn't pay, and You paid my debt that You didn't owe," Jessi repeated, her voice unsteady, her body trembling. "Come into my life. Make me whole. Make me new. Let the old me pass away, and give me new and eternal life in You. I say yes to You, to the gift You offer. Come into my heart and be my God. In Jesus' precious name I pray, Amen."

Jessi knelt quietly for a few more minutes. Peace settled in the pit of her stomach, and she felt washed, clean, new…and full of joy. She opened her eyes and looked up at Jari and smiled, unable to contain the joy that was now flooding her.

Jari had tears dripping off her chin, even as she smiled back. Jari helped her to her feet, and as Jessi looked around, suddenly ashamed, trying to wipe off her tears, all she saw were smiling faces, some streaked with tears of their own. People crowded into her pew, and the kind looking woman on her left reached for her hand. Jari took her other hand and joined hands with the woman beside her. People joined hands until a long chain of people filled the seats of the sanctuary, all of their voices rising up toward the cross at the front.

In the middle of them all was a young mother with dark hair and blue eyes, with a heart that had finally turned to the One who loved her more perfectly than any earthly man could. That day she found the Lover of her soul, the Prince of her peace, the Salvation from her sins, and the Light in her darkness – and although His initials were the same, it was not Joe Colby at all. It was Jesus Christ.

The same God that, a thousand miles away, a young man with pale green eyes and chocolate hair was praying to, weeping before, begging for his lost girlfriend to be saved… just as he had been since six that morning.

Seven

It happened on Bill's way home from the office. He'd had an exhausting day in the senate, and all he wanted was his home, a little scotch and his bed. It had been drizzling all day, as it had for the last week, and his windshield wipers were busy moving the water droplets off his windshield. His suit jacket was damp, and he grimaced as he moved his toes, realizing his socks were sloshy wet from stepping in puddles.

After nearly twenty minutes on the road, he remembered that Jari had texted him a few hours earlier and said Jessica was having contractions. He belatedly lifted his cell phone to check if Jari had texted with any further news. She had.

He clicked on the message to see if he would need to make a U-turn and head to the hospital. The thought of his only daughter lying in a hospital bed giving birth to twins made his mouth press into a thin line. And she was only seventeen. All while that strange Colby boy went on as normal, playing college football and pursuing his degree, as if he didn't have a care in the world. Bill was disgusted, to say the least.

His eyes scanned the text and when he glanced up, it was too late to stop for the red light in front of him. He slammed on his brakes, but the thick layer of rainwater was like ice on the road. The headlights rushing toward his driver's side door were upon him in mere seconds. Horns blared, tires squealed, metal crunched, and then all was quiet.

Bill's cell phone had been flung into the backseat as his car spun, the text message still showing that Jessi's contractions had been a false alarm, and his womenfolk were waiting for him at home.

~~~~~

Jessi was pacing the floor again as she had been for the last twenty minutes. Jari licked her finger and turned the page of her book.

"Sit down, Jess. Your twinsies are already trying to come too early. Lie down and put your feet up like Dr. Corvich said."

"Something's wrong." Jari put down her book.

"With you? With the babies?" she questioned.

"No, with Dad. I keep seeing this picture of his car, and I know something is wrong."

"I told you twenty minutes ago, he's still at work. He said he would be late again. They're still discussing the healthcare bill. The Republicans are objecting to the fact that it covers abortions."

Jessica dropped onto the plush suede sofa. "No doubt Dad supports it." She rubbed her incredibly swollen belly that had long since blocked her view of her lower body. Again the babies were stirring inside, feeling as restless as she was.

"We'll keep praying for revelation for him," Jari answered sadly.

Five minutes later, Jessica was up again. She walked to the window and stared out at the wet, bleak night. It had been raining for days. She again felt the need to pray for her dad. "Jesus, let him be okay. Protect him. Keep him safe. Turn his heart to You. Bring revelation of You, of Your ways, of holiness," she murmured as she continued to stare out at the dark, rainy landscape. She didn't know exactly how to pray, only that she needed to.

Jari yawned and stretched, marking her place in her book and putting it down. "I just read an interesting statement, Jess," Jari said, getting to her feet. Jessi turned toward her.

"What was that?"

"In His great mercy, God uses whatever means necessary to bring us to the cross. Suffering in life can be the best gift if it leads to eternal salvation." Jari's words hit Jessica as being significant, and she mulled over them for several seconds. "I can't keep my eyes open anymore," Jari continued. "I think I'm going to go to bed. Wake me up if anything changes with the girls." Jessi smiled at Jari's affectionate reference to her unborn children, but worry marred her pretty face.

"What about Dad?"

"Did you pray?"

"Yes."

"Then Jesus will take care of it. He knows best, Jess."

"Aren't you worried? What if he's in a car accident? What if he dies?" Jari waited until Jessica met her eyes. Jessi realized that concern showed in the lady's expression, but only concern. There was no fear, no worry. Just concern squeezed in beside a deep peace.

"The LORD is good, Jessica."

"He is," Jessi agreed, feeling small for her weak faith.

Jari crossed the room and put her hand on Jessi's shoulder. "Sometimes the LORD tells us something so we can be prepared."

"Like when He told you that morning that it was my day of salvation?"

"Yes," Jari answered. "If He hadn't told me, I wouldn't have known to be up and ready by seven a.m. to go to church with you – and I wouldn't have received the greatest gift of getting to be with you when you gave your life to Jesus." Jessi nodded.

Was the LORD stirring her heart so she too would be ready for something? She worried about what that something might be.

Jari tugged on a piece of Jessi's dark hair. "When He gives us insight, we are to pray and prepare in any way He leads, but then be at peace. Fear is never his intention. Perfect love casts out all fear. He would not share His workings with you and want them to cause fear in your heart. Cast off fear by trusting in Him completely." Jessi nodded, understanding.

She gave Jari a hug and bid her goodnight. She sat down on the suede sofa, deciding to wait up for her dad just a little longer. She wanted to trust the LORD, but she also wanted to see that her dad was safe with her own eyes.

Two hours later, Jessica heard his key in the many locks on the garage door and looked up just in time to see the door swing open, and her dad walk into the house.

It was very late, and Jessi was curled up on the couch, classical music to stimulate the babies' brain development playing softly from the CD player, a magazine in her hands. She pushed herself up to a sitting position, then stood with some effort and went to meet Bill – something she never did.

"Jessica." His voice sounded strange as he said her name, and he pulled her into a tight hug, shocking her. She let him hug her for what seemed like hours, then pulled back when he finally did. He stared at her, his face pale. "It's late. You were still up?" he asked. She nodded.

"I was waiting for you. I couldn't go to sleep without knowing you were safe. What happened to your car?" she questioned. His mouth fell open.

"How did you know?" he asked, recovering slightly. "Did the police call?"

She shook her head, knowing he wouldn't understand. But then again, maybe the LORD would use it. "I kept seeing your car in my mind and knew something was wrong. I think it was God prompting me to pray for you." Bill stared at her in the strangest way.

"We need to talk," he responded simply. He shook out his umbrella and put it in the umbrella stand, his movements slow, almost robotic. Then he directed her back to the sofa.

She was unnerved by his gentleness.

She couldn't remember a time when they had been in the same room together for this long without one of them saying something mean. Bill sat down in the armchair next to the sofa. He took a minute to grip the arms of the chair and look around his spacious, luxurious home.

"Where's Jari?" he asked.

"She went to bed a few hours ago. She was tired," Jessi answered, curious to hear what he had to say.

He leaned forward in his chair and put his elbows on his knees. "I was in an accident tonight. I ran a red light." Jessi was sad to hear it confirmed, but had been expecting it.

"Daddy, are you okay?" Bill nodded and rubbed the back of his neck.

"Miraculously, yes. But…Jessi, the girl in the other car is dead. She was young and she was pregnant." Jessica's breath caught in disbelief, even as she watched her dad's face crumple. She watched as violent, shuddering sobs began to shake his body.

She had a million questions, wanted to ask him to tell her it wasn't true – that she had heard wrong – that a woman and her unborn baby weren't really dead because of him. She couldn't find the words, though, and if she could have, there was no way he could have answered them.

She crawled off the couch and went to him, slipping her arms around his back, leaning her forehead against his shoulder.

"She's dead, Jessica. The paramedics said she died instantly from the collision. I ran a red light, and a woman is dead. She's dead and I don't even have a scratch!"

The guilt and condemnation in his voice and words caused Jessi to hurt for him even more, and yet what he said was true. There was no disputing or dismissing his guilt. Tears of pain, sorrow, and compassion filled her eyes, and her chest tightened painfully. She wasn't sure what to say, so she just held him as they wept together.

"She should have hit my door, she would have, but she was going too fast. When she hit her brakes, she started hydroplaning. Her car spun around, and she hit the post of the stoplight," he said, barely able to get the words out.

"I ran to her and pulled her out of her mangled car. I did CPR until the paramedics arrived, and Jessica, I tried so hard to make her wake up! I did everything I knew to do, but I couldn't make her start breathing again. When the paramedics got there, I stood there and yelled at them, telling them that they had to bring her back, but no matter how much I yelled, they couldn't." Bill dissolved into more guilty, painful sobs that echoed in the large house.

"Life belongs to God alone. It's one thing we can't control," Jessica murmured softly.

Jari came down the stairs tying her robe, hearing the ruckus. She moaned as Bill retold the story, weeping with them. She sat on the arm of his chair and rocked her usually powerful and mighty husband. He clung to her like a little boy.

"I nearly died tonight. I thought I would never see either of you again. I thought my life was over. But I've been given another chance. Another chance that girl will never have. I rode to the hospital in the ambulance with her – they had hoped they could save the baby. When her family came – her mother, her father, her sisters and husband – they wept and they wailed and then," Bill covered his face and his back shook, unable to go on for a time. "And then, her husband, he walked over to me," Bill continued before sobs shook him again. "He said he knew she was in heaven with Jesus and that he, and the family, forgave me. But…I know I will never be able to forgive myself."

Jessica's breath caught in shock. She was new to the faith, but how could any family, any husband, so quickly forgive the person who was responsible for his wife's death? It was unthinkable. It was incomprehensible.

"Oh, Jesus," Jari murmured quietly. "Jesus comfort

that family tonight. Give them peace. Somehow. Let them know that You were there. That Your eyes were on their woman, that You were with her in that car."

Jessica shook her head, unable to comprehend all that had just happened, all that Jari had just prayed. How could God let such suffering happen? How could He have been in the car as Jari said and still let the young mother-to-be die?

'In His great mercy, God uses whatever means necessary to bring us to the cross. Suffering in life can be the best gift if it leads to eternal salvation.' Jari's words from earlier played across Jessi's mind, and she was struck by their timely significance. Still, her heart and mind wrestled with the events of the night.

"I broke a law, and she paid the price with her life," Bill sobbed in disbelief and intense shame. Jessi looked up and met Jari's eyes. Jari gave her a sad smile. It was an open window – one that came at a terribly high price.

"Bill, that young woman wasn't the first time your mistakes have cost someone their life," Jari told him sadly.

"What do you mean?" he asked, looking up.

As Jari explained the reality of Jesus and His actions to her husband, Jessica watched through watery eyes as her prideful, strong, critical, self-absorbed father crumbled. For the first time in his life, he came face to face with his need for a Savior.

He argued fiercely that Jesus could never forgive him for taking the life of the young woman, but Jari took him to the Scriptures. She showed him the story of Saul, who had orchestrated and condoned the persecution and death of numerous Christians, yet God encountered him, forgave him and used him in a mighty way on the earth.

Jessica was filled with emotion as she watched the desperation in her father's expression turn to hope.

The weight of his sins too great to even stand under any longer, Jessi and Jari knelt beside him as he slid to the floor and asked Jesus Christ for forgiveness, both from the sins of his life, and especially for the fateful decision to run a red light that night.

He confessed his sins to the LORD of Hosts for what seemed like hours, then just lay prostrate before Him and wept at His feet. Jessica led him in a prayer of salvation when Jari nodded to her. When her father looked up, she saw that his expression, his countenance, had been transformed.

In what had been a hard, prideful, tense face, she now saw peace. The hard lines had smoothed out, and his dull and condemning eyes were full of light.

The difference caused Jessi to praise and thank the LORD in awe. He had brought down the proud, the mighty, the powerful Bill Cordel for the purpose of love, of healing, of relationship. She felt small and insignificant before One so great, and she had the sense that she had just witnessed a very real and significant moment, where God had reached down from heaven into the affairs of man to turn one heart toward Him.

Yes, the LORD had allowed great suffering to take place that night, both for their family as they grieved for the young mother-to-be and for the young mother's family. But He had a plan to bring about eternal salvation. The pain and the grief were real, and Jari explained to both Jessi and Bill that while God had not caused Bill to text while driving or to run the red light, He had known it was going to happen. He hadn't caused the accident, but He had brought some good out of something that had been the consequence of Bill's bad decision.

Jessica was convinced that the young believer had asked the LORD to use her life to bring about the salvation of lost souls, and He had – the salvation of Jessica's own father. Never more aware of the reality, the consequences, or the possibilities of what she was offering, Jessi knelt down with her forehead to the ground and asked God to use her life, no matter the cost, to bring true salvation to someone lost in darkness, trapped and enslaved to sin.

That girl from the accident would never know what Bill Cordel had truly been like before that fateful night, but Jessi did, and she saw how he had already changed. If the LORD could use her yielded life to bring just one person out of such deep darkness and into the light, then it was all worth it.

It was only then that Bill remembered to tell Jessi and Jari that the doctors and nurses had been able to save the baby – a little girl. In more ways than one that night, out of death had come life.

Eight

Jessica hurt for her dad during the days and weeks that followed the accident. The press had a heyday with the event. He was constantly worn out from press conferences and dealing with lawyers to try to resolve the issue. Some people were gracious, sticking by their senator, while others flung nasty names and words, calling him a murderer.

The days seemed long and sad, and they went by slowly. Jessica wasn't sure whether to hurt more for her dad, who was beside himself with feelings of guilt and grief while having the accident thrown back in his face every time he turned around, or for the family who was mourning their beloved wife, daughter and sister. Her heart was so full of sadness that she constantly felt heavy and quiet. She could tell that Jari felt the same way.

Jari and Jessi accompanied Bill to the funeral of the young woman. It was an exhausting and grief-filled event, and the three of them found themselves in tears, despite having never known the girl. The evidence of her quiet life of faith and love was overwhelming, and the family asked if Bill would publicly share his testimony of coming to know the LORD through her death. They said it was what Lydia would have wanted – for the gospel to be preached.

In the wake of the accident and the funeral, Jessi couldn't remember a time in her life when Bill was so content to be home. He didn't miss one dinner that week or speak one harsh word. He sat and read with Jari and Jessi in the evenings, and they popped popcorn and watched movies together.

Bill often laid his hand on Jessi's swollen stomach to feel his grandchildren, who were increasingly less active as their space became cramped, and reminisced about when Carla had been pregnant with Jessica. On Sunday, Bill escorted his family to church for the first time in his life.

Jessi couldn't believe how much her family and her life had changed. All because of one Jewish man who had been put to death around two thousand years prior. When she talked to Jari about it, Jari wept.

"I have prayed for this, petitioned the LORD for this so many times," Jari responded. "I begged Him to heal this family that I had broken."

Jari's confession sent a shiver through Jessica. "We were broken long before you came along. Despite how it started, God used you to save us," Jessi had answered.

Now, as Jessi sat on her hospital bed, she reflected on the events of the last few weeks between contractions. They had been the most emotional and transformational weeks of her entire life.

Her dad and Jari were both on their way to the hospital. They had been visiting the family of the young woman again. Bill and Jari had visited them a couple of times since Bill had gone to apologize and tell his story – that their Lydia's death had brought him eternal life. This time they had taken a baby gift for the little girl.

Dr. Corvich walked in and smiled at Jessica, just as another contraction seized her. She breathed through it as she had been told, and Dr. Corvich checked her progress when it was over. She was dilated to seven centimeters.

As she waited for her dad and Jari to arrive, Jessi's thoughts turned to Joe. She wished she could tell him about what had happened. He would be so proud. And so excited. She thought about how wonderful it would be if he was in the hospital with her. If he somehow knew, she hoped he would thank her for what she was doing. She was protecting him, protecting his dreams, and she hoped he would understand that.

Since the first time she had gone to church with Jari,

she had been wondering more and more if she was doing the right thing by not telling Joe about the babies. Was she being dishonest or misleading by not telling him the truth? Was she committing a sin? Recently, she had begun to worry that he would be angry if he knew. She had thought she was doing the right thing – her intentions had been good. She hoped she hadn't been misguided. Either way, she always came to the conclusion that she had gone too far to turn back now.

Looking back, she was certain she had made the decision to leave Glendale for reasons that were greater than Joe. By coming back to D.C., she had found Jesus and reconciliation with her father and step-mother. That was more important than mere happiness, or even young love.

Still, she thought as she settled back in her bed and braced for the next contraction that was coming, it would be really nice to have Joe beside her, holding her hand, encouraging her that she could get through the next several hours. Joe and her mom.

She had told Carla about the girls shortly after Christmas, unable to keep it from her any longer. The conversation hadn't been easy. Carla was shocked and disappointed. More than anything, though, she was sad Jessi hadn't told her earlier. She promised to keep the information to herself and was hurt by Jessi's assumption that she would tell her secret. Now, with the difficult conversation behind them, she was on a plane headed for D.C.

Jessi had texted Carla when she left for the hospital, and Carla had found a seat on a last-minute flight. Checking the clock on the wall, Jessi saw that her mom should be landing in an hour. A contraction rolled over her, and she focused on riding it like a wave, catching her breath as it passed.

Moments later, Jari and Bill rushed in the door of her hospital room as if they were going to miss the birth. Bill's face went white as soon as he saw his daughter in the hospital bed, an IV in her arm. Jari was grinning, clapping her hands and squealing. The exhaustion that had shadowed her pretty face before they left the house that afternoon, was now gone.

"They're coming, they're coming!" Jari sang, doing a little dance as she approached Jessi's bed. Bill took up a stiff residence at Jessi's free side, looking as if he would not be moved for anything. Jessi grinned at her step-mom. "Yes, ma'am, they are!"

Another contraction came. Jari took Jessica's hand and coached her through it as they had practiced at birthing class. Bill lost a little more color in his face.

"What do we do now?" he asked when it was over. Jari shot him a sympathetic smile.

"We wait."

~~~~~

Jessica was dilated to nine centimeters by the time Carla rushed in the door. Jessi was in the midst of a contraction, but gave her mom a weak smile. As it passed, Carla ran to her side and hugged and kissed her as Bill stepped back. Overjoyed by her mom's arrival, Jessi had precious little time to enjoy it as the contractions were less than sixty seconds apart now.

"Mom, Jari's going to be my labor coach – we went to classes together – but please, hold my hand until it's done." Carla shot a glare up at Jari as she gripped Jessica's outreached hand tightly.

"I'm not trying to take your place, I just went to class with her," Jari told the pretty, dark-haired lady quietly. Carla's face relaxed somewhat, and she directed her attention back to Jessica.

~~~~~

"Jess, push. You have to push!" Jari cried, holding Jessica's hand. Jessi's hair was soaked with sweat, her face was red, her eyes closed, and her body rigid with pain. She yelled and pushed, tears rolling out of her eyes.

"Don't let any sound come out your mouth, Jessica, you use that force to push with. Put it behind the baby," Dr. Corvich coached.

"Oh Jesus, please help Jessi. Give her strength, LORD," Jari prayed. Carla slipped another ice chip in her daughter's mouth.

"You're okay, Jess. You're doing a great job! Push again, Baby Girl!" Carla told her. Jessi gave another push.

"Baby number one is crowning!" Dr. Corvich told them happily. Jari looked up and gave Bill, who was now standing outside the door looking anxiously in through the little window, a thumbs-up sign. She saw him visibly relax.

"Rest, Jessi," Dr. Corvich instructed. "Okay, now!" Jessi pushed until her strength was spent.

"Are you doing okay?" Jari asked, brushing the hair back from her eyes. Carla slipped another ice chip between her dry lips.

"I want Joe!" Jessi moaned, crying. She saw her mom and step-mom exchange a glance, as if asking each other if they should call the boy or stick to her previous wishes.

"Get right back at it, Jessi. Push again," Dr. Corvich was saying. Jessi pushed, her hands balling into fists, the scream getting stuck in her throat. "That's it, that's it, keep pushing. Give me everything you've got, Jess."

"Push, Baby Girl, push!" Carla coached, squeezing her only daughter's hand.

After a few more pushes, Doctor Corvich was holding the first baby. It was quickly passed off to a nurse as its twin was right behind. By the time baby number two was born and Jessica was ready to hold her daughters, baby number one was bathed, diapered and wrapped in a warm pink blanket with a pink cap on her little red head.

Jessica eagerly accepted her from the nurse, her hands shaking, tears running unchecked down her cheeks, a bright smile lighting up her eyes. With her first look at her daughter's face, she felt her heart soar.

Jari had not left her post at the side of Jessi's bed, her hand still on Jessica's shoulder. Carla sat up on the bed beside her daughter, her arm around Jessi's shoulders, looking down at her new granddaughter in delight. Bill walked in cautiously and came up behind Jari to get a closer look.

Jessi held her daughter close and covered her face with kisses. She held the tiny little hand, and the baby wrapped her fingers around Jessi's thumb. Jessica squealed, proud as she could be, and brushed another kiss against the little red head. "Look at her! *Look at her!*" The adults watched with huge grins, and Carla ran her fingertips over the baby's face.

"Hello, Sweetheart. We're so glad to have you here!" Jari said, leaning in close to grasp the baby's other hand.

"Okay, Sweet Pea, let's get that little one moved to your left arm, so little girl number two can go in your right," Dr. Corvich said as she helped to position the two babies. The second baby was wrapped in a warm purple blanket with a purple cap on her red head. She was just as beautiful as her sister.

Jessica sat and held both of her girls, her smile huge, her heart overflowing. They were beautiful, perfect, and healthy.

Her family crowded around, holding the babies' little hands and touching their little heads. As wonderful as her family had been, Jessi looked at them sitting around her and wished that Joe was there, too – sitting beside her, holding her close. She needed his grin, the pride she knew she would see in his eyes, the tenderness of his touch and his steady strength. She needed the love that would be pouring out of his eyes, his mouth, his heart, and running over her like cool water. She was sure he would be holding both girls by now, as proud a papa as there ever was.

Jari read her mind and ran her hand over Jessi's hair. "He'll be here in a couple of hours if you'll let me call him." Jessica took a deep, ragged breath and smiled bravely, shaking her head.

"No. Nothing has changed," she answered.

"Except that he's a father," Jari pushed.

"Jari, no," Jessi said firmly.

Jari glanced to Carla then Bill, as if for support, but finally nodded, accepting Jessica's decision.

"What are you going to name them?" Carla asked, changing the subject and smiling as Jessica moved to hand her one of the girls. Carla gladly took the one wrapped in pink, and Jessi turned and settled the one in purple in Jari's waiting arms.

Jessica beamed, her attention back on her tiny daughters. She gave them each a kiss on the head. "This little pink girl is Kelsi Morgan, and this purple girl is Kamryn Montana — after one aunt and two very special little girls in a homeless shelter."

Nine

Joe sat on his bed, his laptop on his lap, looking up information for a history paper that would serve as his midterm. He was supposed to be researching the Aztec civilization, but typed "Jessica Cordel, D.C." into the window of his search engine instead. He drummed his fingers on his keyboard, trying to decide whether or not to hit 'find.'

He was supposed to let her go, and he knew that, but the way he missed her felt like a physical pain inside him. With one click of his mouse, he knew he could find photos if not news stories; one of the pluses of having a girlfriend whose father was in politics. He could at least see her and know she was okay. It was the beginning of March, and he hadn't laid eyes on her in almost a year. It would be comforting to at least see a recent picture, see what she had been doing, if there was any news.

His finger hovered over the mouse, but he finally hit delete and erased her name. The LORD had asked him to give her up, to lay her down, to leave her to Him and lose all track of her. As hard as that was, he was pretty sure searching her on the internet would be a direct violation.

"LORD, she's yours. I'll focus on what's before me. Take her where You will. Do with her what You will. I'll stay out of it. And LORD, if You decide to bring us back together someday, it will be all You. I won't try to make it happen on my own. I won't try to create anything by knowing her business. Thank You for saving both of us through Your great mercy," Joe murmured into the empty room.

He began researching the ancient civilization and in a few hours, had all the information he would need to write a thorough paper. When he went to bed around one o'clock, he was sure he would get an 'A' on his mid-term, ensuring his 'A' in the class.

But as it often did lately, sleep evaded him. All he could think about was a dark-haired, blue-eyed girl in D.C. He wondered how she was doing, what she was doing, where she was. He remembered how hard, cold, and empty she had been when she moved to Glendale, and hoped she hadn't reverted back to that.

When he had first met her, she was all alone in the world, and she knew it. The loneliness in her eyes was sometimes almost more than he could stand. Back then, she was so focused on surviving, trying to fill the emptiness inside of her with anything that could provide temporary fulfillment. And he had been just that.

Again, he asked the LORD to save her, asked Him to open her eyes and let her see what would bring true fulfillment. Despite his prayer and concerns, Joe had a feeling deep down that Jessi hadn't gone back to the way she was before. He had a feeling God had taken away her temporary fix to give her something lasting and eternal. Joe prayed that was the case.

He let his memory drift back through his year with Jessica, and again loneliness filled him as it had since she left. He had tasted of having a companion so deep and connected that they started to feel like one. Without her, he felt as if part of himself was missing. And it wasn't a companionship he could find with any other girl.

Jessica was different. There was something wild and rebellious about her, but underneath that, she was so tender and innocent and loving. The front she put up was one she had been forced to use to survive, but he had fallen in love with her as he watched it fall.

She had been such a mixture of a woman and a girl, so complicated to understand and sometimes tricky to handle. One minute she would be yelling at him, and the next she would throw herself on him, begging him not to break up with her, telling him she was sorry. Sometimes she was so independent, cold and almost snotty, then she would turn around and be loving and kind. He hadn't known exactly what to make of her then, and he still didn't, but he did know that he loved it – loved her. She was a challenge. Not in getting her, that had been easy, but in keeping her, understanding her, helping her to uncurl out of the tight ball of self-defense she had come to exist within.

And it was no wonder she was like she was. Once, when she was mad because he signed her up for something without checking with her first, she had said "We're all kings or pawns, Joe, and I've been a pawn my whole life, being moved around for other people's advancements. I've had no purpose of my own other than to serve someone else's interest, and I'm done." With that mentality, the rebellious attitude, the anger, the emptiness and the way she withdrew made perfect sense. As did her leaving.

He was certain her decision to leave Glendale had been in accordance with the will of God. He believed it was best, even as hard as it was. He was sure she had motives that were good. But subconsciously, he knew she had been running. She had let him closer than she had ever let anyone get before. She had given herself to him, heart, soul and body, and the control she surrendered by doing so had gone against everything she had ever taught herself about staying safe. The repercussions of that last night had shaken her down to her very core.

Again, he was struck with the thought that he was more to blame for her leaving than she was. Despite the forgiveness he had received, his actions had still come with consequences. Unfortunately, the consequence had been losing Jessica, losing the only girl he had ever loved.

~~~~~

Jessi groaned as she saw the front page of the newspaper Jari had just dropped in front of her. They had known the story was coming since the reporter had showed up at the hospital the day after the twins' birth, but that didn't make it any easier to handle.

A picture of Bill trying to keep the media out of Jessica's hospital room was splashed across the front page with the headline 'Senator Cordel's teen daughter gives birth to twins' above it. Jessica skimmed the story, thankful that the hospital had kept her affairs relatively private.

Bill, at the urging of his public relations coordinator, had released several statements about the incident. "Jessica had twin girls. Mother and daughters are doing well and are in good health. We are celebrating the girls' birth. Our family will rally around Jessica and her daughters and the situation is being handled privately," were all sentences the story quoted.

"Hopefully the press will be satisfied that it's not a scandal, there's no family fallout, it's not a secret and just let it go," Jari told her, dropping down in the dining room chair beside her.

"Do you think they will?" Jessi asked hopefully. Jari raised one shoulder and gave Jessica an encouraging smile.

"We can hope."

Jessica had just finished feeding Kelsi and Kamryn and was still patting Kelsi's small back, hoping to get out any uncomfortable bubbles that may be trapped in the baby's tummy. Jari reached out and ran her thumb across the baby's soft cheek, then looked around for Kamryn. Jessi had her lying on a blanket on the floor beside her. Jari bent and scooped her up, careful not to wake the sleeping girl.

"How many papers do you think will run the story?" Jessi asked, unable to dismiss her worry.

"Well," Jari paused. "I don't know. It will for sure run in the D.C. papers, and may make it on the news."

"I never thought about the fact that Joe could find out through the media," Jessi said miserably. If he was going to know, that was not how she wanted him to find out.

"Maybe you should tell him yourself rather than letting him find out from the press," Jari suggested. Jessica considered the option, but then shook her head no.

"He may find out, but there's a chance he won't. If I tell him, he certainly will. I want him free to follow his dreams, Jari."

"But what if his dreams include you?" Jari asked, sounding frustrated.

"Jari, I'm not telling him!" Jessica responded firmly, hoping it was love and not fear that fueled her determination. They were both quiet for several moments.

"Do you think he'll read it in the paper?" Jessi asked, glancing down at the newspaper again.

"Maybe he will, maybe he won't. Trust that the LORD knows best," Jari said simply. Jessi nodded.

Throughout the next week, several of the local papers ran the story, but without a scandal to report or a fight to expose, the story died down. Hungry for some sort of tragedy or outrage, the news stories concerning the Cordel family were turned back to the accident. While she wished they weren't in the news at all, she was glad her teenage pregnancy was a spent story.

For the next month, Jessica felt as if she was holding her breath, but there was no word from Joe or the Colby family. Finally, in late May, she relaxed. If they had found out about her secret, she was sure she would have heard from them, and if they were going to find out through the media, they would have already.

Her secret was safe. Joe was free to go on following his dreams. She was free to make the best of things and carve out a new life for her and her little daughters.

Ten

Three years later...

"Joe Colby!" The feminine voice pulled Joe from his thoughts, and he nearly couldn't hide a grimace as he turned. Class had just let out and he was in a hurry to get to football practice. The blonde-haired girl running down the hall after him was one he didn't recognize. A newby.

Reaching him, she held out a marker and pointed toward the front of her shirt. Barely able to put up with yet another overly eager fan, Joe shook his head. "I don't autograph shirts." The girl started to pout, then smiled.

"I'm Clarissa. I'm in your history class. I'm going home for fall break and I want to show my friends I know you. You are like a hero where I come from!"

It always started this way. Her flirty smile reminded him of a hundred other girls. Hoping to be as kind as possible in the process, he was determined to nip this in the bud before it went any further. He knew what would come next – he'd heard all the lines before.

"Clarissa, I'd be happy to sign your history test when we get them back tomorrow in class or your notebook."

"Well, if you would want to walk with me back to the lounge, I could—" Joe held up a hand. He had known the last plea was coming.

"I don't date, Clarissa. At all. No exceptions. Not one dinner, not one drink, not one walk." He turned and walked away without waiting for her reply.

He had been harsh, but now in his fourth season as a collegiate star quarterback, he had wised up. He knew all the ploys, all the tricks, and all the games some girls played to be able to say they were dating one of the football players. He also knew that something as harmless as a walk could turn into something more in the mind of a girl, as well as starting rumors that were nearly impossible to dispute. And while some of his teammates enjoyed the constant feminine attention their uniforms ensured and milked it for all it was worth, he wasn't interested.

He hurried out of the building and down the stairs, shoving his textbooks back in his bag, jogging toward the locker room. Practice started in fifteen minutes, and he didn't want to have to run the laps required if he showed up late.

In the locker room, he shoved his bag into his locker and grabbed his pads and practice jersey. He put on his football pants and cleats, then pulled off his t-shirt and replaced it with an athletic shirt, which he topped with his pads.

"Colby!" Joe looked up and grinned at his number one receiver who was walking toward him with one of the offensive linemen.

"Hey boys. How's it going?"

Andrew Michaels, the third best receiver in the league, leaned against the locker next to Joe's. "Not too bad. Not too bad at all." Joe shoved his clothes into his locker and shut it, turning to the grinning man next to him with a knowing look.

"What is it Michaels? Spit it out already," Joe said good-naturedly.

Michaels suddenly became animated, the lineman behind him nodding his agreement before Michaels even started talking. "There's a new club opening tonight downtown, and it's going to be smashing. Come with us! We can have a few beers, chase a few girls, have some fun. What do you say?"

"Not tonight, boys," Joe responded instantly.

"Oh, come on, Colby! You never come out and have any fun with us," Michaels said, his voice taking on a bit of a whine.

For just a moment, Joe hesitated. He was growing weary under the constant battering from his teammates, his classmates, his friends. They were always asking him to do things with them, to do what they were doing. It wasn't as if he sat in his dorm room all the time without having any fun – he did things, lots of things. But they were always asking him to go further, to do the things they were doing – things they knew he didn't agree with.

However, he had learned a valuable lesson in high school, one that he wouldn't soon forget. He couldn't plow into a dangerous situation expecting he could withstand the temptation and bring those around him to salvation without being prepared and constantly on guard. He was a man of flesh and bone, just as subject to temptation as the next one, and without the pride that had misled him in the past into thinking he wasn't.

He didn't think going to a new club was a way to bring glory to God or that it was overly wise. Drinks and girls, Michaels had said. Joe wasn't interested in either, yet he was not foolish enough to believe he was above temptation.

Since Jessi left Glendale, he had learned a lot about who he was, who Christ was, and how to protect his convictions and positions, while still reaching the world around him. He had learned that sometimes bringing in the lost meant going to where they were in order to reach them. Sometimes, he went places or into situations that he normally wouldn't, for the sake of being with someone who was there. But that was different than simply going for a night out.

Jesus had hung out with sinners, but He had done so with a clear understanding of who He was and what His purpose was. The outing Michaels was describing didn't seem like one that was purposeful, nor one that would accomplish anything of worth. Instead, it could put Joe in a compromising situation unnecessarily. He would go merely for entertainment and choosing the easy way out rather than putting forth the effort to say no one more time. But again, he had learned a lot since Jessi left, and sometimes 'no' was the answer that came with the least amount of heartache.

Jessi. Her image flashed before him now and brought a smile to his face. If she were at the club, he would be there before it opened. Unfortunately, he was sure she wouldn't be. *Jessica.* He said her name slowly in his mind. She was the only girl he wanted, the only girl he had room in his heart or mind for.

"Sorry, boys," he said again. "Not tonight."

"Oh come on, Joe. Beer, girls – what's not to like? And the girls will be especially nice if you come along! We need you, Man!" Michaels pressed.

"Two good-looking guys like you don't need my help to get girls," Joe pointed out with a grin. Still, his words did little to dissuade them. They must have taken his contemplative silence a few seconds earlier as a real encouragement. Scrambling for an excuse, he gave them the one that felt the truest. "I'm a married man, Michaels. I don't want any girl other than the one I'm already committed to."

He may not be married legally, but he was in every way that mattered to him. He had vowed one girl – one girl for his entire life – and he knew who that one girl was. Now, it was just a waiting game.

He grabbed his helmet and left his teammates staring after him, their jaws sagging from the news he had just shared. Leaving the locker room, he pushed thoughts of anything but football out of his mind and ran out onto the field.

Hours later, after practice and dinner with his teammates, he walked across campus to his dorm, every muscle in his body aching. As he climbed the stairs to his floor, his legs burned, and as he opened the door to his dorm room, he was glad to see that his roommate was gone. Over the last three years, he had become good friends with his roommate, Jackson, who was also on the football team. They had a lot of fun together, but tonight he wanted to be alone.

He took a hot shower and drank as much water as he could stand. Then he laid down on his bed and let his mind go to the place he had been fighting to keep it from all day, just as he had to every day.

Jessica.

"How is she today, LORD?" he asked into the stillness of his room. "Safe," was the answer that came, and Joe was glad. He spent the next thirty minutes praying for his girlfriend, whom he hadn't seen in years. When he ran out of words, he came back to the place where he found himself day after day after day.

"She belongs to You, LORD. I lay her down again. If it's Your desire that we be together someday, then let it happen. If it's not, keep her away. Let Your will, not mine, be served in her life. Let Your will be done."

Every day since Jessica left, he had prayed that prayer or one like it. Every day he had submitted his will to the LORD's, particularly where Jessica was concerned. Every day he made it known that he was committed to the LORD first and foremost, before any woman, man or activity – as much for his own knowledge as the LORD's. Joe was pretty sure God, who knew the thoughts of men, knew where his commitments lie whether he told Him or not. He was the one that sometimes had to be reminded.

Feeling once again at peace and able to think about other things, Joe sat up and pulled out his textbooks. It was already eight o'clock and in twelve hours he had a test he had neglected studying for. He couldn't afford to be distracted any longer. He pulled out his physics book and got to work.

When his phone rang an hour and a half later, he was

thankful for the break. He was even happier when he saw his dad's number. Answering, he chatted with his dad for almost an hour, catching up on all that was happening at home and filling him in on what was going on at school. His parents were coming to his game on Saturday, and Joe was looking forward to seeing them.

After hanging up, Joe convinced himself to study one more hour, then after texting Kara back and forth for several minutes to check in, went to bed. About an hour later, Jackson came into the room, waking him up with his usual ruckus. The running back didn't have a quiet bone in his body.

When Jackson hit him with a pillow, Joe answered with a groan and tried to push him away. He wanted to sleep. The pillow thumped him on the back of the head again, and this time Joe rolled over. As usual, he didn't have to wonder what Jackson was thinking for long. "Man, Michaels said you said you was hitched. Were you messin'? I told him you were, but he swore you was as serious as ever."

Joe groaned. Why had he ever said that? As if he didn't get enough questions about his love life. "It's complicated," he said, still groggy.

"Well, I figured that much, considering you've been living with me for the past three and a half years, and I ain't never seen or heard nothin' 'bout your wife! Is it true? Tell me what you was talking 'bout!"

Joe looked at his friend out of one half-closed eye. "Go to sleep, Jackson."

"C'mon, Man! Okay, fine. At least tell me her name. And tell me if you're married." Joe considered it for a brief moment, then simply groaned again and rolled over.

"I'm going to sleep. I have a physics test in the morning and unlike some people in this room, I want to get good grades."

"Hey! I never said I don't want good grades," Jackson told him. "If they fell in my lap, I'd say *sweet*! I just ain't gonna put *my* time into getting them." Joe pulled his pillow over his head. "Okay, fine, you go on to sleep then, but we'll be talkin' 'bout this in the mornin'!" Joe didn't respond.

Eleven

Eighteen months later…

Jessica sipped her coffee slowly, watching the girl across the table from her. Tacy had matured and changed since high school. Her red curls were still charmingly wild and her skin just as tanned, but she seemed wiser and more at peace.

Jessi set her coffee down and wrapped her hands around the cup. "You must like it up in Idaho. You look fantastic." Tacy nodded.

"It's great." She stopped and blushed. "Although, I'm pretty sure Guatemala would be great if Trae was there."

Jessica's eyebrows lifted in question as a smile spread across her face. "Trae?" Tacy nodded, a smile threatening to stretch out her face.

"He's an architect. Twenty-seven. Dark hair, dark eyes, his mother is Italian."

"An architect? Impressive. How long have you known him?"

"We met my sophomore year of college, but we've only been going out for about a year now," Tacy hesitated, suddenly shy. "Rumor has it that he was seen in a jewelry shop last week making a very small and expensive purchase."

Jessica's face was animated as she leaned forward in her seat, grabbing her friend's hand. "Tace, are you serious? That's amazing! What will you say?" Tacy broke into another bright smile.

"Heck yeah! He's incredible, Jess! He is one of the best men I've ever met. He's kind, loving, and he's such a gentleman! He opens doors for me, and always picks up the check – that's hard to come by these days. He actually reminds me a lot of Joe Colby."

In her excitement, Tacy had slipped up, exposing the elephant in the room. Now, she fell quiet as she watched the brief look of pain and regret flicker across Jessi's face.

"Sounds like a keeper," Jessi said smiling, her eyes sad.

Since the subject had already been opened, Tacy decided to get the answers she had been curious about for the past five years. "Is he why you left?"

Jessi took a drink of coffee and tried to think of how to explain. "Partly," she finally answered, not coming up with any great explanation.

"Do you ever talk to him anymore?" Tacy probed.

"Not since I left." Jessi gave a small laugh. "I used to watch him play football on television, but since he graduated, I've lost track of him. I don't know where he is these days, what he's doing or even if he's married."

Tacy was quiet for a moment, then shook her head. "I haven't heard. I did hear that Kara married Justin Troyer last summer. I got an invitation but couldn't make it – my cousin was getting married the same weekend in California."

Jessi's eyebrows shot up in surprise, her smile quick. "Are you serious? That's perfect! I knew they would get married – they were so right for each other."

"Yeah, it was never a big mystery who they would end up with. From the time she entered high school, they were inseparable." Jessi nodded, and looked out the window of the café thinking back to the pixie-faced blonde.

She had missed her over the years. So much that she often thought about calling, but never had the nerve. Now she had missed one of the most important days in Kara's life. Regret filled her.

"Kind of like you and Joe," Tacy continued softly, pulling Jessi back from her thoughts.

"Some things change, Tacy."

"Why? He didn't want it to. That much was obvious. He missed you so much. So did his whole family." Tacy winced as she continued. "So did I." The pain was obvious in her voice, and Jessi sighed as she reached across the table to cover Tacy's hand with her own.

"I'm sorry I left without saying goodbye." Tacy diverted her eyes.

"So, Jessi, what have you been doing since the end of our junior year? You just disappeared," Tacy continued, breezing over the serious turn in the conversation.

Jessi started to bite her fingernail as she looked at Tacy. She had been hoping the conversation wouldn't come to this. "I got pregnant." The news hit Tacy as hard as Jessica had expected.

"You're serious?"

Jessica nodded slowly. "You can't tell anyone."

Tacy shook her head. "I won't, Jess. When? After you came back here? What happened?" Jessica hesitated for a moment, realizing Tacy didn't understand.

"I had twin girls. Kelsi and Kamryn – they're four now."

Tacy narrowed her eyes and tipped her head in thought. "Those names together sound so familiar," she paused. "Oh, that was Joe's older sister. Kara used to talk about her some. She died when she was little, though."

Jessica gave her a soft smile and quietly said, "I know. I thought it was fitting."

Understanding suddenly dawned on Tacy, and her shoulders slumped. "Wow." Jessica nodded but stayed quiet. "Do you have pictures?" Tacy asked softly after a moment. Intense relief washed over Jessica, and she nodded and pulled her wallet out of her purse with a smile. She held the pictures out to Tacy, and Tacy smiled as she flipped through them. "They're beautiful, Jessi." Jessi took them back when Tacy finished and paused to smile at the pictures of her two girls.

"Yeah, they are."

"You can definitely tell they're Joe's – they look just like him."

"Yes, they do," Jessi agreed.

"So, did you finish high school?" Tacy asked.

"My step-mom homeschooled me actually, so I could finish. She has helped so much with the girls over the years. I couldn't have done it without her," Jessi paused. "I took a heavy course load, and graduated with my bachelor's last year."

"Wow! I'm impressed. I just graduated with mine in May, and I don't even have kids. What are you in?"

"Disaster relief. I work with people who have gone through traumatic events such as natural disasters, school shootings, etc. I also work with local human services agencies to place children who have been orphaned by disasters into temporary families."

"That's a life-changing job."

"For them and for me," Jessi agreed with a smile.

"What made you decide to do that?"

Jessi smiled again. "A little girl at a park told me I was alive to help people, like Jesus was helping me. After I watched a horrible tragedy lead to a powerful salvation, I asked the LORD to use my life to save the lost and hurting. Through this line of work, He has."

"I knew you were different," Tacy said triumphantly, as if she had uncovered a secret. The red-haired girl couldn't hold back a smile. "I knew Joe would get to you eventually." Jessi shook her head, even as she smiled.

"He provided the information, but Jesus saved me, not Joe." Tacy let that settle as she sipped her mocha. "So, Tacy, what have you been up to? You said you just graduated?"

"Yes, I graduated in May with my Bachelor's of Science in Nursing. I'm working in the cardiovascular unit at a local hospital. I really love it!"

Jessica laughed. "You always were the one who offered to dissect the hearts in biology, weren't you?" Tacy laughed too.

"I guess I have always been pulled to finding out what makes it tick. I'm going for my master's this fall."

"Will you attend a program there in Idaho?"

Tacy nodded. "I don't want to leave Trae, and there's a good one in Boise."

"Trae and Tacy," Jessi paused with a grin. "It sounds good."

"Trae and Tacy Koerner," Tacy added, her eyes sparkling. "You'd like him, Jessi, I know you would."

"I would like to meet him someday," Jessi answered.

"Fly out to my wedding," Tacy suddenly said, reaching across the table and taking Jessi's hand imploringly. "You can bring the girls, come a few days early, and help with wedding preparations! It would be so fun!"

A smile spread across Jessi's face. "I thought he hadn't asked you yet."

Tacy blushed. "Alright, well, if he does, come to my wedding!"

"You mean when he does," Jessi teased. "Send me an invitation and I will."

Tacy leaned back in her seat and shook her head. "I can't believe we're sitting here talking after all these years. What are the odds that we would have both stopped in here for a coffee at the exact same time?"

"Or that you just happen to be out here visiting your aunt?" Jessi added. "I don't believe it was a coincidence."

Tacy smiled, still shaking her head in agreement. "Me neither. And now you're coming to my wedding! I can't wait." She checked her watch. "I have to go, Jessi, but it was so good to see you." Jessica stood with her as Tacy grabbed her brown suede jacket.

"I'm sorry we lost contact," Jessica said, her eyes moist as she reflected on the years of her friend's life that she had missed.

"Me too. You have my number now," Tacy said, embracing Jessica. Jessi smiled and pressed her cheek against Tacy's.

"I'll use it," she promised.

"You'd better!" Tacy said, grinning as she shrugged into her jacket and grabbed her purse. "I'll be expecting a call soon!"

Jessica waved. "Have a safe flight."

Tacy hurried out of the café. Jessica watched her go before sitting back down and resting her chin on her hand. She felt as if she had been hit by a train. Since she left, her life in Glendale had never collided with her present. The effect was dizzying, pulling her back into the most magical year of her life.

Her heart was assaulted by memories of dearly loved people, places, and times – all things she could never go back to. Too much time had passed, too many things had happened. Joe was gone. It had been five years. She had to move on.

She stood, grabbing her purse and tossing her empty coffee cup in the trash. She had only meant to stop in for a moment to grab a cup of coffee on her way home, but saw Tacy and stayed to chat.

She was sure Jari wouldn't mind. Jessi checked the clock and realized her step-mom was probably just picking the girls up from preschool. She would meet them back at the house.

When she pulled into her Dad's drive and used her key to let herself in, the house was still and quiet. She wandered into the living room, sat on one of the plush sofas, leaned her head back, and let her mind drift over the last several years.

Her dad's career had recovered from the car accident that sent it reeling for several months. During that time, he had changed his stance on a lot of things and, for the first time, stood for justice and righteousness in the senate and in the country. As a result, he was re-elected, but his supporters had changed. His political persona had done a complete one-eighty. Now, he was flourishing, even if he was known by both parties as being narrow-minded and non-negotiable when it came to upholding truth, liberty and freedom – for all. The thought brought a smile to Jessi's face. Her dad had changed so much in the last four years.

One of her favorite memories was what had transpired between her mom, dad and Jari. Carla had moved back to D.C. the fall after the girls were born to be close to her daughter and granddaughters. Jari, whom Jessi had anticipated to cringe at the move, welcomed Carla with open arms.

In fact, before Carla even moved, Bill and Jari went to Glendale to apologize for what they had done and ask for her forgiveness. Reconciliation, though it had taken time, had followed. As odd as it was, Carla and her new husband, Tim, shared nearly every holiday with Jessi and the girls and Bill and Jari, as well as at least one Sunday lunch a month. Just a few short months after Carla moved to town, Jari had been given the gift of leading her, too, in the prayer of salvation.

Jari had wept as she told Jessi about how it happened, weeping mostly out of gratitude to the LORD that He had taken the greatest mistake of her life, the most hurtful thing she had ever done, and used it for good.

She confessed to Jessi that in the beginning she had felt so dirty, so unworthy to even be a Christian. When she finally gave in to the promptings of the Holy Spirit, He placed the dream in her heart to see the entire family, including Carla, reconciled to one another and serving Him.

She said even the thought was hard at first, wondering if she would still have a place in the family and what it meant for her relationship with Bill. She had to overcome her own selfishness and forgive over and over when hurtful things were said. But, she continued on in hopes of seeing Bill, Carla, and Jessi reconciled to one another, and she fell more in love with Jesus throughout the process. Jari said the outcome had been so worth the pain of her obedience.

Thinking back to the conversation with Jari brought tears to Jessi's eyes. The woman had so freely poured out her heart and confessed how wrong her attitude was in the beginning. Jessi knew it had been a painful struggle for her friend, but what a joyful reward had come. Jessi's family was healthy, happy and whole because of the goodness of the LORD and one lady's selfless obedience.

For the past five years, Jari had been constantly at Jessi's side. She had watched the girls while Jessi took college classes and now watched them while Jessi worked, sometimes for several weeks at a time when Jessi was called to a disaster. Sometimes it felt as if Jari was raising the girls as much as she was, and she didn't mind one bit. If there was anyone she could have chosen to raise her sweet girls in her stead, it was her step-mom. Jari had become her closest friend and anymore, the decade separating them in age didn't seem to matter.

The door from the garage opened, and two precious little girls ran in calling for her, with Jari following behind carrying coats and backpacks. Jessi stood and caught Kelsi and Kamryn up in her arms, hugging them close, before returning them to the ground. They both exploded into conversation, telling her all about what they did at preschool. She laughed at the four green eyes staring eagerly up at her, their mouths moving in constant chatter.

After staying for lunch with Jari, Jessi loaded the girls up in her SUV and took them home for naptime, then spaghetti and a game of Candy Land. When she went to sleep that night, her dreams were full of a green-eyed boy who looked so much like her daughters. A boy she still missed and loved.

When she woke up at three in the morning, her dreams

of him still fresh, she reached for the picture she kept in the drawer of her nightstand and smiled as she studied it. She and Joe were holding up the ugliest fish Jessi had ever seen. It was raining, and he was grinning – it was the picture from their first date. She sighed and laid back in her bed. She prayed for him again as she had so often since getting saved. When she fell asleep, she was still holding the tattered picture in her hand, unable to let go.

Twelve

"Jessi! Jessica Cordel!" Jessi froze where she was, stopping midstride. Her fitted black coat swung around her knees at her abrupt stop, her tall boots slipping a little on the sidewalk. People streamed around her in every direction, and she scanned the crowd for the one voice that had caused her to stop short. Suddenly, the pedestrians parted as a man pushed his way through the crowd, and she saw a face she loved – the face of a man she had spent five years trying to avoid.

The five years since she had seen Joe Colby seemed like a lifetime, yet as his eyes met hers, and he crossed the remaining distance between them, pulling her into a tight hug, it felt like only yesterday that she had left him at the airport, beating against the window with his fists as her plane taxied away from the terminal.

He suddenly released her and stepped back, hoping he hadn't overstepped unspoken boundaries. They both stood there for a second, unsure of what to say. He finally threw up his hands and broke into a grin. "You look great, Jess." She smiled and nodded, her eyes never leaving his face.

His laugh lines were a little deeper than they were the last time she saw him, and he had filled out. He looked more like a man and less like the boy she had known. Still, his green eyes were stunning in his tanned face, his chocolate brown hair fell just right, and his build was even more athletic. After living in a city, traveling the country and doing some work internationally, Joe Colby remained the most handsome man she had ever seen. "So do you, Joe."

For a moment, concern and sorrow clouded his face, and she held her breath, worried about the questions that would come. Just as quickly it passed, and his smile returned. "Jessi, come and get some coffee with me. I'd love to catch up."

After five years of being strong, she now felt weak with him in front of her. If only he knew of all the times she had thought of him, missed him, longed for him, and now, here he was. All she wanted to do was say yes and stay with him forever. Yet the situation was more complicated, and she knew the right thing to do was decline.

"I would love to, but I just returned from Kentucky and I haven't slept in twenty-six hours. I'm afraid I would be poor company and wouldn't make any sense," she said, reaching up to hold the strap of her laptop case, keeping it from sliding off her drooping shoulders.

By the set of his jaw, she could see he was not going to be deterred. His smile in place, he continued, "Well, I don't fly out until tomorrow morning. Go home, sleep and meet me tonight for dinner." She checked her watch – it was eight thirty a.m. She would have plenty of time to get some sleep before dinner. Still, she hesitated.

His pale green eyes were nearly begging. Without thinking, she quickly pulled out a pad of paper and wrote down her cell phone number, trying not to think about the repercussions that would follow.

Surely it had been long enough. Surely things had changed. Surely they could go to dinner as old friends, then go on as if nothing had happened. Surely.

She tore off the paper and gave it to him. "Call me around five and we can decide where to meet."

His face broke into an excited grin. "That sounds great!" They stood there for an awkward moment, with so much to say, but without the nerve to say any of it.

Finally, she stepped around him. "Well, I'll wait for your call then. Have a good day!"

He turned and watched her walking backward away from him, then gave a short wave. "Sleep well, Jess."

She hurried to her apartment building and ran up the six flights of stairs, trying her hardest not to think of Joe or any of the memories he brought up. She was exhausted, and the last thing she needed was to lie awake thinking through every detail of the encounter or worry about what it might mean.

Once she was inside, she kicked off her tall boots and dropped her jacket on the chair. She went to the kitchen to get two sleep aids and a glass of water. After washing the pills down, she drank the rest of the water. Then she lie down on the couch, dragging a blanket off the back and letting it fall over her. She closed her eyes and began to pray, taking the entire situation to the LORD and laying it at His feet. When she finished praying, her mind wanted to race over the events of the last hour and the last six years, but her exhausted body won. Within seconds, she was asleep.

As she slept, she had the most detailed dream of her time in Glendale. It seemed as if every major day or event played across her mind as if her memory had put that year on a movie screen. The dream was slow and sweet and even as she slept, she smiled, enjoying the tender memories, people and days that were so precious to her heart.

Hours later, Jessi woke slowly, fighting her way out of the fog of her dreams. She rubbed her tired eyes, and they felt gritty. She yawned as she pushed herself to a sitting position. She was on her black suede couch, the shades were drawn tightly, and the apartment was dark and quiet.

Pictures of Kamryn and Kelsi lined the top of the entertainment center, their four-year-old faces shining brightly with their sunny smiles and sparkly eyes. Jessi felt happiness well up within her as she went to inspect the pictures. She stood, her hands in the pockets of her jeans, and smiled at them for awhile, taking a moment to soak in the beauty of her daughters. She had missed them while she was gone. She was glad they had found the kids, and she had been able to fly home early.

Her mind ran over the relief of finding the missing children, the joyful reunion between the kids and their grandparents, the sorrow of having to tell them their parents had not survived, her last few hours in Kentucky, the flight home, the ride on the bus, the walk from the bus stop, and... Joe. She spun and checked the clock. It was almost four. She was suddenly nervous as she looked at the telephone. After so many years, would he call?

She grabbed her cell phone and hurried into the bathroom to take a shower. Whether he called or not, she needed to pick the girls up from her dad and Jari's. She took a long, hot shower, then put her makeup on, fixed her hair, and got dressed. She unpacked her suitcase and was sorting her dirty clothes into piles of laundry when the telephone split the silence. She reached for it with shaking hands, an odd sense of the past settling over her.

"Hello?"

"Hey! Jessi?" Her heart raced. It was a deep familiar voice that made her stomach flop.

"Yeah, this is Jessi." There was a pause.

"It's Joe."

"Hi," she said, taking a deep breath to try to calm her heart, which was now thumping wildly against her chest.

"Hi." She could hear the smile in his voice. "How did you sleep?"

"Good," she answered, choosing not to tell him about her vivid dreams. Let him think she had moved on, and his presence had no effect on her.

"Good. I'm glad. Where would you like to have dinner? Can I come to your house and pick you up?"

"No," she answered quickly, thinking about the numerous pictures of the girls that decorated her home, their toys in the toy box in the living room, their colored drawings covering the refrigerator.

If this dinner with Joe was going to be pleasant and uncomplicated, if afterward he would be free to go his way, and she would be free to go hers, there was one thing that he absolutely could not know – Joe couldn't know he was a father. Jessi was more certain of that than anything else. She couldn't consider any other option – it was too hard and un-wise...at least she wanted to think it was wisdom and not fear that kept her from telling him the truth.

"The truth will set you free." The subtle voice was kind and familiar, but she pushed it away. After all this time, the last thing she wanted to tell Joe was the truth.

"I can pick you up. I know the city, so it makes sense for me to drive," she continued.

"Sounds good," he agreed. He gave her the address of his hotel, and she knew just where it was. They agreed on a time, and hung up.

She immediately dialed the phone again as she ran into her closet. "Hello?"

"Jari!"

"Hey Jess! Did you get some sleep?"

"Jari, Joe's in town, and I'm picking him up for dinner in half an hour." There was stunned silence on the other end of the line.

"How did that happen?" Jari finally asked.

"I don't know! We bumped into each other on the street today and he asked me to dinner, and I don't know, I just said yes!" Jessi was freaking out as the reality that she would soon be trapped in a car, then having dinner with Joe Colby, hit her. She had thought about him so many times in the last five years, but being with him petrified her.

"Okay, you're okay, Jess," Jari said, going into sup-port mode. "It's going to be nice to catch up with him – see how his family is, what he's up to now." Jari's voice had smoothed out to a comforting, motherly tone as she recov-ered from her shock. "We'll just keep the girls a little bit longer. Maybe we'll have a movie night. Just come get them whenever you're done. They're fine here."

"Jari?"

"What, Hon?"

"What should I wear?"

Thirteen

Jessi was pleased she hadn't underestimated the dinner when Joe stepped out of the hotel elevator dressed in a button-down shirt and a tie. He looked more handsome than she even wanted to admit. Her heart began to flutter even more wildly than it had on the way over.

She saw appreciation flicker in his eyes as he took in her black one-shouldered dress, loosely curled hair and silver hoop earrings. His slow-growing smile made her happy she had dressed up.

"You look beautiful, Jess."

"Thank you," she answered shyly. Joe searched her face just a little too long for comfort, and she turned away feeling flustered. "Where do you want to eat?" she asked.

"What's good here? You're the one who knows the city."

She smiled as he followed her through the lobby. "I know just the place."

Once they were both shut in her SUV, she headed to a Chinese restaurant near her house that she frequented. It was nice enough that they wouldn't look out of place, but casual enough to feel relaxed.

Stuck in the car with him in the passenger seat, Jessi felt her heart hammering against her chest again. She glanced over at him. He was staring at her. She felt completely unnerved. "I watched your games on TV. You had a great college football career," she blurted, searching for something to say.

"You watched?" He was grinning as if it somehow satisfied him that she had watched his games.

"I like a little football now and then," she answered,

not about to admit that she hadn't missed a game.

"I got an offer to play in the pros," he said casually.

"I heard. I was proud when you turned it down." He was grinning again. "I wasn't keeping tabs on you – it was all over the news – college star turns down draft pick to go to seminary…it's definitely not the norm," she explained, irritated that she was showing exactly how over him she wasn't. He nodded, still grinning.

"I talked to Tacy a few months ago, and she's getting married up in Idaho next month. The girls and I are going." Jessi stopped abruptly, her mouth going dry. This dinner was already going horribly and they had barely left his hotel. "Tacy really wants her girls around right before she gets married, so some of us who have been friends with her over the years are going to fly out," she continued, praying that the LORD would forgive her for misleading him while at the same time praying he wouldn't think anything smelled fishy. Joe just grinned.

"I hope she'll be happy. Tacy was always a great girl. I lost track of her after graduation."

"She's a nurse in a cardiovascular unit," Jessi offered.

"That's perfect for her," he responded with a laugh.

"I know."

It was quiet again. It was almost as if he enjoyed the silence, knowing how she felt the need to fill it. She decided she wouldn't – she would wait for him to talk. But when he opened his mouth to say something, she was suddenly nervous about what he might say…or ask.

"I heard Kara got married!" He was grinning again.

"She did. Last summer. It was a beautiful wedding. I'm the only one of my siblings who isn't married now. Even my baby sister married before I did." He gave her a pointed look, as if it was her fault. Her heart gave a wild kick.

"So, you're not married?" she asked. He laughed now.

"No." His expression dropped. "Are you?"

"No!" She thought she saw relief wash across his face, but she couldn't be sure. "I just heard...well...again, it was on TV that you were married, but I wasn't sure if it was true or just a rumor."

Joe cleared his throat. "That was a misunderstanding. Is there anyone special in your life?" he asked casually, changing the subject back to her.

"I work a lot, Joe," she answered carefully.

"Like your mom." She smiled.

"I guess in a way. What about you? Anyone special in your life?" When he didn't say anything, she glanced at him. He was looking straight ahead out the windshield.

Obviously, that was a closed subject. That made Jessica curious and more than a little concerned, which irritated her as they were simply old friends who were meeting for a casual dinner. Still, jealousy kept her from asking anything more.

They were both quiet until they arrived at the restaurant. After parking, Jessi reached for her door handle, but Joe grabbed her arm to stop her and raised his eyebrows. "You forget so quickly."

"It's been five years," she reasoned.

"Five years, one month and fourteen days. But some things never change." Her breath caught. What all hadn't changed?

Feeling thoroughly reprimanded by the look on his face, she sat still until he circled the SUV and opened her door. She hurried to the restaurant ahead of him, trying to have a private moment to get her nerves under control.

He knew exactly how long it had been since she left? Maybe he had casually calculated it since bumping into her earlier that day just as she had. Either way, she couldn't afford another slip-up like the one in the car.

It was hard to maintain her composure, though, when she felt so unnerved. Everything felt so distant and yet so familiar. She hadn't had anyone open a car door for her since she left Glendale. Memories and emotions were racing back, filling her mind. How did she casually have dinner with an old friend when it was someone she had loved deeply and been intimate with? Someone she had children with? Her heart was hammering and she felt lightheaded. Taking a deep breath, she blew it out slowly, forcing herself to calm down.

It had been a long time. A very long time. Things were different now.

Joe jogged lightly to fall into step beside her and swung the door of the restaurant open before she reached it. After they were seated across from each other, she could feel him watching her. She continued to study the menu, despite the fact that she wanted what she always ordered. When the waitress came to take their order and their menus, she had no choice but to meet his eyes. She folded her hands on top of the table.

"So, what brings you to D.C.?" she asked brightly. She felt transparent under his piercing stare, as if he were reading her as easily as he always had. He leaned forward.

"You believe now, don't you?" Her eyebrows drew together in confusion. "In Jesus. You're a believer now, aren't you? I can see it – you're different. You seem... peaceful," he paused and gave her a lopsided grin. "Under all the nerves, that is." She returned his grin and threw up her hands.

"It's just been a long time, Joe. I'm sorry. I'm usually not this jittery." He gave her an understanding smile.

"Just answer my question." He looked as if he couldn't wait another minute to hear what she had to say.

She laughed. "Yes, Joe! Yes, I'm a believer now!" His face grew animated with excitement and relief.

"I knew it! I prayed you would be! I prayed it every day for months. And then one day I just stopped praying it – I knew you already were. Will you tell me the story?"

Jessi felt her own face brighten. This was a subject she

loved and one she was comfortable with. She spent the next hour sharing her testimony and that of her family.

More than once, Joe's eyes filled with tears that he made no attempt to hide. When she was finished with her story, he shook his head slowly, his eyes shining.

"That is amazing, Jessi. Absolutely amazing. I prayed for that so many times. It is so…man, it grips my heart to hear how it all happened! That is a powerful testimony, Jess – a powerful testimony of forgiveness and reconciliation!" He slapped the table, making her jump, reminding her of his dad. "Man, that's why I want to be a pastor. More people need real encounters with God! Powerful encounters like the ones you just shared. If there is any way my life can lead just one person into an encounter with Him, then it's all worth it. Every sacrifice will be worth it."

Jessi's eyes were soft as she smiled at him. "Don't you see? You already have."

"I made so many mistakes," he protested softly. "Jesus saved you in spite of me. I was no aid to Him in that process."

"You awakened my heart to love and longing. It's like He used you to work the ground of my heart and plant the seeds. The planter is no less instrumental than the harvester."

Joe reached across the table and wove his fingers between hers. "Thank you for saying that. I know Jesus forgave me for the mess I made of things, but it is huge to hear it from you."

"There was nothing to forgive," she told him, swallowing at a painful lump that had crept into her throat. She knew to what he was referring. If only he knew what a gift she had been given through what he referred to as a mess.

"Tell me what your college years were like – what was it like to play collegiate football? And what is seminary like? It's your turn to talk and my turn to listen," she said, leaning back and taking her hand from his to finish the last bites of her sesame chicken.

As he talked, she found herself studying his face, his every feature. She had forgotten the little details over the years. Of course both girls had his eyes, and Kelsi his chocolate brown hair, but she now realized that Kamryn had his nose and Kelsi his smile. His physical qualities now not only made him handsome, but endeared him to her even more as she recognized them as being ones she saw every day on little freckled faces that she loved more than anything.

They talked for three hours before Jessi yawned. Joe's eyes were gentle as he said, "I'd better let you get home and to bed. It sounds like you've had a pretty full week."

"I've loved catching up, Joe," she conceded, unable to hide the fact that she was wilting fast. "It's been really wonderful." His eyes held hers for a long moment.

"Yes, it has." He reached for the bill. She moved to stop him, but he held up his hand. "Please, Jess. This has been such a treat for me." She nodded and let him pay.

The trip back to the hotel was quiet as they both realized the evening was coming to an end. The vehicle was filled with a sad tension, as if they both had so much more to say, but were unwilling to say any of it.

"So, I guess I fly out in the morning and you'll… probably go back to work. Or do you have a few days off?" Joe asked as Jessi pulled up to the hotel entrance.

"I have two days off, and then it will be the weekend, so I don't go back to work until Monday."

"That will be nice to have a break." He was stalling.

"I'll walk you to the door," she offered. He nodded and got out.

As they reached the hotel entrance, Joe turned her by her shoulders to face him. "Why did you leave, Jessi? Why? I know it was for the best, and I know it was the LORD, but I have to know, why did you leave?" His voice was hoarse with pain – pain that was still as fresh and raw as it had been five years ago. Her reasoning had never seemed more empty or silly as it did at that moment.

"I wanted you to have everything you always wanted – a college football career, seminary, a church of your own." Her voice was small and she couldn't meet his eyes. He picked up both of her hands in his.

"Jessi, I wanted *you*."

For a moment, she thought he was going to kiss her and she hurried to speak before she found out if he was. "We don't always want what's best for us, Joe," she said softly. "And that was a long time ago." His expression was unreadable, but he stepped back.

"Yes, it was." She felt a strange loss at the distance he put between them. She mustered up a smile that she hoped was convincing.

"It's been really fun tonight, Joe. Thank you…for everything." Still, his expression was unreadable. He only nodded. "Good luck in seminary!" She took a step back.

"Bye Jess," he answered softly. "May the LORD bless you and keep you."

She walked around to her door of the vehicle, got in and pulled away. She tried to steel her heart against the myriad of emotions raging within her as she drove to her dad's, and stuffed them down deep inside as she pulled up in the driveway. When she went in, Jari didn't ask any questions and, after a subtle elbow to the ribs, neither did Bill. They simply helped Jessica buckle the sleeping girls into their car seats. "Call me in the morning when you wake up," Jari told her before shutting Jessi's door.

Once home, Jessi positioned a sleeping girl in each arm, draping them over her shoulders, and shut the door of the SUV with her foot. She was thankful for the doorman who held the front door open for her and was even thoughtful enough to summon the elevator.

As she struggled to keep the sleeping girls from slipping off her hips and onto the ground, she found herself daydreaming about what it would be like if she and Joe had simply been out on a date and he was with her now, holding the girls, helping her put them to bed.

Instead, she exited the elevator alone, juggled things around enough to unlock her front door, kicked it shut behind her, turned the deadbolt with her chin and carried the girls in to bed. After the way things had ended with Joe earlier that night, she was sure that was how it was always going to be.

"That's okay. It's best this way," she told herself as she smoothed the hair off of Kelsi's face and covered the girl's skinny little body with her lavender comforter before turning to do the same for Kamryn. Now if only she could convince her heart.

Fourteen

Jessi slowly woke to distant knocking. Confused from her deep sleep, she rubbed her eyes, hoping to clear the fog. Her time in Kentucky had been exhausting and despite her long nap the day before, she had slept hard. The knocking continued, and she looked to her bedroom door thinking it was one of the girls coming to tell her good morning. But her bedroom door was open and there were no sleepy-eyed little girls in sight.

She heard the dead bolts flipping on the front door of their apartment. "Girls!" she cried, jumping out of bed. They knew better than to open the door without permission! She raced down the hall and made it into the living room just in time to see Kelsi swing the door open wide, Kamryn still standing on the chair she had used to reach the dead bolts. Joe was standing in the open doorway with two cups of coffee and a dozen red roses in his hands.

Jessi stopped short, the blood draining from her face, and stumbled back until she found the wall, using it for support. Joe didn't even see her – he was staring at the two little faces in front of him.

~~~~~

Joe couldn't believe what he was seeing. Four pale green eyes stared at him from inside Jessica's apartment – eyes that were identical to his, his sisters', his dad's. The girls were young and small – four or five at the most. One of the girls had thick, dark brown hair, the other light blonde. Their hair was messy, as he had obviously woke them, and they still wore their long, silky nightgowns.

His heart, which had seemed to stop as soon as the door swung open, gave a lurch, then began to thump wildly.

The two girls looked at him, and he stared back, studying them with disbelief.

He wanted to believe that Jessi was babysitting or had brought some kids home from work that needed a place to stay, or even that she had adopted. But no matter how much he wanted to believe that, he knew the truth. He knew that these little girls staring up at him with their wide green eyes that matched his own, were his daughters – his and Jessi's.

He dragged his eyes away from the girls to look up at Jessica where she stood pressed back against a wall, and he couldn't hide the anger, the accusation, or the hurt in his eyes. The guilty, fearful expression on her face confirmed his suspicions. He stood for a brief second, trying to put some semblance of order into the chaos that was filling him.

Finally, he shook his head, dropped the coffee and roses on the ground, and walked away. He got in the elevator, half-praying she would run after him, half-praying she would stay where she was. He had no idea what he would say to her. She didn't come.

He rode the elevator to the ground floor and stormed out the door in search of his rental car. Unsure of what to do, lacking confidence in the emotions banging around inside of him, his instinct was to flee. He checked his watch. If traffic wasn't bad, he could still make his flight.

As he drove, his mind raced over what had just happened and what it meant. He had four-year-old daughters, if his math was correct, and he didn't even know their names. Their quiet curiosity toward him had been no more than if he was just a delivery man. But then again, how were they supposed to know he was their father? He had never met them, never been at a Christmas or a birthday, never even called to say hello. How could he if he hadn't known they existed?

He remembered the guilty look on Jessica's face. She should feel guilty! She had avoided him for months when she was pregnant with *his* children, *their* children. She had hidden them from him for four years. *Four years.* He had been playing football, going to college, hanging out with friends, all while she had been raising their daughters by herself – a job he gladly would have shared if he had been given the chance.

Daughters. His heart pounded against his chest as the word registered. He was a *father.*

"*LORD!*" he railed aloud, his voice filling the cab of the car. "You knew! You knew I was a father, and you never told me! You said to let her go! You said to seek *You,* and that You would take care of Jessi, which I did, but God, I have *daughters!* By giving up Jessi, I gave up my *children!* Children I didn't even know about! How could You let that happen? How could You keep them from me? Father, You know how I've cried out to You day and night for Jessica!"

"*And your prayers have been answered – she knows Me.*" The quiet answer seemed to fill the car.

"You know how I've longed to be a husband, to start a family," Joe continued as if he hadn't heard. "Only, one has started, it just doesn't include me!"

"*Go back.*"

"No! If she doesn't want them to know me, if she doesn't want me to know them, then fine! I'll leave and never go back."

"*Go back.*"

"I won't!" he vowed, anger coursing through his veins. Anger toward Jessi, anger toward God. How could she have done that? How could the LORD have allowed it? How could they both have kept him in the dark for four long years?

"*Go back, Son.*"

His anger mixing with a hurt so deep it came with a physical ache, he shook his head at his unseen God. "I can't. It's too hard. It hurts too much, God. This is worse than before. She misled me, God. She kept herself and the girls from me. She didn't go away for me or for You – she went away because she didn't want me in her life anymore."

Joe returned his rental car, grabbed his suitcase, checked in, and ran through the airport. He arrived at his gate just in time to walk on the plane. As he sat in his seat waiting for take-off, he reflected on the hours he had spent with Jessica the night before. Never once had she brought up the subject. She must have been determined to go out to dinner with him as an old friend, then go on with her life without him being any the wiser.

No wonder she had been so nervous. He had chalked it up to the jitters one expected to have after seeing someone they hadn't seen in years – the same nervousness he had been feeling – but now he knew it was more than that. Much more.

He shook his head as he realized she was never planning to tell him. If there was ever a good time, it would have been last night, and yet she hadn't said a word. Well, now he wished he didn't know.

As the plane taxied down the runway and took off, he was more resolved than ever that he wasn't going back. If he wasn't welcome in her life, then he wasn't going to be a jerk and push his way in. If she wanted her freedom, if she thought they were better off without him, fine. He would leave them alone.

~~~~~

"Mommy, who was that?" Kelsi's innocent question pierced Jessica's heart as she stood looking at the empty doorway.

Joe had left. He had known the truth. She had seen it written all over his face – and he had left. Just as he should have. And that hurt.

She had always thought that if she told Joe about the girls, he would marry her and spend the rest of his life doing what his family needed, instead of achieving what he wanted out of life. But she could see now that she shouldn't have worried.

Joe was as dedicated to his dreams as she was and hadn't wanted to get tied down. She was glad that he understood so quickly. Yet her chest and throat ached.

"That was just an old friend of Mommy's from high school," Jessica answered, drawing in a deep breath, stepping forward to kiss Kamryn on the forehead as she swung her off the kitchen chair and set her on the ground. "Why did you girls open the door without permission?" she asked, heading off any further questions.

"Mommy, we knew you were tired, and we didn't want the knocking to wake you up!" Kamryn said, hugging Jessi's leg, peering up at her out of innocent green eyes.

"That was very dangerous. It might not have been one of Mommy's friends. It could have been a bad person. Even if I'm sleeping, you have to get my permission before you *ever* open the front door. Even if you think you know who it is. Kapeesh?" Kelsi came to hug her other leg, their upturned faces sporting bright smiles.

"Kapeesh!" they answered in unison.

Jessi smiled down at them and pinched their cheeks. "You two are so stinking cute. Do you know that?" They both nodded, giggling. Kamryn stepped up on Jessi's foot, and Kelsi followed suit.

"Walk with us on your feet, Mommy!" Kelsi requested, and Kamryn nodded enthusiastically. Jessi laughed, put her hands out for balance, and walked the two girls to the kitchen table, letting them ride on her feet. Even with the girls in tow, her feet didn't feel nearly as heavy as her heart.

The girls laughed as she pretended to wobble, then climbed into their chairs, happy and chattering, excited about Jessica's promise of breakfast. Jessi got the girls started with cereal, then went out into the hall to clean up the mess Joe had left. She picked up the now-empty coffee cups and sopped up the brown liquid with a dish towel. Thankfully, the carpet around the edges of the hall was already dark, so the coffee hadn't made a stain. As she bent to pick up the discarded roses, she found herself kneeling down and grabbing a card that had fallen from them onto the ground.

Reading it, she sat back hard against her open door, tears springing to her eyes. *'I wanted you then and I want you now.'*

"He didn't even say anything, LORD," she whispered. "I wanted this for him for so long – for him to follow his dreams – so why does it hurt so much?" Jessi sniffed. "I know it's what he should have done but how could he just walk away? Didn't he want to know them? Even just a little? How could he not see how beautiful they are? How wonderful they are? LORD, they're my whole life, and they didn't appeal to him in the least? What am I supposed to tell them someday?" She glanced back at his note.

"LORD, he wanted me. He found where I lived, and came back for me. Am I less desirable because of my children? *His* children?" Her emotions were spiraling wildly, and her chest ached with pain. What she wanted for Joe hadn't changed, but it still hurt that he had left.

"*Wait.*" The quiet command calmed her, and she let out a deep breath.

"I don't want him to come back, Jesus. I didn't mean that. Keep him away. Keep him where You want him. I've taken him from You once, I don't want to take him again."

"*No one can snatch him out of My hand. He is mine.*"

"Maybe so," she answered, pushing herself to her feet. "But he belongs where he is, not taking care of us."

"*My way is the perfect way.*"

She went back into her apartment, shut the door and locked it. She put the roses in a vase and set it on the kitchen table where all three of them could admire the beautiful flowers. After turning on an educational cartoon for the girls, she slipped the card from Joe into the drawer of her nightstand, right beside his picture. As much as she wanted him to stay where he was, doing what he was born to do, it made her heart glad that, even for a night, he had wanted her back in his life.

Fifteen

Jessica stood in the bridal shop waiting for Tacy to try on her wedding gown one last time before getting married. The wedding was the next afternoon, and Jessica and the girls would fly home the morning after. They had been in town for three days already, helping with flowers and last minute details.

Tacy came out, and Jessica's breath caught as she clasped her hands together. "*Tacy!*" Tacy was laughing.

"Do you like it?"

"I love it! It is stunning!" Jessica raved, going to her high school friend.

The dress was an eggshell color to complement the tones of Tacy's light skin and auburn curls. The bodice was covered with what looked to be thousands of tiny glass beads, and the skirt was billowing and full. Although Tacy had always been slender, the dress made her waist seem positively tiny, giving her a true hour-glass figure.

Jessica felt a tug on the hem of her shirt and looked down at Kamryn. The little girl pointed at Tacy. "She looks like a princess, Mommy." Everyone in the room started laughing, and Jessica bent and swung her blonde daughter up onto her hip.

"She does, doesn't she?" Kamryn nodded.

"May I touch a bead on your dress?" Kelsi asked, characteristically the bolder of the two.

"Yes, you may," Tacy told her happily. Kelsi walked forward and carefully ran a finger over the beading before smiling up at Tacy, and returning to stand beside Jessica.

Tacy turned to the mirror and took a deep breath, pressing her hands against her stomach. "I love it! I'm getting married!" she suddenly squealed in excitement. Jessi, the dressmaker, and Tacy's mom all laughed.

"Yes, you are, Honey! Tomorrow!" her mom said, clicking another picture of her daughter.

"So, it's all good? You're pleased?" the dressmaker asked.

"Absolutely," Tacy and her mom said in unison.

After the dress was carefully laid flat in the trunk of Tacy's car, they took it straight to the church and hung it in her dressing room. Then they supervised the set-up and decorating, stopped at the florists' to look at Tacy's bouquet, and went back to Tacy's apartment to change for the rehearsal dinner.

Tacy had asked Jessica to be her personal attendant, so Jessi and the girls went everywhere Tacy went to assist however they could. After the rehearsal dinner and part of the bachelorette party, Jessi went home early to get the girls to bed and escape a portion of the party she wasn't comfortable with.

She went to bed exhausted, but as she lay in Tacy's spare room, she could not stop thinking about Joe. She told herself it was only because she had known Joe during the same time period that she had been friends with Tacy, so naturally, Tacy reminded her of Joe. She would like to think that was the reason, at least, so when she got home, she would be able to return to life as normal. Either way, she couldn't stop thinking about him.

He hadn't called, hadn't come, hadn't written. She knew that he knew Kelsi and Kamryn were his, but she hadn't heard from him in a month and a half. Not since the morning he had shown up at her door.

She was glad...mostly. She was glad he was staying focused, glad he was using common sense, glad he was making the hard decision and saving her the heartache. But as she looked at her sleeping daughters, beautiful, sweet, and innocent, the two emotions that filled her most were surprise and sorrow.

Joe Colby must be very different than he had been in high school if he would find her, find out about his daughters, and then just walk away. The young man she had dated in Glendale never would have done that – which was why she had avoided him for the past several years. Obviously, she was not the only one the years had changed.

What puzzled her most was if he still wanted her, as his note had indicated, why did children, *his* children, change that? Was he not ready to be a father? Was he scared? Did he think he would be too tied down?

Jessi watched her girls sleep and couldn't imagine someone not wanting them. Being a mom made some things more difficult for sure, but what her two little girls added to her life far outweighed any inconveniences. She loved them so much that she couldn't imagine life without them. From the moment they were born, they were the two most important people in her life, second only to God. From the moment the nurse had put them in her arms, her world had ceased to be about herself and had revolved around them. The love she felt for them continued to grow every day. They were her everything. Now, she wondered, how could their father not want them?

But, she reminded herself, Joe hadn't had all of the same experiences with them. He hadn't been given the opportunity to grow to love them. Maybe if she had told him sooner, if he knew them, maybe he would want them now. Still, even with all of her reasoning, she couldn't reason away the surprise and sorrow she felt when she remembered how he left.

The first week after he came she had been on edge, jumping every time there was a sound in the hall, expecting it to be him. The next week had been better, but still, she found herself expecting him to show up. Even right before she left for Idaho, she had been half-anticipating his arrival out of the blue. But he hadn't come.

"It's best this way," she told herself again, rolling over on to her stomach and stilling her mind against the hurt and confusion that had distracted her over the past six weeks.

~~~~~

Jessica hugged a girl under each arm and smiled as she watched one of her best friends pledge the rest of her life to another. After meeting Trae, she understood what Tacy saw in him and had to agree that he was like Joe in a lot of ways. A gentleman through and through, Trae was obviously as smitten with Tacy as she was with him. Jessi was happy for them both.

Her gaze drifted from the happy couple to the attendants, the decorations, the crowd. The wedding was truly beautiful. It wasn't as elaborate as most she had attended in D.C., but it was beautiful in a simple way and fit Tacy and Trae perfectly.

She studied the brown tuxes, the turquoise dresses of the bridal attendants, and the brown, turquoise and cream colored flowers. She gazed through the church windows at the turquoise lake and the mountains surrounding them, and she smiled. Tacy had picked the perfect colors and the perfect setting for her fall wedding.

Before she could stop herself, Jessi was thinking about her own wedding – where she wanted it, the colors she would use, the season in which she wanted it to take place. She wanted it in the spring with a profusion of brightly colored flowers. She wanted it outdoors, where fresh green leaves could provide the backdrop.

Kamryn began to wiggle beside her, bringing her back to reality. She was about to scold herself for daydreaming, telling herself there was no wedding in her future, when Kamryn stretched up to whisper something.

When Jessi leaned down, Kamryn said, "Mommy, I want pink at my wedding." Jessica almost laughed, realizing that no matter how likely a wedding was or wasn't, attending someone else's wedding made girls think about their own. "And I want a dress just like Tacy's," Kamryn continued, looking up at Jessi expectantly.

Jessica smiled and nodded. "You would look beautiful in a dress like Tacy's," she told her four-year-old, a twinge of sadness piercing her heart as she realized that one day her own girls would be grown up and getting married.

She wondered sadly if they would have a father to walk them down the aisle. If not, she had no one to blame but herself. And she was sure her own father would be honored to perform the task.

After the ceremony and reception, Jessica and the girls hurried to Tacy's dressing room to help her change out of her dress into something more suitable for travel. The couple was catching a late night flight to Jamaica, where they would spend their honeymoon.

While Jessica unzipped, unbuttoned and unlaced to free Tacy from her dress, she had the girls run around and pick up all of the makeup, shoes and clothes scattered around the room. While Tacy changed into her street clothes, Jessica sorted through the pile the girls had collected and pulled out the items that belonged to Tacy. Jessi hurried to pack all of it away, and Tacy's suitcase was ready to go by the time she was. She gave Jessica a long hug.

"Thank you for coming, Jess," Tacy told her, still embracing her.

"I wouldn't have missed it," Jessica replied sincerely. "Thank you for inviting us." Tacy stepped back and met Jessica's eyes.

"It hurt when you left, Jessi, but this makes up for it. Promise me it won't be another five years until I hear from you again." Jessica laughed.

"I'll call as soon as you get back from your honeymoon. Now go! Your husband is waiting for you!"

Tacy's face lit up. "My husband! That has a great ring to it!" Jessi laughed again.

"It sure does. You're a married woman now."

Tacy clapped her hands in excitement, then bent down to hug each girl goodbye. They hugged her neck and planted warm kisses on her cheek, then came to hold Jessica's hands.

"Have fun, Tacy!" Jessica told her friend, handing Tacy her purse. "We'll walk you out."

Jessi let go of Kelsi's hand so she could pull Tacy's suitcase, and followed her friend out of the dressing room, the girls right behind her. Tacy and Trae walked together through a cascading wall of bubbles, while Jessica went around to put Tacy's suitcase in the trunk of Trae's car. Her task completed, she watched Kelsi and Kamryn chase the shimmering bubbles, trying to catch them in their hands.

Once Tacy and Trae left, Jessi and the girls helped clean up, then went back to Tacy's to spend the night. In the morning, Jessica cleaned the apartment so it was spotless for when the honeymooners returned, took out the trash and left a bottle of sparkling cider and a 'welcome home' card on the kitchen counter.

During their flight home, as the girls watched a movie, Jessica's thoughts turned to weddings again. She had often been a bridesmaid or personal attendant over the last several years as her friends got married, one after another. After the last month, she was more convinced than ever it was the only role she would ever play in a wedding. That knowledge was the one thing that marred the otherwise perfect trip to Idaho.

Sixteen

"We have granddaughters?" Hannah Colby's face was full of shock. Confusion and shock. Joe had just finished relaying the details of his trip to D.C. to his parents and sister.

"Jessi had a baby?" Kara's voice was choked with emotion.

"Two," Joe corrected matter-of-factly.

"Son, you went to D.C. two months ago. You've known where Jessi lives and that you have twin daughters for two months, and you haven't been back?" Chris Colby asked incredulously, leaning forward to set his elbows on his knees and stare intently at his only son. Joe couldn't believe what he was hearing.

"Dad, she *betrayed* me," he defended, his voice full of hurt and anger.

"And you know why!" Chris countered. "She told you plain as day when she left you at the hotel! Women are complex creatures, Son – she told you why before you knew the what. She wanted you to understand."

Joe shook his head. "I don't know what you're talking about." Chris shot a glance at his wife and daughter, but they were hugging, tears running down their faces. They would be of no help. He stood and pointed toward the patio.

Joe led the way, annoyed that his dad seemed upset with *him*. He settled into a lawn chair and waited for his dad to pick up the conversation. Instead, Chris Colby smiled and leaned back, surveying the fall colors. "The leaves are pretty this year." Joe bobbed his head in agreement, caught off-guard by the change in subject and by his father's pleasant demeanor. "It doesn't seem like that long ago that we sat

127

out here and you told me you were thinking of dating the new neighbor girl."

Joe thought back to that time as well. Jessi had been so different then. She was so hard, so cold, so empty. Not at all like the woman he had spent an evening with a couple of months ago. His heart rejoiced at the change that had taken place in her – a change she said he had helped facilitate. He praised the LORD for His wondrous ways and His ability to change hearts. But like a pin in his balloon, he remembered another way she had been different in high school. Back then, she had loved him. She had wanted to be with him constantly. He almost snorted. Obviously, that had changed, too.

"You had a real good college football career, Son," Chris observed, settling into his chair as if he planned to have a long, leisurely talk. Joe wondered what his dad was getting at, but respected him too much to demand he state his point.

"Yes, sir."

"It made me proud as punch to watch you play every Saturday, either on TV or from the stands." Joe nodded and leaned forward to clasp his hands between his knees.

The hardest part of his college years had been the fame and admiration that had come with them. In a season of learning and rejoicing in true humility, all of the praise had felt distasteful, as it did still. He loved the game, had enjoyed leading his team to victories, and treasured the relationships he had formed with his teammates, but the fame and glory held no sweetness as it once had. Even now, it made him uncomfortable. Even coming from his own father.

"I bet Jessi sure enjoyed watching you, too," Chris commented casually. Joe wanted to retort that he wasn't so sure she had watched, but then remembered she had told him she had, so he stayed quiet. "I bet every Saturday she watched you, proud that you were really playing college ball with half of America on the edge of their seats, waiting to see if you would make that winning connection," Chris paused. "And I bet every game, as she changed a diaper or fed one of those girls a spoonful of baby food, she thought the only way you were able to play the game you loved was because you thought you were a carefree college student."

Joe started to protest, but Chris held up his hand. "You and I both know what a full schedule you had during college. Between games, practices, travel, classes, and homework you barely had time to stay sane, much less take care of a family."

"I would have given it all up if I had known. In an instant, Dad."

"I know you would have, Son," Chris replied quickly. "And so did she. That's why she didn't tell you."

"That's ridiculous! I didn't want any of that. I wanted her."

"But she wanted what was best for you. Joe, don't you see? She was willing to sacrifice so you wouldn't have to."

"So I wouldn't have to? Dad, I've sacrificed the first four years of my daughters' lives!"

"Do you think these four years have been easy for Jessi? Easier than if you had been there?" Chris continued. "She was an unwed teenage mother of twins. Try raising one child, and then you'll be able to imagine what twins must be like. Yet, she earned her diploma, then her degree, and has made a career for herself – a career helping other people. Do you think she hasn't sacrificed to keep you where you are? Do you think she hasn't been lonely? Tired? Overwhelmed? Scared? Do you think she hasn't asked herself a hundred times if she's doing the right thing? And yet for five years she chose to put your needs above her own. I don't think she selfishly betrayed you. I think little Miss Jessica did the most selfless thing I've ever seen."

Chris held up his hand to stop Joe's argument before his son could even start. "I'm not saying it was right. I'm not saying I'm not sad for you, for us, for the girls and for Jessi. I'm saying that if you think about it, you'll understand why she did what she did. Maybe some of that anger you're holding on to will clear enough to allow you to see the situation through her eyes and eventually forgive her for the years she stole from you."

"That's just it. She stole years I can never get back," Joe answered, sounding just as angry as he had when the conversation began.

Chris stood and looked down at his son. "I knew a boy once who made a bad decision," he paused, letting his words sink in. "You've come a long way, Son. You have matured and grown in the LORD. You have humbled yourself and sought His face. Don't let the enemy take what might be your three sweetest gifts this side of heaven and use them as a stumbling block again."

The wind went out of Joe's sails, and he slumped in his chair. "I don't know what to do."

"Well, I suggest asking the One who does…and then obeying what He says," Chris said, winking at his grown son, then squeezing his shoulder before going back into the house, leaving Joe by himself to think.

Joe put his head back against the chair and calmed his troubled heart. He listened to the wind rustle the dying leaves and breathed deeply of the scent of fall. Somewhere nearby, a neighbor was burning his fields and the smell of dying vegetation mingled with the smell of damp earth and the scent of baking apple pie coming from his mom's oven.

In the quiet solitude, Joe heard again the gentle command he had heard so many times in the last two months. And this time, after his conversation with his father, he had no more excuses.

He needed to go back.

~~~~~

Jessica stopped short as she stepped out of the elevator onto the sixth floor of her apartment building. She stopped so abruptly, both girls bumped into her. Wearing matching black wool coats and hats, with only different colored scarves to distinguish one twin from the other, Kelsi and Kamryn looked up at her curiously. They followed her gaze to the two women who had just stood from their waiting positions at her front door.

"Who are they, Mommy?" Kamryn asked, taking Jessi's hand.

"Jessica!" Kara called, running the few yards that separated them. Jessica wanted to run and hide before Kara's familiar smile registered, as did her open arms and the tears on her cheeks. Catching Jessi, Kara hugged her close for a long time. As soon as Kara released her, Hannah swooped in for an equally long hug.

"We have missed you, Honey," Hannah said into Jessi's hair as she pressed her face to Jessica's head. "So much." She held Jessi at arm's length, and Jessica noted that Hannah's face was covered with tears, as was her own and Kara's. She looked from one beaming face to the other, and started to laugh as joy overtook fear and self-condemnation.

These women she had loved and missed for five years, women she had wanted to call but didn't because she was too afraid they would shun her, had come to Washington, D.C. to find her. With warm smiles, they had greeted her through their tears, embracing her and reassuring her. Not only had they neither condemned nor rejected her, they had sought her out. Her heart soared.

"Come in! Come in and join us for dinner," Jessi invited, grasping both of their arms, her smile warm and sincere. "Later, once the girls are in bed, we can have tea and talk." Kara and Hannah both nodded, their smiles bright, before turning their attention to the two little girls who were now peering out from between Jessica's legs.

Laughing, Jessi pulled the girls out from behind her and knelt down to their level, as did Kara and Hannah. "Girls, this is your Grandma Hannah and your Aunt Kara –

the ones I've told you about. Ladies, this is Kelsi and this is Kamryn."

Hannah's breath caught, and more tears streamed down her face. Self-consciously, Jessi shrugged her shoulders. "I thought it was fitting. Joe asked one time if we ever had a daughter if we could name her Kelsi Kamryn, so..." She let the sentence trail off. Hannah nodded, trying to wipe away the tears that just kept coming. Kara bent down and said hello, talking to each girl for several minutes while Hannah pulled Jessi up and gave her another long hug.

"Thank you!" Hannah told her softly when she had regained her composure. "Thank you for honoring my daughter, my son, and our family like you did."

"You were my family, too," Jessica answered softly.

"Are," Kara corrected from the floor. "We *are* your family, too...even if we've been separated for a long time. It doesn't change anything."

There was another round of hugs before Hannah reached down and, after asking permission, boosted Kamryn up to her hip while Kara did likewise with Kelsi.

Jessica let the ladies get acquainted with the girls while she put together a quick dinner of grilled salmon, wild rice and steamed asparagus. As she worked, she attempted to calm her whirling mind.

How had Hannah and Kara come to be waiting for her at her door? How had they known about the girls? If they knew, then it must mean one thing – Joe had told his family. But where was Joe? Had he known they were coming? She certainly hoped he wasn't about to pop out from around some corner as well. She wasn't sure how many more surprises her heart could handle.

For five years, all had been quiet and she had been free to live her life as she saw fit, no matter how empty and disconnected parts of it seemed. Then, Tacy showed up at the coffee shop. Just a few months later, Joe spotted her on a busy sidewalk. The next morning he was at her door, and her secret was out in the open. For the last three months, all had been quiet again with no word from Joe and no collisions with Glendale.

The first month she had been on guard, waiting and wondering what would happen next. Even the second month, she was cautious, but in the last several weeks, she had relaxed, thinking it was over. But then, just when things were getting back to normal, Hannah and Kara showed up on her doorstep.

She murmured quietly to the LORD about it as she fixed dinner, asking Him to prepare her for whatever came next and to give her poise and wisdom. She also asked that He would give Hannah and Kara grace when they had time to talk later. For five years, the fear of telling these two special women what she had done, facing them, had been enough to keep her from them – her two dearest friends. Now, they were in her living room.

"I am with you always."

The gentle reminder brought her peace as she put the platter of grilled fish on the table.

"Dinner's ready!" she announced. Kara and Hannah followed the girls to the table, and everyone sat down.

Jessica watched her girls carefully as they looked over the dinner table, waiting for any signs of complaining. They had been working on table manners lately, and if ever there was a vegetable that would bring out the girls' complaining sides, it would be asparagus. But both of them were perfect ladies and didn't even make a face.

"I'll say grace," Jessi said, holding her hands face up on the table. Kara took one, and Kelsi the other.

"Heavenly Father, thank You for this day that You have given us. Thank You for the food we're about to eat, and we ask that You would let it nourish our bodies and keep us strong and healthy. And LORD, thank You for bringing Kara and Hannah here safely and for giving us this time together. It's been a long time. Thank You for being a

God of restoration. In Jesus' name, Amen."

A chorus of amens rose from around the table, and Jessi smiled as both little girls surveyed their dinner and went straight for the wild rice, obviously deeming it the lesser of the evils on their plates. She took a bite of salmon.

"Kara, I ran into Tacy a few months ago, and she told me you and Justin got married!" Jessi remembered after swallowing her salmon. Kara grinned, her face as pixie-ish as it had been when Jessica first met her.

"Yes, ma'am!" Kamryn giggled at Kara's response. Kara shot her a charming smile before continuing. "We'll celebrate our eighteen-month wedding anniversary next month!" she declared proudly.

"They count in months," Hannah told Jessi, her eyes laughing.

"And celebrate every one," Kara added. Jessica's smile was wide.

"You like being married, Kara?" she asked, already seeing the answer in her friend's face.

"I *love* it!" Kara answered enthusiastically. "It's the best! I can't get over how wonderful it is to have my best friend with me all the time – and to know that we'll always be together, have a family together and grow old together. It's amazing." Jessi tried not to show how much she longed for the same thing.

"That sounds great! You should get married too, Mommy!" Kamryn interjected, matching Kara's enthusiasm. Jessica was speechless. She was glad when Kelsi picked up where her twin left off.

"Are you married, Grandma?"

Hannah shot a sympathetic look at Jessi and then a warm smile at her granddaughter. "Yes, Sweetheart. I'm married to your Grandpa." Kelsi frowned.

"Grandpa Bill? I've never seen you with him before." Kamryn elbowed her sister.

"Grandpa is married to Jari, Silly," Kamryn said.

"No name calling," Jessica reminded. Kamryn patted Kelsi's arm as an apology.

"Grandpa Chris is who I'm married to," Hannah explained.

"Have we met him?" Kelsi asked, turning to Jessica.

Jessica felt as if all eyes were on her as she shook her head. "Not yet, Hon." Kelsi put her palms face-down on the table.

"Well, then I would like to meet him soon." All the adults smiled.

"He would like that very much," Hannah answered.

"How is Chris? And Kaitlynn and Kimberly?" Jessi asked.

The conversation flowed easily in the new direction, and Jessi was excited to hear that Kimberly was expecting her fourth child and Kaitlynn her second. All the grandchildren were boys...until now, Hannah added with a smile aimed at the two little girls who were now spooning in their pudding dessert. Hannah's eyes shone with tears again, but she didn't let them fall.

"Funny that your girls have had boys, and your boy had girls," Jessica observed.

"That's what I told Mama on the way here," Kara agreed. "Funny how that happened."

After dinner, Kara insisted on cleaning up, and Hannah asked if she could help Jessica put the girls to bed. Jessi readily agreed, glad for the help but even more persuaded by the look of longing in Hannah's clear blue eyes. Jessi sent Hannah in to pick out pajamas while she ushered the girls through the shower.

Giggling, they ran to their bedroom, their towels clutched around them, and slipped into their nightgowns with their grandma's help. Jessi handed Hannah a brush and untangling spray, and Hannah brushed through the girls' long hair. Jessica leaned against Kamryn on the bed as Hannah read a story, both of her granddaughters cuddled close.

One book turned into four, and when Jessi could tell that Hannah would keep reading to the girls all night, she finally cut it off. Then there were goodnight hugs and sweet kisses on the older woman's cheek. The girls said their prayers, and after Jessi tucked them in and met Hannah and Kara in the living room, she found tears running down Hannah's face again.

Jessi stood behind the couch and looked across the room at the woman in tears, feeling nervous. "I'm sorry, Jessi, I didn't expect to cry this much," Hannah sniffed. Kara burst out laughing.

"Oh mom, *I* knew how much you were going to cry," Kara said lightly. Hannah ignored her daughter's teasing.

"I don't mean to say they don't look like you – I see so much of you in them, but," Hannah paused, "but I look at them and I see my children." Jessi nodded, understanding completely.

"They're Colbys through and through," she agreed. At that, more tears streamed down Hannah's face.

"Jessi, we understand why you ran away. We really do. We're just sad you did, that you felt like you couldn't even come to us – to Mama and me," Kara said, grabbing Jessica's hand and pulling her around the couch to the spot beside her.

"I wanted to," Jessi told them honestly. "I almost called both of you so many times that first month…that first year, I just…." Jessi paused, ashamed. Her head dropped, and her shoulders sagged. "I was afraid. I knew I had hurt Joe – hurt you all – and I didn't know how to explain. I'm sorry." Kara wrapped an arm around her shoulders.

"We understand, Jess. Truly, we do. We just missed you so much."

"It's true," Hannah affirmed, coming over to sit with the young women on the couch. Mother and daughter both looped their arms around Jessica and held her close as if they weren't letting her escape again.

"Does Joe know you're here?" Jessi asked cautiously, finally asking the one question she had wanted to ask all night. Kara and Hannah exchanged sheepish, almost guilty glances, and Jessi knew their answer without them having to utter a word.

"We just couldn't wait any longer," Hannah explained in a rush.

"Once we heard where you were and about the girls, we had to come to you. We had to meet the girls and let you know that you are welcome in our family," Kara explained.

"Not just welcome, you *belong* in our family, Jessica Cordel. You've been a part of our family for a long time, you just didn't realize it," Hannah added.

"I realized it," Jessi said through a teary smile. "It's what made me want to belong to the family of God." Hannah tucked her in close under her shoulder as if tucking a chick under her wing.

"Will you tell Joe you've come?" Jessi asked after awhile.

"We don't know," Hannah admitted slowly.

"At some point, yes," Kara added.

"Maybe just not at first," Hannah finished.

"It's alright if you do," Jessi felt obliged to say. "I don't think he'll be upset. He was wise to leave. I'm glad he's committed to what he's doing. Choosing the LORD is the right choice, even if it doesn't feel good. I'm just glad it wasn't a hard decision for him, and that he's going after what he's always wanted. I want that for him, too."

Hannah looked shocked. "Oh, Jessica, you have it all wr—"

"Mama, do you want some tea?" Kara interrupted. Hannah fell quiet and then she nodded.

"That sounds nice. Thank you, Dear." Jessica looked from one lady to the other, not understanding what had just taken place.

"If you'll point me in the direction of your tea bags

and kettle, I'll make us all a cup," Kara told Jessi, standing. Jessi waved her back down.

"You sit. I'll get it."

Settling back down into the couch fifteen minutes later, each with a mug of green tea, Hannah was the first to speak. "I like how you've decorated your apartment, Jessica."

Jessi looked around, trying not to notice the dress-up things that still lay in the corner of the living room or the stack of mail that was on the coffee table. Instead, she looked at the color of the walls – cream, with a carpet that was several shades darker – and the black themed wall hangings. Over the fireplace hung a large black and white photo of her and the girls playing in the leaves. On each side were one of the girls' four-year-old pictures.

The couches were plush black suede with cream throw pillows, and the deep red armchair popped in the otherwise black and cream room. A flat screen TV was tucked into a black armoire with closing solid doors and a myriad of red candles were set around for decoration. The kitchen table was stylish with its sleek lines and black painted finish, and the cream placemats and napkins fit well with the rest of the décor.

"The furniture was a gift from my dad and step-mom," Jessi explained.

"Well, it's beautiful," Kara answered. "How did it go with them? I know you were nervous about coming."

"Well, it was difficult at first, especially with my dad, but it ended up being wonderful."

"Will you tell us about it?" Kara asked, dragging the throw off the back of the couch and spreading it across their laps in preparation for the story. Jessi did and they talked late into the night.

Kara and Hannah stayed for the weekend, and on Sunday, they all went to church with Bill, Jari, Tim, Carla, and Maybelle, then went to Bill and Jari's for Sunday lunch.

Jessi and the girls drove their guests to the airport to catch their plane mid-afternoon and told them goodbye with lots of hugs. Hannah and Kara promised to visit again soon and made Jessi vow to pray about visiting Glendale in the near future. Jessica knew they were hoping for Christmas, but she could never do that – she wouldn't risk distracting Joe, and they all knew it.

Hannah gave Kelsi and Kamryn one last squeeze each, then allowed Kara to pull her toward the boarding gate to avoid missing their plane. Jessi stood and waved with the girls until Hannah and Kara were out of sight.

"Mommy," Kamryn said, taking her hand and swinging it back and forth. "I hope they come back soon!"

"Did you like them?" Jessi asked, smiling down at her blonde-haired daughter.

"Very much!"

"Me too!" Kelsi added. "To think we never even met them in our whole lives! And they're our grandma and aunt! We've never had an aunt! And now we have aunts and uncles and another grandpa and..."

"*Cousins!*" the girls cried jubilantly in unison.

"We're rich!" Kamryn added, thinking of all her new family members. Jessi chuckled and ruffled Kamryn's hair.

"That you are."

Seventeen

Jessica had been in south Texas for two weeks working with families whose town had been devastated by a strong hurricane and the ensuing flood. She was tired, dirty, and sore as she finally boarded her return flight home from Houston.

Earlier that day, she had joined in the disaster relief efforts by working alongside one of her families as they dug through the soggy wreckage of their home in hopes of finding personal belongings. The family had lost a three-year-old son to the storm when he was swept away in the flood waters. It was much more than photographs, clothing and toys that Jessi was helping them find by digging through the rubble – it was closure.

As she tried to stuff her hand luggage into the very full overhead compartment, a man to her left offered to help. She sat down with a thankful sigh as he rearranged the compartment to fit in her small black suitcase with the red ribbon tied around the handle. When he was finished, she thanked him and settled back in her seat to get some rest. She slipped on her sleep mask and put in her ear plugs, but sleep wouldn't come.

Instead, she found herself thinking about the kind man who had offered to help with her luggage. It reminded her of something Joe would do. *Joe.* She still hadn't been able to stop thinking about him since he came to town at the end of summer. She expected it to get better with time, but here it was, two weeks before Christmas, and still he consumed her thoughts more than ever.

Where was he? What was he doing? Did he ever think of her and the girls? Did he ever want to know more, like his mom and sister? The mother and daughter had been very tight-lipped when it came to Joe, but Jessi had expected as much – the Colbys weren't ones to break a confidence or gossip.

Jessica thought of the date and wondered how Joe's finals were going. She wondered if he had enjoyed his semester at seminary and what he was learning. She wondered which book of the Bible he was studying and what kind of revelations he had gotten. She would love to sit down with him and listen to what he had learned.

She thought of the worn, soft, brown leather Bible that was in the front pocket of her suitcase. She had learned to love the Word of God and looked to it for the inspiration and strength she needed. She wanted to understand it more and would love to be in a school where class time was devoted to studying the Scriptures.

She pulled herself from her thoughts of Joe and Scripture, and tried to sleep again. But soon she found herself making a checklist of things she needed to do when she got home.

With so many lengthy trips over the fall, her supervisor had gladly granted her request to take off the rest of December, and she had big plans for her vacation time. She needed to do all of her Christmas shopping and pull out the Christmas decorations with the girls. There were cookies to bake and gingerbread houses to make. Her mom and grandma would come over for the decorating of the gingerbread house, and Jari and Carla would both likely be around for the rest of her festivities.

Jessi had kept the gingerbread house as a special activity she did with only Carla, Maybelle and the girls. It was a tradition her mom and grandma had started in Glendale, and they had so precious few traditions, she wanted to continue it.

She had already planned an afternoon of Christmas shopping with Jari on Wednesday, and Saturday night was the Cordels' annual Christmas party. Her dad's work Christmas party was the following week, which he always insisted she and the girls attend, as was Carla and Tim's.

Her mind drifted to Joe again, and she wondered what his plans were for the holiday season and how his schedule looked. Was it as busy as her own? She thought back to the Christmas she had shared with the Colbys – how it had been the first holiday of her life that really felt like a holiday.

She was so young and immature then. She had thought she enjoyed it only because Joe was there; now she saw that so much had happened that Christmas. Christmas at the Colbys' was about family, food, laughter and games, but mostly it was about Christ. It was the first time she heard the account of the birth of Jesus read.

It was also the last Christmas she had with her grandpa. Pops passed away from a heart attack the following spring. Although it wouldn't have been a big deal to her during the first fifteen years of her life, it was at the time of his death.

Pops had become as close to her as she had let any adult get at that point in her life. With his witty sense of humor and relentless determination to be involved in her life, he had wiggled his way into her heart. His death had devastated her.

She could still remember him sitting up in the bleachers at every one of her track meets that spring, timing her races. On several occasions he argued with the official's time, and at least once, Jessi had moved up a place because of it. She smiled sadly. She missed him and wished she hadn't wasted so many of her years with him.

She was thankful Maybelle had moved to D.C., and that her grandma was now happily living in a retirement community not more than ten minutes away from Jessica's apartment. It was nice to have her so close. Maybelle came over for dinner at least once a week and she often watched the girls on days that Jessi had to work and Jari was busy.

Although she hadn't approved of the circumstances at the time of their conception, Maybelle had been enchanted with the baby girls from the moment she met them. She had arrived at the hospital just three hours after they were born. More than four years later, she was just as in love with her great-granddaughters, if not more so. The thought made Jessi's heart swell. She was glad that her daughters had the chance to be close to their great-grandmother – a privilege she never had.

And Maybelle was sure, she had said over and over, that Pops would have loved the girls as well – they would have been his pride and joy. Hearing that always made Jessi happy.

Maybelle had assured her that Bert was a believer, so Jessi was excited to spend eternity with him. She wondered sometimes if he was watching from heaven, and if he was, what he thought of how things were turning out. She hoped she was making him proud.

She smiled. One thing she knew he would be proud of, was how Maybelle was doing. She had struggled, understandably, at first. In fact, Jessi and Carla had first convinced her to move, afraid that the soft-spoken lady would die simply from a broken heart. The couple had been so much a part of each other that it was as if Maybelle truly did not know how to live without her husband.

Their love for each other had been so great that she had no longer been a complete person once Bert died. But over time, Maybelle realized that the best way to honor her husband was to continue to live the way he had always encouraged her to – unhindered and without fear. She put away her grieving as if it were a garment, and although she still missed him, she now glowed when Bert was brought up in conversation. She had learned that loving and honoring him in this season of her life meant moving on. He would want her to be happy and she knew that.

Thinking about the kind of love her grandparents had

shared made Jessi's heart ache and fanned a desire that had steadily grown in the past six months, a desire she had spent years pretending didn't exist. But it seemed as if it was not to be ignored any longer. She dragged her thoughts from Joe, what it would be like to share that kind of love with him, to grow old together, to raise their children together, and turned them again to her grandparents.

She was glad her grandmother would be coming over to help with the gingerbread house. She had missed her during the last couple of weeks.

Still unable to sleep, she pulled a writing pad out of her purse and started on her Christmas list. When she was satisfied with her list of gifts to find for her loved ones, she was finally able to catch an hour of sleep. When the plane touched down on the runway, she woke up and collected her belongings. The kind gentlemen from the seat behind her got her suitcase down before she had a chance. She thanked him and walked off the plane.

In the terminal, she heard someone calling out for her to stop – not by name, but by 'Miss' – and the voice was getting closer. She turned to find the man who had helped with her suitcase, running toward her. She was confused until he held out her sleep mask.

"I would have brought your ear plugs, too, but someone stepped on one right before I got to it," he said apologetically. She laughed and took the mask.

"I didn't realize I had forgotten them."

"I think you took them out when you started writing your Christmas list," he admitted sheepishly.

"You were spying on me?" she accused with a smile – the man had been nothing but kind.

"I accidentally saw it when I was on my way to the middle of the plane," he explained. "The big 'Christmas List' title wasn't too hard to make out." She gave him a knowing look while tucking her sleep mask into her purse.

"Were you down helping at the flood site?" he quickly

asked when she started to turn away. "I recognize you from there," he continued. "I was down with my church helping with the relief efforts, but had to come back because of an emergency at my office."

Jessi's mind was quickly putting together pieces. He was a Christian man who was interested in serving, had proven himself a gentleman not once but twice, was ruggedly handsome and was from D.C.

"Yes. I work in disaster relief," she answered simply. He nodded.

"It was something down there, wasn't it? I've never seen anything like it."

"Was it your first trip out?" she asked. That would explain his slightly shell-shocked look.

"I've been on mission trips to other countries, but never for a natural disaster like that. I can't—" he paused as he reached out and moved Jessi to the side as a running woman nearly ran her over.

"Sorry! Got to catch my plane!" the woman called back over her shoulder.

Jessi offered the man her first full smile of the conversation. "Thanks. That would have put on a few more bumps and bruises for sure." He started to talk again, then hesitated.

He smiled. "Are you hungry?" She checked her watch. She had an hour and a half before Jari was going to meet her at her apartment with the girls.

She looked up at the man in front of her and smiled. "Starving," she admitted. He smiled back.

"My name's Jason."

~~~~~

"Go to her." Joe let his forehead rest on the kitchen table.

"I can't, Dad. I walked away without a word four months ago. *Four months ago.*"

"It's unfortunate you didn't go sooner," Chris agreed,

"but it's no excuse to stay gone."

Joe was home for Christmas break and seemed more relaxed than the last time he was in Glendale. Chris was glad the anger had subsided, but couldn't understand why his son had yet to go back to D.C. to see his family.

"How do I go back?" Joe asked.

"On a plane. In a car. It doesn't matter, just go." His son gave him an exasperated look.

"That's not what I meant." Chris took a deep breath to curb his own frustration.

"Son, I've watched you go there once a year for the last four years to look for that young lady. Now you know where she is, you've talked to her, you've learned you're a father...and you're still sitting around here on your keester. I don't get it."

Joe pushed his chair back and stood. Chris folded his arms, preparing for the kind of conversation Hannah had with Joe right after Jessi left. Chris could only hope the outcome would be as good today. But his son's expression wasn't angry, only sad.

"It's not that, Dad!"

"What is it? Help me understand," Chris said, unfolding his arms and putting them on the table, hoping to appear more approachable.

In the past it was his girls that had perplexed him. With every tear, every tragic drama, he became a little better at comforting the finer members of his household. He and Joe had waded through the rapids of living with four women together, but now it was his boy he couldn't understand.

"I got her pregnant, Dad! I got her pregnant, and then I got mad at her for leaving and went off and did my own thing. I didn't have a care in the world while she was supporting herself and my children. I left her alone. I should have searched for her harder! I should have forced her to be with me! I should have been there for her!" Joe grabbed a quick breath. "Then, when I found her and was about to tell her of my undying love for her, the minute something didn't go as planned, I ditched."

For the first time in weeks, Chris understood. Joe was no longer angry; he was ashamed.

"I'm not fit to go back to her," he continued. "What would I say? How would I explain my behavior? How do I make excuses for being immature? I'm not fit to be a husband or a father. My love, which I thought was deep and unending, has proven to be fickle and selfish."

"Now hold on just a minute. You've loved her since you were seventeen. You've loved her for over six years – five of which she's been gone. You didn't even look at another girl through college. No matter how many girls throw themselves at you, you continue to have eyes for only her. That doesn't sound very fickle to me." Joe shook his head, obviously not convinced. "And as for selfish, you've never been that. A little self-absorbed, maybe, in your younger years," Chris said with a wink, "but you've matured into a humble and selfless young man. I'm proud of who you've become, Son."

Joe was quiet as he stood looking out the patio doors. Chris prayed he had taken hold of the truth in his words. Joe turned back toward him, and Chris felt hopeful as he saw that the guilt and hopelessness in Joe's face had been replaced by determination. Was it determination to go to Jessi and his children? Chris could only hope.

"Well, then let this be my selfless act. She's been sacrificially thinking of me for the last five years, now it's my turn to think of her. I'm going to leave her alone and give her the space she wants. No matter how much I want to show up on her doorstep again, I'm not going to do it. I'm going to think of her this time – of the girls."

Chris groaned. "What if that's not what she wants, Joe?"

"How do you know that it isn't?" Joe challenged. Chris wisely kept his knowledge acquired through his wife's visit to Jessica's to himself. "She's given no inclination that she wants it to be any other way than how it is. She barely even accepted my invitation to dinner."

"She was keeping a secret, Joe."

"She hasn't called."

"She wants you to focus." Joe shook his head.

"I'm not going to interfere unless she wants me to. I've been pursuing her for the past six years. I'm not going to do it anymore. Out of respect for her, if she wants me in her life, she's going to have to let me know."

"I know your intentions are good and noble, Son, but that's a bunch of hogwash. Go to your family!" Chris ordered.

"I can't this time, Dad," Joe said, swinging back toward the window.

Chris took several deep breaths to calm himself, tempted to give his son a good shaking. "What is it going to take, Joe? Are you going to pay penance for the next five years? Pay her back day for day? And in the meantime, miss out on the next five years of being with her and your girls?"

"If that's what she wants."

"You don't know what she wants!"

Joe didn't respond, and Chris stood, unsure how much longer he could resist knocking some sense into his son. He washed the dishes he and Joe had used to have Christmas cookies and milk. As he approached the kitchen doorway, he turned to his son with one last thought.

"In five years, your daughters will be almost ten. Ten Christmases, ten birthdays, three thousand six hundred and fifty days you will have missed...and you still won't even know their names." He walked out and shut off the kitchen light, headed to bed.

Eighteen

Jessi traced the outline of her lips, then filled them in with lipstick. She fluffed her softly curled hair and pulled her swooped bangs to the side just a bit more. One final shot of hairspray, and she headed into her closet. She stepped into her nylons and pulled on her fitted black turtleneck dress, folding the collar down until it hit the perfect spot on her neck. She added jewelry and perfume, then stepped into her black heels.

Her heels clicked on the wood floor as she walked into the kitchen for a glass of water, drawing the attention of the man sitting with her daughters on the couch, watching Christmas movies.

She had asked Jason to come an hour early to sit with the girls while she got ready. Now, he let out a soft whistle.

"You look amazing," he said, coming to his feet. She shot him a smile, thankful for his affirmation.

It certainly wasn't everyday she received a grown-up's vote of confidence on how she looked before leaving the house. Usually, her only critics suggested more pink lipstick and something sparkly.

She went into the living room to make sure the girls still looked good, and they did. They looked exactly as she had left them before showering. That was, no doubt, thanks to Jason. She was glad she had thought to have him come early to watch them while she got ready.

She had curled Kelsi and Kamryn's hair and swept the top up to fall in a cascade of curls down the backs of their heads. Their red dresses were velvet, their tights were new and white, and their shoes, black and shiny.

Jason looked festive, too, in his black suit and red tie.

When he first arrived he was sporting reindeer antlers, which had drawn laughter from the girls, but Jessi saw they had been discarded as the party was close at hand.

It was important for Jason to look his best tonight, and Jessi was thrilled to see how he had risen to the occasion. He was going to be meeting some very important people.

"Are we ready?" he asked as Jessi lifted Kamryn, then Kelsi off the couch and set them carefully on their feet. She clicked off the television as he held the front door open.

"Yes, sir!" Kamryn and Kelsi said together, picking up their very ladylike white sparkly purses and heading toward the door. Jessi grabbed her own purse and followed. Jason took the girls to summon the elevator while Jessi locked her apartment door.

The girls were all smiles as they stepped out of the elevator and ran to inspect the giant Christmas tree in the lobby for the fifth time that day. Jason offered Jessica his arm, and she took it, letting him steer her toward the front door of the building.

"You look great tonight," she told him, smiling up into his eyes.

"Really?" he asked, revealing just how nervous he truly was.

"You're going to do great," she encouraged. He shot her a worried look.

"This is an important night," he said, and she smiled – as if she could forget.

"I know." She patted his arm.

Jason walked them to her SUV and buckled Kamryn into her car seat while Jessi buckled Kelsi. He waited as she got in and shut the door behind her. Then, she waited as he went to get in his own car and was careful not to lose him as she drove to her dad's.

The last thing the poor guy needed tonight was to get lost. She found herself smiling again. She hadn't seen any-one so nervous to meet her family since…well, Joe. But then again, she wasn't sure who was more nervous the day Joe met her dad and Jari – him or her. Definitely her, she decided. She pushed aside the sweet memories. That was in the past, and tonight the future took precedence.

The girls were clapping and shrieking in the backseat, enjoying the Christmas lights as they drove through the city. Jessi pointed out pretty houses for them to look at.

"I love Christmas, Mommy!" Kelsi cried out from the backseat.

"Me too! It's the prettiest time of the whole year!" Kamryn chimed in. Jessi laughed.

"I like it, too! And I'm so glad to be home with you girls for it!"

"Us too," they answered together.

"And now we're going to Grandpa and Jari's party, then Christmas is in *one* week!" Jessi told them.

"Yay!" was the resounding cheer from the backseat.

It was then that Jessica noticed the set of headlights that came careening down the sidewalk, took out a sign and burst into her lane. Jessica swerved sharply, but there was no escaping it – the car plowed into the back passenger side door.

Metal screeched and then crunched, glass seemed to explode from everywhere. Frightened screams split the air, and then all was silent.

~~~~~

Everything was dark and foggy, and Jessica felt as if she was swimming in something heavy and thick. She fought to get to the surface. When she opened her eyes, all she saw were bright flashing lights that gave her a terrible headache. They were yellow, red, blue and white, and she couldn't make out anything past their wild flashing. Slowly, she started to hear sounds around her. There were shouts and a scurry of activity.

"Ma'am, I'm a paramedic and I'm here to help you. Can you hear me?"

Suddenly the party, the drive, the wild car, it all came back and panic overtook her. She tried to turn to see in the backseat, but she couldn't move her head. She reached up and felt a neck brace. She started ripping at it.

"My girls! Where are my girls? Are they okay?" she asked frantically, her words sounding thick, her own physical pain forgotten.

"They took them in the last ambulance. You will meet them at the hospital. Sit still and let me get you out." The paramedic's tone was smooth and comforting, yet his words did little to stop Jessica from trying to unfasten her neck brace. Changing course, she began jerking on the door handle. She had to get out. She had to get to her girls.

"Are they okay?"

"Hold still," he said again.

"Are they okay?" she practically screamed, hurting her throat. If they took them first, it meant they were in worse shape than she was. She grabbed the man's shirt when he didn't respond. "Answer me. Are my daughters okay?"

He met her eyes and said the words she was desperate to hear. "They're alive." She sank back against her seat, relieved. Broken bones, punctured lungs, bruises or cuts they could deal with just so long as they were alive.

"Jesus," she whispered, just needing to hear His name. "Jesus, Jesus, Jesus. Jesus, please be with them. Heal them, please. I beg You! You are the ultimate Healer! A long time ago, I told You that if it would bring You glory, You could have my life, and You can! But please, please heal my daughters!"

The paramedic gave her a sympathetic look as he continued to work to free her from the wreckage, but she didn't see it – her eyes were closed as she lost herself in prayer. Suddenly, she opened them. "Where's my cell phone? Do you see my cell phone?"

"We have more important things to do than finding your cell phone," the paramedic told her, impatiently.

"You don't understand! I need my cell phone! Please! Just give it to me and I'll sit still and do whatever you ask as soon as you give me my cell phone," Jessi pleaded. There was a phone call she had to make.

Sighing, he searched around for it, and miraculously found it on the seat beside her. She flipped through the contacts one-handed and found the number she sought. As the phone on the other end rang, she prayed he would pick up. If he didn't, she would call his family.

"Hello?" He sounded surprised, and no wonder – it was the first time she had called him in five and a half years.

"Joe, you need to come to D.C. As fast as you can."

~~~~~

When Joe burst into the hospital waiting room, Carla, Jari and Bill all jumped to their feet. Bill crossed the distance first with his long stride, and caught the young man in a hug. Joe wanted to break past him and start demanding answers, but the older man was surprisingly strong.

"They're alive," Bill said, holding Joe still. "Calm down. You're not going to help any of them if you burst in looking like you might faint."

"I'm not going to faint," Joe told him, angry at the additional delay.

"They're alive," Bill said again.

This time Joe relaxed some, truly hearing the words he had been praying to hear for the past four hours since Jessica's call. The ride to the airport, the flight, the taxi ride to the hospital – it had all felt like a lifetime, not knowing how Jessica or his daughters were doing.

Finally, Bill released him. "Where are they?" Joe demanded, his voice choked with emotion.

"Jessi's getting dressed and will be out in a minute. She suffered a bad concussion, but she's going to be fine," Jari said, standing beside Bill, her pretty face drawn with worry. Still, she smiled as she relayed the news about Jessica.

"Thank God," Joe murmured.

"Absolutely," Carla agreed, wrapping her arm around Joe's waist. He wondered if it was as much to keep herself from collapsing as him. He had never seen her so pale.

"How are the girls?" he questioned. Concern flickered on all of the faces around him, and his breath caught, bracing for their answer.

"Kelsi is doing okay. She's in the pediatric intensive care unit now, but should be taken to a room on the pediatric floor within the hour. Her right arm is broken and she, too, has a nasty concussion," Carla told him.

"And the other?" Joe asked, not having known either of the girls' names.

"Kamryn," Jari hesitated, "hasn't woken up yet. The doctors are doing MRIs now. Until those come back, they won't know how severe the brain injury is."

"She's on a ventilator – she isn't breathing on her own yet," Carla added. Joe took that information in slowly, feeling sick to his stomach.

What they were saying was that she may never wake up. His daughter might die in this hospital tonight, and he would have never even spoken to her.

Still, he played their names over in his mind. Kamryn and Kelsi. He allowed a small smile. Jessica had honored the request he had made so many years ago – back when everything was different. "What are their middle names?" he asked, needing to know.

"It's Kelsi Morgan and Kamryn Montana," Carla answered. Joe was speechless for several seconds.

"The girls at the shelter?" he finally asked.

Jari nodded, knowing to whom he was referring. "They made a big impression on Jessi," she told him with a sad smile. He nodded, remembering.

"So, what do we do now?" he asked.

Bill gave him a sympathetic smile and echoed what he had been told the last time he was in a hospital with Jessi and the girls, the night the twins were born. "We wait."

"And we pray," Maybelle added, stepping into Joe's line of vision. She gave him a long hug and held on tight. "Just as we prayed you would all be back together again someday. The LORD has a funny way of answering prayers."

Joe tried to smile, but couldn't. What if he was only there to say goodbye?

"Trust in the LORD, Son, and lean not on your own understanding," Bill said, squeezing Joe's shoulder before returning to his seat. Jari followed him after giving Joe a brief hug, and Carla squeezed his hand, then returned to her seat beside a man Joe didn't know. It must be her new husband.

Joe then noticed a younger man – closer to thirty in age – sitting on the other side of Jari. He had a bandage on his forearm. "That's Jason," Maybelle whispered, the only one left standing with Joe. "He's a friend of Jessi's." Joe felt his heart lurch at Maybelle's explanation. He wanted to ask what kind of friend, but didn't. What right did he have? "Why don't you pace a little. It helps a man deal with his nerves. At least that's what Bert always said." Maybelle patted his arm and went back to her seat beside Carla.

Joe was about to do what she had suggested when Jessi walked down the hall. She was dressed in a black dress and heels. Other than some nasty bruising on her face, she looked as if she was still on her way to a Christmas party. Even here, after being in a car wreck, she was beautiful. Everyone stood, but her eyes fell on Joe.

For a moment it looked as if she would run to him and let him hold her, but regaining her composure, she closed the distance between them in measured steps. She stopped in front of him, just out of reach. She didn't meet his eyes.

"I just talked to the doctor, and I can go see Kelsi. Do you want to come?" He willed her to look at him, but she didn't.

"Yes," he managed to say, wishing he could take her in his arms and just hold her. He had been shaken to the core by her phone call. He had been sick with worry for the past few hours, and he wanted to physically hold her to be certain she was truly alright. He wanted to keep her in his arms where she was safe, and he could protect her.

Jessi turned to her family and mustered up a smile. "They said when they get her moved out of ICU, you will all be allowed to go in, too. Right now, it's only parents."

"We'll be out here waiting and praying," Bill told her firmly.

"Any news on Kamryn?" Jari asked. Jessi shook her head, looking down. Then she walked out of the room, and Joe hurried to follow.

He glanced back at Carla. "My parents will be here in an hour or so. If they come, and I'm not back, will you fill them in?" Carla nodded.

"Absolutely."

"I'm glad Chris and Hannah are coming," Bill added, earning an elbow in the ribs from his wife. Joe didn't have time to wonder about the familiar way Bill mentioned his parents. As far as he knew, they had never met.

Following Jessi down the hall, he jogged to catch up with her. She didn't look back. Reaching her, he grabbed her arm and spun her around.

"Jessica." He didn't know what else to say except her name. He was too full of emotion to come up with anything else. She finally looked up and met his eyes, and he saw then what had kept her from him in the waiting room – she was full of guilt.

He pulled her into his arms and she willingly came. She wrapped her arms around him and held on for dear life, her tears coming like a flood. He held her, enveloping her in his arms and pulling her closer, burying his face in her hair. She didn't say anything for a long time and neither did he. For the moment, he was content to simply be holding her.

He breathed in the scent of her perfume, her hair, her skin – smells that he had dreamt about and tried to remember for five long years. She felt just as right in his arms as she had in high school. They fit together like a puzzle.

As her sobs subsided, he ran his hand over her hair, over her back, calming her. "Are you okay, Love?" he whispered against her hair. She stiffened and stepped back, staring up at him.

"My daughters are in ICU, and Kamryn is fighting for her life. Do you think I'm okay?"

"They're my daughter's, too," he said softly, reaching for her again, hoping to bring her close. She side-stepped his reach.

"You don't know them or love them like I do."

Emotions banged around inside his heart. She had crushed him with her response. Feeling wounded and shot down, he responded in anger. "Whose fault is that?" She turned and started walking down the hall again. "Do you think I don't want to know them? You didn't tell me, Jessica! How am I supposed to know them like you do?" She didn't stop, and he jogged after her. "Why did you finally call, Jess? Why now? Did you finally call me so I could at least say goodbye?"

"She's not going to die!" she cried.

"You don't know that! What if I never even get to see her awake because you never got around to telling me I had a daughter?" Joe accused, his emotions getting the better of him. She spun on her heel and faced him, her eyes snapping.

"You've known for months, and you haven't bothered to call or to come see them once. The first four years were my fault, yes, but the last four months, that's all you." Jessica whirled and started walking again, scanning the numbers on the signs by each door.

Joe stood still. He thought of a million mean things to shoot back at her, but he couldn't even open his mouth. She was right. The fact that he had been trying to do the right thing didn't matter. He may have just wasted the last four months of his daughter's life.

~~~~~

Jessica walked into room 408 and ran the remaining distance to the bed. Her little girl looked so small in the big hospital bed. She had a cast on her arm and oxygen in her nose. Her forehead had a bandage on it, and she was bruised on her left cheekbone.

"Mommy!" Kelsi croaked out of a hoarse throat, and Jessi tried to hold back tears as she carefully climbed up onto the bed beside her.

"Hi Baby," Jessi said, her voice wobbling. She carefully slipped her arms around her little girl and held her. Kelsi clung to her with her good arm.

"What happened, Mommy?" Kelsi asked, sounding scared. Jessi knew from what the nurses had told her that Kelsi had just woken up and didn't remember anything about the crash.

"We were in a car accident, Honey. We were on our way to Grandpa and Jari's for their Christmas party, and a man hit his car into ours. Do you remember any of that?"

Kelsi shook her head, looking sad and frightened. "Did we miss the party?" she asked, clearly disappointed.

"The party was cancelled, Baby," Jessi told her, smiling at Kelsi's question. "But maybe, if you ask Grandpa and Jari when they come in later, maybe they'll reschedule it." Kelsi smiled and nodded and Jessi impulsively pressed a long kiss against the girl's forehead in relief.

Sitting in the mangled car, she had wondered if she would ever see her daughters' bright smiles again. Seeing Kelsi smile now was one of the most beautiful sights she had ever seen. Now if only Kamryn would do the same.

"Who's that, Mommy?" the small girl asked, her gaze drifting to the doorway. Jessi turned and saw Joe standing just inside the room. She held out her hand to him, all ill feelings forgotten in the presence of her daughter. He came to the side of the bed and took Jessica's hand.

"Kelsi, this is your daddy," Jessi said, barely able to get the words out past the emotion in her throat.

Kelsi looked up and studied the man out of curious green eyes. "You're the man who dropped coffee in the hall." He nodded. She tilted her little head and continued to study him. "I saw you on TV." He broke into a grin.

"Oh yeah?" She smiled up at him and nodded. "You were playing football. Your number was eight. Mommy recorded all your games so we could see you play." Joe shot Jessica a look that made her feel warm inside.

"That was nice of your mommy."

Kelsi nodded and motioned to the chair beside the bed. "Sit and stay awhile," she said, sounding so grown-up that Joe and Jessi both laughed.

Joe pulled the chair close and sat down in it, reaching up to hold on to Kelsi's fingers that were sticking out the end of the cast. Jessi crawled over to sit on Kelsi's other side and propped herself up with her elbow. The little girl looked from one parent to the other and smiled. Then she searched the room as if looking for something.

"What is it, Baby?" Jessi asked.

"Where's Kammy? Where's my sister? She wants to meet Daddy, too."

Jessi blinked back tears and swallowed hard. "She will."

"Where is she?" Jessi didn't know if she could explain where the little girl's twin was without completely falling apart. Thankfully, she didn't have to try.

"The doctors have Kamryn in a different room," Joe told Kelsi, his voice even.

"Tell them to bring her in here," Kelsi answered, ever bossy.

"She's still very sick," Joe told her slowly. Kelsi looked worried for just a moment before her face cleared, and her charming smile returned.

"She'll get better faster if she's in here with us – if we're all together – you and me and Mommy and Kamryn."

For the first time, Jessica saw how truly wrong she had been. As Kelsi looked at Joe with adoration filling her green eyes, Jessi realized that her daughters had longed for their father as much as she had.

She had thought that if their lives were full enough – if they had enough family around – it would be okay. She thought they wouldn't really notice that they didn't have a father. After all, she practically grew up without one.

She saw now that she had been very wrong. In their little girl hearts, they had been wishing he would come. Joe looked up and caught her eye, and she glanced away, ashamed.

Nineteen

Jessica's knees felt weak as she stood gazing at the still form in the bed in front of her. Unlike her sister, this little girl was not happily chattering and giggling. Machines purred and beeped all around her, and Jessi watched as those machines kept her daughter alive.

Kamryn's face was several shades of purple, some of the bruises so dark they were almost black, and so swollen that Jessi barely recognized her daughter. She had casts on both arms and one leg. Her soft blonde hair was blood-stained around her ears – hair that would be shaved off if the swelling in her brain didn't go down in the next twenty minutes. Even now, the doctors were scrubbing up for surgery.

Jessi put her hand to her mouth in horror and took a step closer to the bed. She touched Kamryn's face, but the child didn't even flinch. Jessi had an eerie sensation that her daughter no longer occupied the little body.

Joe was on the other side of the hospital bed. He reached out and carefully picked up the little hand with an IV in it and broke into a spontaneous and emotional prayer, asking God to save the little girl in front of them, to heal her body and her mind, and to take away the swelling in her brain. Jessica swiped at unwelcome tears and added her own prayers after Joe's.

"She may not be awake, but she can hear you. Keep talking," the nurse said casually from behind them. Cautiously, Jessi leaned over the side of Kamryn's bed and started out slowly.

"Hi, Kammy." She brushed back a piece of blonde hair from the little girl's face. "I want you to know that Mommy's here...and your daddy is, too. Your Grandpa Bill and Jari, and Tim and Grandma Carla and GG Maybelle and Jason are all in with Kelsi. Your Grandpa Chris and Grandma Hannah are on their way from the airport. Remember how you and Kelsi said you wanted to meet Grandpa Chris? Well, now you'll be able to!"

Out of the corner of her eye, Jessica saw Joe shift. Never mind what he overheard.

"And they're all out there praying for you. Praying that you'll wake up and get better. Daddy and I are praying for that too, Baby Girl. There are more Christmas lights to look at, all those presents under the tree to open, and we still have to make cut-out cookies with Jari next week. We have tea parties to have and…" Jessi stopped, unable to go on. After a moment she continued. "You need to wake up, so we can do all of those things. And don't forget – next August you start kindergarten, and you've been looking forward to that for so long. There are lots of reasons to wake up, Kamryn."

"One more is that I want to meet you," Joe added, leaning forward over the bed, too.

Jessica and Joe continued to talk and pray over their daughter for the next twenty minutes until the doctors came in to take her for more tests. If they didn't like what they saw, they would take her straight into surgery. It was time for Joe and Jessi to say goodbye and hope they would see their daughter again shortly.

"We can't come with you, so we're going to wait right here for you to get back, Baby Girl," Jessi said, kissing the girl's forehead. "We'll be right here, so don't worry. As soon as you get done with your tests, you'll come back to us."

Joe said his goodbyes, too, and the nurses wheeled Kamryn out of the room. The doctor stayed just a moment longer, his face grim.

"I'll let you know as soon as we know something," he said, then turned and left. Jessica wrapped her arms around herself, knowing by the grim look on the doctor's face that she may have just told her daughter goodbye for the last time.

Her bottom lip trembled and she was shaking, both inside and out. She felt sick to her stomach and her knees were weak. Trying to compose herself, knowing she needed to be strong for her girls, she turned and stared out the window at the city lights. Christmas lights twinkled from every building, and tears threatened to fall as she remembered how she and the girls had enjoyed them just hours before.

"Who's Jason?" Joe's quiet question sounded both edgy and defeated. She turned, distracted and confused.

"Jason?" He nodded, his green eyes serious.

"You said Jason was in with Kelsi and the others. I saw him in the waiting room. Who is he?" She waved her hand as if it were nothing.

"He's my friend." Joe came to his feet.

"How good of a friend?" Jessica suddenly realized how it must seem, and her face relaxed into a smile, the lines of worry temporarily erased.

"I met him on my way home from Houston last week. He had been working at the disaster site, just like me." Joe looked even more worried than before, as if he didn't like the sound of things. "He was struggling with being out on the field for the first time, so I went to dinner with him and helped him debrief. That's what I do, Joe, I help people who are somehow involved in disasters," she explained. He didn't look so sure. "I found out he was single and a Christian and—" Joe held up a hand to stop her midsentence.

"I get it. You don't need to explain."

She had never seen such intense pain in his eyes before. "No, you don't understand. I was taking him to Dad and Jari's party tonight to introduce him to Jari's friend, Layla. She's single, and I think they would really hit it off."

Joe's mouth fell open. "You were setting him up?" Jessi nodded.

"As a favor, he came to my house early to watch the girls while I got ready for the party. I offered to lead him over to Dad and Jari's, so he didn't get lost. He was so nervous about meeting Layla, the last thing he needed was to get lost along the way. After the accident, he was the one who called '911' and got to Kammy first. He started CPR and rode with her to the hospital. He's the one who called my family."

Joe strode purposefully toward her. He stopped right in front of her, so close she could feel his breath on her face. It made her shiver. His eyes were serious, begging her for the answer he wanted. "You aren't dating him?"

She laughed. "No." Her expression turned serious. "I couldn't ever be with anyone but you," she finished honestly.

Before she knew what was happening or could step back, Joe was slipping his arms around her waist and pulling her close. He covered her lips with his own and kissed her slowly as they both remembered their way. By long-forgotten instinct, her arms wrapped around his neck, pulling herself in closer, drawing herself into his steady warmth. The kiss was sweet and more comforting than it was passionate. Joe drew back and brushed his thumb across her cheek. "Then be with me."

Drawing on all the willpower she had, Jessi stepped back. "No." He followed her.

"Why?"

"So much has happened."

"It doesn't matter."

"You have school."

"I'll transfer to one here. Or you and the girls can come live with me." She shook her head.

"We'll get in the way."

"Is that what you think?" he asked, sounding as if the idea was unthinkable. She shrugged, not being able to nod under his intense gaze. His smile was so tender it made her heart hurt. "You'll be anything but in the way. For the past five years it's been a challenge to keep my mind off you. I'm always wondering what you're doing, how you're doing, praying for you constantly. It would be such a relief to be with you – to already know." He traced her jawline with his thumb. "I want to be with you, with the girls. We could really be a family, Jess – you, me, Kelsi and Kamryn...and any other children that might come."

Trembling, she stepped back again. These were words she had yearned to hear for so long, yet her mind warred against them.

How did she change so suddenly from picturing her life without Joe, being committed to allowing him to achieve his dreams, to suddenly allowing him in, including him in her little family? How did she go one direction for so long and then suddenly switch and, in one night, go the opposite? She didn't know how. It would change everything. But then again, a lot of things had changed suddenly in the last few hours.

~~~~~

Joe watched the struggle playing on Jessica's face, and his heart warmed to her even more. She wanted to say yes to him, he knew she did, but she couldn't...not yet. He let her keep her distance, but reached out and touched a dark curl.

"Do you love me?" She looked away, and he tipped her chin back toward him. "Do you?" She finally let out a defeated sigh.

"I could never stop." He tugged on the curl he had touched.

"That's good enough for now. We'll figure the rest out later," he promised.

He wanted to kiss her again, but didn't – this night was emotional enough without adding anything else into the mix. He didn't want to push her too far.

"Tell me about the accident. Who hit you?" he asked, easing back a step to give her some space. She recounted the drive, the Christmas lights, the wild car.

"Turns out it was a teenager on drugs who had just

robbed a house. The family was out of town for the holidays, but the neighbor called the cops. He was running from the police."

Joe shook his head. One senseless young criminal could cost his daughter her life.

Jessica sighed. "Years ago my dad was in an accident and a woman was killed. The incident ended up leading to his salvation. I told the LORD then that I would trade my life for the furthering of His Kingdom," Jessi paused, "but I didn't mean Kamryn's."

Joe shook his head, suddenly sure of the one thing he had been asking the LORD all night. "Kamryn is going to be okay. She'll wake up. You'll see."

Jessica's look told him she wanted to hope, but was afraid. He smiled. He would have faith for the both of them. Their daughter would be alright. "Want to go check on Kelsi?" Jessica nodded, and he led the way.

~~~~~

There was a light tap on Kelsi's hospital room door, then the doctor walked in. Joe looked up from where he was sitting on the edge of Kelsi's bed, and Jessi turned from where she was talking with the others. The doctor, still in scrubs, looked weary, but smiled.

"The swelling's going down. We don't have to operate." Happy shouts went up around the room. The doctor held up a stilling hand.

"We don't know to what extent her brain has been damaged yet, or even if she'll wake up. We'll run more tests in the morning and hopefully know more."

Joe followed the doctor out, hoping to convince him to move Kamryn into Kelsi's room as the dark-haired sister had been insisting for the past couple of hours.

Family members slowly filtered out for the night, promising to be back first thing in the morning. After many hugs, Carla and Tim departed with Maybelle, and Jari and Bill took Chris and Hannah home with them. Jason had left earlier.

Jessica was certainly staying the night, and Joe had made it clear he was as well, so Jessi thought through options for sleeping arrangements in the small room. She decided she would sleep on the bed with Kelsi and give Joe the recliner.

She crawled up onto the bed with her sleepy daughter and brushed the hair back from her eyes.

"Mommy?"

"What, Honey?"

"Will Kamryn be here soon?"

"If your Daddy can convince the doctor, then yes, hopefully so."

"I think he can." Jessi studied the little face in front of her that she loved so much.

"What do you think of him? Your dad, I mean."

Kelsi's smile was sleepy as she cuddled into Jessi's side. "He's just what I always wanted."

"Yeah?" Kelsi nodded. Jessi kissed her face. "You know what?"

"What?"

"I think we're what he has always wanted, too." Kelsi smiled, and Jessi kissed her daughter's face again, her own words settling over her. "I love you, Baby Girl," she said, turning her attention back to the little girl she was cuddled up with.

"I love you, too, Mommy."

Kelsi was asleep within minutes. Joe came in a little later and Jessi was thrilled to see nurses wheeling Kamryn and her machines in right behind him. He stopped and smiled, a smile meant just for her. She smiled back.

She watched as they got everything situated, motioning for quiet and pointing to her sleeping daughter. The nurses finished and left. Again Jessi was struck by just how fragile and broken her Kamryn looked. But at least they would all spend the night together.

"Thank you," she told Joe softly. He smiled and came to her.

He slipped off her heels and dropped them over by the recliner where she had put his jacket. Then, he came back and got one of the extra blankets a nurse had brought in. He settled it over her.

"How are you feeling?" he asked, standing above her.

"Stiff and sore," she admitted.

"I'm sure. How's your head?" He brushed a tendril of hair out of her eyes, rubbing it between his fingers to feel its silkiness.

"Throbbing," she told him honestly.

"I know tonight has been about the girls, but I want you to know I was just as worried about you." She appreciated his comment.

"Thank you."

"I'll sleep in the recliner. Wake me if you need anything," he told her gently. She nodded, enjoying being taken care of. He leaned down and pressed a kiss to her temple. "I'm glad you're safe." She hesitated, wondering if she could say what came to mind.

"I'm glad you're here," she finally answered.

He gave her another tender smile – so utterly different from his usual cheerful grin, but just as capable of making her heart flutter, if not more so. He leaned over her to kiss Kelsi's cheek, then went to the bed beside Kelsi's and held Kamryn's motionless little hand for a long time.

Joe began to pray quietly, and Jessica listened to the soothing sound of his voice, the passionate words of his prayer, the way he spoke to God as if He was his best friend. He thanked the LORD that He had kept them all alive and for Jessica and Kelsi's safety. He prayed fervently for Kamryn's complete healing and thanked God that the swelling in her head was going down.

As he prayed, peace seemed to flood the room, and Jessi found herself pulled into the comforting, peaceful presence of God. Starting her own silent dialogue with Him, it continued into her sleep.

~~~~~

Joe stood between the two beds and thanked the LORD for the females around him. He studied every little detail of his daughters, down to picking up their hands and looking at their small, slender fingers.

He ran his fingertips softly along Kelsi's delicate eyebrows and wondered how the girls had looked as babies, as one-year-olds, as two-year-olds and last year. He would have to convince Jessica to get out some photo albums.

He stood over Kamryn and prayed and prayed, then simply just stood there, feeling as if the LORD was standing beside him. He pictured her as she had looked the first morning he saw her – delicate and beautiful, looking almost exactly like her sister but with blonde hair instead of brown. It was hard to remember exactly as she looked so different now.

Again, the thought came that he might never get to know her. What if she slipped away during the night? Or if she never woke up? Or if she did, and the brain damage was so severe that she was never again the girl she had been – the girl he had never known?

He pushed the troubling questions aside. He would stand on faith and believe the LORD for a miracle. Joe knew God was free to do as He wished, but Joe would pray for and believe the LORD for a miracle up until Kamryn's last breath if it came to that. Then, once he got past his flesh, he would understand that the LORD's ways were good, even if they're mysterious, and he would praise His name. Just as he had for the past five years.

"LORD, she was Your daughter first. Have Your way," Joe whispered. Still, he hoped and prayed that the LORD's will was to restore his daughter to full health.

Joe turned from his daughter to look at the girl who had stolen his heart in high school. She was a woman now – she had grown up. He stood looking at her, his chest filling with emotion. He was still fiercely attracted to her, just as he always had been, but now he felt a connection to her on an even deeper level. It was no longer simply physical or emotional, it was spiritual, too.

And he was so proud of her. He thought back to how she had been with the girls that night, and a smile tugged on the corners of his lips. She was great with them. It was obvious how much they adored her, and that it was mutual. She had become a wonderful mother.

He laid his hand softly on the gentle rise of her hip and peered down at her. Even as she slept, even with bruises on her face, she was beautiful. He ached to climb on the bed behind her and tuck her in against him, but knew better. She may have let him take care of her tonight, but he knew from past experience that she had an independent streak a mile wide, and if she felt he was getting too close too fast, she may bolt. And he might have to spend five years getting back to where they were now.

Standing in the room with Jessica and his daughters, he finally felt like things were as they should be. He was ashamed of how foolish he had been the last several months. Jessica had been right – it was his fault that he had missed the past four months with them. The LORD had told him to return, and he hadn't listened. He had been a fool again, and this time it had nearly cost him everything.

But it hadn't, he reminded himself cheerfully. "I'm done being childish," he promised Jessica quietly, then quirked a smile. "Well, at least hopefully to the same extent."

He watched her sleep, hoping she had pleasant dreams and that she wouldn't have to relive the crash. He drew the long dark hair off her shoulder and neck, then pressed a kiss to her temple. With that, he sat down, pushing his recliner back to get comfortable, and prepared to fall asleep. Here. In a room with his daughters and their mother...whom he hoped would become his wife.

Twenty

Jessi woke slowly to the hum of machines and the quiet murmuring of a man's voice. Opening her eyes, she remembered suddenly where she was and why.

Kelsi was still sleeping, curled up against her side, the oxygen tube still attached to her little nose. Jessi turned her head and saw Kamryn lying in her hospital bed, as still as she had been the night before. Joe sat at her side, holding her little fingers, his Bible open between him and his daughter. Jessi realized the voice that woke her was him reading Scripture aloud. He was on Psalm 116, and she wondered how long he had been reading.

She smiled as she turned back to Kelsi. There was something so comforting about having Joe there. She felt a warmth start to spread through her as she remembered the conversation they had the night before and the kiss they had shared.

Her mind started spinning as questions about the repercussions of the last twenty-four hours came to the forefront of her mind, but she stopped them. Today was not a day to think about Joe, herself or what may or may not lie ahead of them. She needed to focus on getting her girls healthy and home. That had to take precedence right now. There would be time for everything else later. Still, she closed her eyes and listened to the familiar, comforting words for just a few minutes longer.

"LORD, thank You for letting me wake up this morning, that my girls are both alive. Father, thank You for bringing Joe here to be with us. No matter how short our time with him is, we'll be thankful that You brought him here for this moment in our lives. And most of all, thank

You that You were with us in that car last night. LORD, I believe You cushioned the blow to Kelsi and me and mostly to Kamryn, saving us as You always do, in one way or another. As little as she is and as hard as we were hit, she shouldn't even be here, but she is. So Father, I'm asking now that You heal her. That You make her whole again. Father, she is Yours, and I will trust You with her." She thought of Joe. "We will trust You with her."

Following what she was hoping was the prompting of the Holy Spirit, she disengaged herself from her sleeping daughter and slipped out from under the covers. She sat on the very edge of Kamryn's bed, afraid to get too close and disturb the tubes that were keeping the girl alive.

Joe looked up, surprised, and she smiled. "Good morning."

"Good morning," he answered, his face lighting up as he smiled at her.

She ignored the instant butterflies in her stomach and turned to her daughter. She ran her finger along the side of her face. Nothing. Her heart fell. Jessi felt close to tears, but pushed them away. Her daughter always responded to her touch, even if it was just a smile in her sleep. But the LORD had given them one miracle when the doctors didn't have to operate – He could give them another and let her wake up.

"I've been reading through the psalms, reading them to her," Joe told her.

"I know. I heard you."

"Her eyelids fluttered at Psalm 103." Jessi turned to him quickly and found him grinning with excitement.

"Are you serious? Psalm 103?" Jessi asked, trying to think of the words.

"Bless the LORD, O my soul; and all that is within me, bless His holy name!" Joe recited from memory. "Bless the LORD, O my soul, and forget not all His benefits: who forgives all your iniquities, who heals all your diseases, who redeems your life from destruction."

Joe pointed to Kamryn, and Jessi quickly turned her eyes from him to her daughter. "Who crowns you with lovingkindness and tender mercies, who satisfies your mouth with good things, so that your youth is renewed like the eagle's."

Joe was right! Some kind of movement was happening under her eyelids. Jessi watched, holding her breath, not wanting it to stop. But it did.

Nothing more happened, and she didn't wake up, but it was enough. Regardless of how the tests came back later that morning, Kamryn's spirit was still connected to her little body. It was more than just machines and doctors keeping her alive.

Joe was grinning when Jessica looked back at him. "I don't feel as scared of those tests as I did when I first woke up," Jessi admitted.

"The LORD heals and redeems. His Word is powerful," he told her. Jessica nodded.

"I guess I never knew just how powerful," she said. She had often experienced its power to still her troubled heart and bring peace, joy, understanding, and even conviction, but she had just witnessed it reach through a coma to catch hold of a little girl who was still very much alive. Jessica was filled with awe, gratefulness and excitement.

Jessica picked up Kamryn's hand and kissed her little fingertips. "You're going to be okay, Baby. We're all here with you – Mommy and Daddy and Kelsi. We're all waiting for you to wake up. Later, the doctors and nurses are going to take more pictures of your head to see how they can help you."

"I like how you explain things to her. To them both. You're a good mom, Jess," Joe said casually, smiling at her. Her own smile faded, and she looked away.

"A good mom doesn't get in car accidents that leave her kids fighting for their lives," she told him.

"Mommy!" Kelsi cried out from the next bed over.

Jessi jumped off Kamryn's bed and hurried to her dark-haired daughter, hearing the panic in her voice. Kelsi was ripping at the oxygen she still wore. Jessica grabbed her hand and gently pulled it away from the tubing.

"It's alright, Sweetheart, I'm right here." Kelsi's eyes calmed noticeably, and she reached her arms out to Jessi. Jessica smiled, leaning in to hug her and hold her close.

"Good morning to you, good morning to you. We're all in our places with bright shiny faces, is this a good way to start the new day?" Jessi sang softly against Kelsi's head, singing the song she sang to the girls every morning. The little body in her arms relaxed.

"I was scared when I woke up," Kelsi told her.

"Did you not remember where we are?" Jessi asked sympathetically, rubbing her back. Kelsi shook her head. "That's okay. It took me a little while, too."

After Kelsi calmed down and was smiling again, Jessica started into the topic she was dreading. Right now, she was blocking Kelsi's view of her sister, but she wouldn't always be able to shield her.

"Kelsi, remember how you asked your dad to bring Kammy to you?" Kelsi nodded. "Well, he did. But, Kelsi, Kamryn is still very sick, and she doesn't look like she normally does. In fact, you may not even recognize her. Kamryn was hurt very badly in the car accident." Kelsi's bottom lip stuck out.

"Will she be okay?"

"We hope so, but we need to pray and ask Jesus to heal her." Kelsi nodded solemnly.

"I will. Can I see her? Can I see Kamryn?" Jessica hesitated, not sure if her little girl was ready for the sight that still made her sick to her stomach.

It was Joe that answered. "Yes, but you need to know that this is just on the outside. Kamryn's face looks different, but it's only because of the swelling. The swelling will go down, and she'll look normal again. If it's a little scary, it's okay to cry. Just remember that inside, she's still the same. And soon, she'll get better and look like you remember her looking."

"Will she talk to me?" Kelsi asked. It was Joe she reached for to take her to her sister and not Jessi.

Joe collected her in his arms, holding his daughter for the first time. He made sure he had enough free line for her oxygen. "No. She's in a coma – kind of like she's sleeping, but we can't wake her up…yet." Kelsi looked nervous. "Are you ready?" Kelsi nodded bravely. Joe turned and took the few steps between the beds. He held Kelsi against his chest as she looked down at her sister. Her green eyes were large, and she started to whimper.

Joe cradled her against him and spoke calmly. "Something, probably the airbag, hit Kamryn in the face and it made the blood vessels under her skin pop. That's what makes all the bruises. You have some on your face, too. So does your mommy. Because it all happened so fast and the car hit so hard, lots of extra fluid, kind of like water, collected under the skin in her face, so it looks puffy like that. The glass from her window broke and got all over her. That's why she has so many cuts and scratches. And look, she has broken arms, just like you, and a broken leg." Kelsi seemed to relax as Joe explained why her sister looked the way she did.

Jessi watched from Kelsi's bed as Joe handled the situation. Part of her felt hurt that Kelsi had chosen to go to him instead of her, while the other part of her warmed as she watched him talk Kelsi through the scary moment, now letting her touch her sister's hand.

Jessi had a strong urge to go and take over, make sure Kelsi was doing okay and ensure it was being handled properly, but she forced herself to stay where she was. She needed to give Joe the freedom to take his place in the girls' lives. And he truly was doing a good job.

A knock came on the door and as Jessi stood, Jari

poked her head in. Seeing they were up, she smiled and swung the door open wide. "Good morning!" She came in carrying sacks of food that instantly made the whole room smell good. "I brought you a change of clothes, Jessi. And shoes."

"And I brought yours, Joe," Hannah added, entering behind Jari. Bill and Chris followed, looking as if they had just been having a very enjoyable conversation.

Jessi gave Jari and Hannah long hugs.

"How are they?" both women asked, glancing to where Kelsi was now sitting on the bed beside Kamryn, talking to her. Joe stood with his hands on Kelsi's little shoulders, listening. Jessi smiled.

"Kelsi is much better. Her eyes are sparkling again. And Kamryn's eyelids were moving earlier when Joe read Psalm 103!"

"Praise the LORD!" Jari exclaimed, hugging Jessi again.

Hannah was beaming. "That's great news!"

The grandparents went to join the girls and Joe, crowding into the small space. Jessi took the clothes Jari offered and went to change.

She was thankful that Jari had thought to grab jeans and a sweater, her toothbrush, toothpaste and a ponytail holder. She changed, brushed her teeth, and pulled her hair into a low side ponytail before going out to join the others.

She saw that Carla and Maybelle had arrived, and that the nurses were preparing to take Kamryn away for testing. The oxygen had been removed from Kelsi, so the little girl was free to move at will. Joe was getting her dressed in clothes Jari had brought.

Seeing Joe complete the everyday task that she usually performed, made Jessi feel both sad and happy. She realized it was going to be hard to give up the right of being the sole parent – the one the girls always needed.

As the nurses prepared to wheel Kamryn out, and Jessi

hurried to tell her goodbye, she realized that the girls having a dad would also have its perks – like not having to wait for news alone. Jessica came up along Kamryn's bed and told her exactly what was happening, and that they would be waiting for her to come back. She kissed her bruised face and told her goodbye. Jessica started to tell the nurses about Kamryn's activity that morning, but Joe had already told them.

Once Kamryn was wheeled out, Jari and Hannah opened the sacks of food. The breakfast burritos the women had made before coming smelled good, but Jessi couldn't bring herself to eat. She couldn't muster up any kind of an appetite when her daughter was fighting for her life. Instead, she sipped coffee while watching Kelsi eat her mini-burrito and drink her cranberry juice while sitting on Joe's lap. Joe was talking to his dad and Bill, but made comments to Kelsi frequently, drawing giggles from the little girl.

Kels was enraptured. That much was obvious. Jessica worried about what would happen to her daughter's heart when Joe went back to school.

"Jessi?" Jari looked as if she may have already said her name once or twice.

"I'm sorry," Jessica said, bringing her attention back to the women around her.

Carla gave her a knowing smile. "It's a good scene, isn't it?" Jessica nodded.

When the door opened awhile later and the nurses wheeled Kamryn into the room, the doctor right behind them, silence fell over the group. Jessica stood and handed her coffee back to Jari, wiping the palms of her hands on her jeans. Across the room, Joe stood too, handing Kelsi to his dad, who accepted her with open arms.

Joe came to stand beside Jessi, his hand on her back for support. Her knees were shaking and her heart was racing as she waited for the news. Different scenarios and what -ifs flooded her mind, but she pushed them aside as the doctor began to speak.

"The swelling on Kamryn's brain continued to go down throughout the night; enough so we could get clear readings of what has been damaged." The doctor went on to describe Kamryn's condition.

Jessica was trying to make sense of it all when her dad stood up in the back of the room and spread his hands out to the doctor. "I'm just a humble politician; please tell us what all that means in words we can understand." By the way the doctor smiled at Bill, Jessi was ninety-nine percent sure he had voted for her dad in the last election.

"It means," the doctor shifted his attention back to Joe and Jessi, "your daughter is one lucky little girl." Jessica didn't dare let out the breath she had been holding just yet. "Anything she's learned so far, she'll likely have to relearn, and she may be a little slower to learn than she would have been otherwise. However, the damage was not nearly as extensive as we would have thought. When she wakes up, she'll likely be weepy, which can last for six months to a year, but she should eventually return to normal, or at least close."

Jessi felt lightheaded. "She'll wake up?" she asked, holding her breath. Joe slipped his arm around her waist and hugged her. The doctor smiled kindly.

"We believe so."

"When?" Jessi asked, shooting a quick glance at her daughter. The doctor shrugged his shoulders.

"There's no way of knowing. It could be today, it could be a week from now or even several months down the road."

His answer was a little disappointing, but the important thing was that she would be waking up someday, and when she did, she would be herself. "It's truly a miracle," the doctor was saying. "I honestly didn't think she would make it, then to see her with so little brain damage...it's truly a miracle," he repeated.

In the next instant, Joe was shaking the doctor's hand, Bill was going forward to thank him, Jari and Hannah were hugging, as were Maybelle and Carla, and a very happy Chris was listening to how Kelsi could sing her alphabet. Jessica walked to Kamryn's bed, leaned down and kissed her forehead.

"Do you hear that, Baby Girl? You're going to be okay! You're going to wake up!" she whispered to her small daughter, tears of joy stinging her eyes. "You can relearn your numbers, your alphabet, and even how to write your name. It was easy for you the first time, and we can do it again. The most important thing is that you'll be waking up. You're going to wake up, Kammy! Mommy's so excited! Wake up soon, Baby! Wake up soon!"

Twenty-One

Joe was sitting beside Kamryn's bed reading Scripture. He had just read the sixth chapter of Mark when her eyelids began to flutter and a moaning sound escaped from between her lips. Joe jerked his head up, studying the little girl.

It had been three days since the accident, and her black and blue bruises were fading to greens and yellows. The swelling had gone down in her face, and the true shape of her features had returned.

Her eyelids were still fluttering, then suddenly she opened her eyes and looked around the room. He started to call for Jessica, but remembered she had taken Kelsi down the hall to get a glass of milk.

Instead, he stood and leaned over his blonde-haired daughter. "Hey Sweetie." Her eyes found his face, and the most beautiful smile transformed her bruised features.

"Daddy."

Her one word caused tears to collect in his eyes. She knew him. Not from before, but from his hours at her side, reading to her, talking to her, singing to and over her. She knew him.

For one glorious minute, he had her all to himself. "How are you feeling?" he asked, perching on the side of her bed.

"I hurt," she said, wincing as she tried to move her arms. He nodded.

"I'm sure you do. But you're alive, Kamryn. Don't ever forget there's a reason you woke up – a plan for your life," he told her, making use of these first few moments he had with her.

"Daddy?"

"What, Honey?"

"I like it when you read to me."

Nurses rushed in with Jessica and Kelsi right on their heels. "We saw the monitors, her brain activity is increasing," the closest nurse told Joe. He moved aside so they could see the little girl.

"She's awake."

He thought he saw jealousy flash in Jessica's eyes, before she looked away from him and rushed to Kamryn's side. She leaned over her. "Kammy?"

"Mommy!" Kamryn's delight was obvious. Jessica carefully hugged the little girl for a long time, burying her face in the pillow. By the way her back was shaking, Joe was fairly certain she was crying. He wanted to watch the entire emotional, tender moment between the mother and daughter, but Kelsi was tugging on the leg of his jeans.

"Lift me up, Daddy! I want to see Kammy." Joe swung Kelsi up so she could see her sister. Kamryn caught sight of her and, struggling against the weight of her casts and her idle muscles, held up her arms.

"Kelsi!"

"Be careful," Joe told Kelsi firmly, setting the squirming girl down on the side of the bed. Jessi sat up to let Kelsi in, and they hugged Kamryn together. Joe wanted to somehow join in but wasn't sure how, or if he was completely welcome. He went to alert the others instead.

Carla had gone into her office that morning, and Bill, Jari, his parents and Maybelle were all set to arrive any minute. He dialed Carla's number first, hoping to tell her the news. He had to leave a message, but knew how excited she would be when she got out of her meeting and heard the update.

After he left the message, he heard his mom's voice in the hall leading from the elevator. He ran to meet the group. They knew as soon as they saw him – he didn't even get the joy of telling them about Kamryn.

His mom burst into happy tears. Jari danced around until she found Bill, then threw her arms around him in an exuberant hug. Chris left his wife, crossed the distance quickly, and pulled his son into a hug. Joe returned it warmly. Maybelle was off like a bullet to the girls' hospital room to see Kamryn for herself.

The group followed Maybelle, and there were hugs, kisses, laughing, crying and praying. Joe watched, hanging back to allow room for those who had not yet seen the little girl awake. He remembered his few moments with her earlier when it had been just him and his daughter. He felt warm again inside, just remembering how she had known him. It was a beautiful start to their relationship.

He looked for Kelsi and found her sitting proudly on her twin sister's bed. Joe grinned. Kelsi was a bossy and spunky little girl, with all the charm and beauty of her mother. From what he had gathered, Kamryn was much the same. He was going to have his hands full, that was for sure, but it was a load he would not pass up for anything.

His gaze slid to the girls' mother, who was standing back, but still close enough to reach Kamryn and be in her line of sight. Joe wondered about the jealousy he had seen in her eyes earlier. Was she upset he was there instead of her when Kamryn first woke up? If so, it made sense. Jessi had been by the girl's side nearly every moment since the accident happened, not wanting to leave for fear she wouldn't be there when Kamryn opened her eyes. Then, the moment she left, the little girl awoke. He had those first moments with Kamryn instead of her, and he could see how that was something to be jealous of. If only she knew how important those moments were to him.

He watched the happy group milling around the room, talking to the two girls. Carla came rushing into the room almost forty-five minutes later and made a beeline for Kamryn. There were more hugs, more kisses, more tears.

Joe looked expectantly to his mom who stood beside him, and saw she was crying again, just watching the exchange between Carla and Kamryn. He grinned.

His mom hit his arm. "What? They're happy tears," she told him. He held out his hands innocently.

"I didn't say a word." Chris winked at him over Hannah's head.

"Leave your mother alone. A grandma is entitled to a few happy tears." Joe grinned back at his dad and watched as Chris slipped his arm around his wife. Chris stepped behind her, putting his chin on her shoulder, and talked to her in a low, quiet voice that was meant for her ears alone. Whatever he said earned him a look of pure adoration from his wife.

Joe found his gaze back on Jessi. She was beautiful, just as she always was. She looked stylish in a long black shirt, dark jeans, tall black boots and a wide belt settled over her hips. Her dark hair flowed long and straight over her shoulders. Her blue eyes were moist. He found himself wishing he was free to go to her and rejoice with her privately as his parents were. This should be a moment they celebrated together, a mile-marker in their lives. Instead, he was watching her and the girls from across the room.

Somehow knowing his thoughts as he always did, Chris stepped close. "The first step is yours for the taking, Son." Giving his dad a grin, Joe started for Jessi. Seeing him coming, she shot him a warm smile, but subtly moved to position Kelsi between them.

Seeing his opportunity slip away, he sighed. He wanted to be alone with her for awhile. He wanted the chance to talk with her and see how she was doing. Still, he was amused by how she was so subtly avoiding him. "I'm a patient man," he told her in his mind. He'd waited for her for over half a decade. He certainly wouldn't stop now.

A sweet little voice stole his attention. "Kamryn, this is Daddy. Daddy, this is my sister, Kamryn," Kelsi was saying, looking as proud as could be. Kamryn smiled at him, and he smiled back.

He wasn't sure if she remembered their conversation from earlier or if she had forgotten as the fog continued to lift from her mind, but he knew one thing for sure – no matter how many years went by, he would certainly never forget.

Kelsi continued chattering and Joe reached behind her and took Jessica's hand. Jessi jumped, obviously surprised, but didn't pull her hand away. She didn't look at him or even actively hold on, but that was okay. He ran his thumb back and forth. He had missed the feel of her hand in his.

Twenty-Two

The morning was cold. The bright sun didn't seem to be giving off any warmth at all. Jessi shut the car door and zipped her coat all the way to her chin. She began picking her way through the cemetery, weaving between tombstones until she found the one she sought.

There was a Christmas wreath leaned up against it. Jessica smiled. It had been almost five years since Lydia O'Connel was killed in a car accident, and still her family brought a Christmas wreath to her grave…just as she would have done if Kamryn had not made it.

She knelt down beside the grave, giving no thought to her clothing, and sat looking at the stone marker for a long time. Finally, she let out a heavy sigh. Tears came unbidden.

"I often come here to do exactly what you're doing." The gentle voice startled Jessi, and she turned quickly. She had been so focused on her walk to the grave that she hadn't noticed Lydia's mother sitting on a bench just a few feet away. The older lady patted the empty seat next to her, and Jessi rose and went to sit beside her.

"I saw the story about your car accident on the news," Joselyn Doughtery said as Jessi sat down.

"We got the flowers you sent. Thank you." Joselyn nodded.

"I heard Kamryn woke up."

"She did. She's going to be fine." Jessica almost felt guilty relaying the wonderful news to this mother who had endured the opposite outcome to her own child's tragedy.

"Praise the LORD," Joselyn said, closing her eyes for a brief moment.

Jessica appreciated her sincerity and the grace she extended. The Doughterys were the most grace-filled people Jessica had ever met. Over the past four years, they had continued to both amaze her and convict her of her own lack of grace for others.

"Are you back home yet?" Joseyln asked.

"No. We're still at the hospital. Joe, the girls' father, offered to stay with them while I got some fresh air." Joselyn nodded but didn't ask the question Jessica knew she must be thinking – on Jessica's first trip out of the hospital, why had she chosen to come here – to Lydia's grave?

Jessi was glad the woman hadn't asked; she wouldn't know what to tell her. She didn't know why she had sought out the quiet cemetery.

Jessica and Joselyn both sat quietly for several moments. "My daughter died, Jessica, but it hasn't been in vain." Jessica looked over at the woman beside her.

"I don't understand how you can say that," Jessica told her honestly. Joselyn smiled sadly, looking back at the Christmas wreath.

"Lydia used to tell me, 'Mom, I want to make a difference. I want to change the world for good. I want to promote heaven on earth.' What she didn't accomplish in life, she accomplished in death."

"With my dad?"

"Yes. Bill Cordel's salvation is truly a miracle. But aside from what it meant for him personally, look at all your father has accomplished since he changed his entire outlook on life. Look at the truth he's stood for, the justice he's fought to obtain. He used to sit back and let all sorts of lawless and foolish things take place. Now, he stands for what is good and right. And our state, our country, will feel the effects. Through Lydia's death, the LORD used her as a catalyst to promote change in our national government," Joselyn paused. "I will *never* stop missing my daughter, and I don't think I will ever understand why the LORD took her instead of bringing her back, as He did your daughter. But I do know that He has a plan, it is good and it is about the advancement of His Kingdom, even when we don't understand it."

Jessica nodded, looking down at her folded hands, feeling guilty. Joselyn reached out and put her hand on Jessica's knee. "Lydia was a willing participant. She told the LORD to use her in whatever way would bring Him glory. And He honored her request."

"The night of Lydia's accident, after watching my dad accept Jesus, I knew she must have told the LORD that – or at least wanted it in her heart. I knelt down, and I told the LORD the same thing. But my heart wasn't pure, Joselyn. I wasn't speaking the truth. Over and over, I go to the ends of the earth to help those who are hurting, to bring Christ to dark situations. I say, use me to bring You glory, but I was so offended with Him when I thought he was going to take my daughter. I told Him I had offered myself, not her – that He couldn't take her."

Joselyn took Jessica's cold hand in her mittened one. "We are but flesh and blood, Dear. The LORD knows your heart, even when you respond out of your flesh. He understands that you are a mother, and He gave you the very love, the very instincts that caused you to say that. He understands. Just as He understood when I wept and railed at Him, got angry and yelled at Him after He took Lydia. I didn't respond how I should have, yet He was gracious and kind and compelled me to return to Him until I could stay away no longer. I took all my anger and pain and grief to Him...there are days I still have to. He understands our flesh, Jessica. Jesus was a man. If He had stayed a God, then perhaps He wouldn't understand. But He became a man that He might walk with us, experience what we experience, and endure what we endure." Joselyn took a deep breath. "He was no more surprised by the accident than He was by the outcome...or by your reaction."

Joselyn gave her a calm smile. "Don't waste time beating yourself up about your response. He is waiting even now for you to return, to repent and to offer yourself, your life, those you love, for His glory once again. There's no time-out period in the Kingdom, Jessica. His mercy extends beyond our concept of time and punishment."

Joselyn checked her watch and stood. "I pick Rachael up from preschool in half an hour, so I'd better go." Jessica stood, too.

"I'm sorry I interrupted your time here with your daughter." Joselyn cupped her mittened hand to Jessica's cheek.

"Don't you know? My daughter is not here in this place of death – she's alive! I came today to meet with you." Jessica was speechless, and Joselyn's eyes were merry. "It's not only in death that we can be obedient and bring Him glory, Jessica."

Jessica's eyes filled again with tears. "Merry Christmas, Joselyn."

"Merry Christmas," Joselyn answered with a tender smile. Jessi embraced the dear lady, then watched her walk to her sedan. When she sat back down on the bench, she lowered her forehead to her knees and thought over what Joselyn had said.

She grew grateful as she realized the LORD had sent exactly the right person at exactly the right time to meet with her and speak into where she was. He never ceased to amaze her.

With her head bowed, her teeth chattering from cold, she repented and again dedicated herself, her life, and all she had, to Him and His glory.

~~~~~

"Jess?" Jessi looked up from the crossword puzzle she was doing to where Jari sat reading a book. "Are you scared?" Jessi looked to Kamryn who was sleeping on her bed.

"Less scared than I was the night of the accident, or even the morning after," she answered. Jari shook her head, her smile kind.

"Are you scared that Joe's here – and very much a part of your life now?"

Jessi put down the booklet of puzzles Hannah had brought the day before. Jessi had already completed four.

"Yes," she told Jari honestly.

Jari nodded. "I thought you were. Want to talk about it?" The woman sounded hopeful.

Jessi shrugged. "I'm scared he'll leave…and I'm scared he won't. It's hard to hand over some of my parenting rights and the girls' affection, and it scares me how deeply I feel for him."

Jari considered her for a long moment. "All these years, if you were the one who kept him away, you were in control, but now he could leave you, is that it?" Jessi thought through what Jari had said.

"I guess so."

"You have a wonderful dad who loves you very, very much, but you and I both know it wasn't always like that." Jessi nodded, not knowing where her step-mom was going with the conversation. "I know you started out wanting to do the right thing, Jessi, and I know you have wanted to give Joe the freedom he needed to be able to do what he's called to do, but you have places in your heart that are broken. You've kept Joe away for the past five years because you were scared he would eventually hurt you the way your father did, and you didn't know if you could endure that." Jari held up her hand to silence any argument.

"You know how much I love you, Jess, and how well I know you, so know that what I say is only meant for your benefit." Jari hesitated for just a moment, then charged the subject head on. "You are terrified of being rejected and abandoned. I saw it over and over that first year you were with us, before everything changed. You always were so quick to fight, so quick to hurt your father, and then so quick to retreat and hide. You thought that maybe, if you could hurt him first, maybe he couldn't hurt you. Or maybe if he did, it wouldn't matter so much because he would simply be retaliating and not actually coming after you. You so often threw the first dart in hopes that by the time he recovered and could throw one of his own, you could be long gone." Jari took a quick breath before continuing.

"You were even more like that the first time I met you. And no wonder. Jessi, you have been hurt, abandoned and rejected so many times in your life. I know it's scary to let someone close enough to hurt you again. But you can't live the rest of your life protecting yourself against ever getting hurt...if you do, you'll never be able to let someone love you or love someone else in return. Joe isn't perfect, no one is, and you might get hurt, but you need to allow the LORD to heal your heart enough that when you do, it's a pin prick, not the uncovering of a gaping and festering wound."

"That's a lovely visual," Jessica said dryly. Jari smiled.

"I know your dad hurt you every time he chose work over you, every time he chose a meeting over time with your family, every time he chose golfing with his associates over your gymnastics meets. It was like the final dagger to the heart when he chose me over you and your mom. I know that. While you've forgiven your dad and have a restored relationship, you have not allowed Jesus to heal the rejection and abandonment in your heart. I think the real reason you left Glendale was because you wanted Joe to be free, but I think the reason you stayed away is because you wanted to be free yourself. If you're not in a relationship with Joe, then you can't be hurt by him, right?" Jessi looked away.

"But look at what your freedom has cost, Hon. Do you see how Joe is with your little girls? He's in love! He dotes on them. You can see how badly he wants to be a father –

and what a good father he'll be. And do you see how he looks at you? He loves you, Jessica. Like really, truly, from-the-bottom-of-his-heart loves you. It's written all over his face. He has waited for you for *five* years. Think about that. Think about what it had to be like for him in college. Think about the girls he passed up for you." Jari paused, and Jessi sat still and quiet.

"You may have spent your junior year of high school seeking approval from him, but you've spent the last five proving to him and the world that you don't need him and never will. But there's a difference between finding your identity in him, and allowing yourself to love him, to be loved by him. You can love the LORD and love Joe at the same time. But it's going to take you being willing to be vulnerable and to take the chance of being hurt. Until you do that, you will never be able to receive his love and fully love him in return – Joe or Jesus. And I know you want to. I know you want to say yes to him, you're just too scared to let yourself. Fear debilitates a person, Jess. As you have sought freedom from Joe, you've only paid homage to fear. Perfect love casts out fear – but you have to open your heart to receive that love." Not waiting for an answer, Jari stood and hustled out of the hospital room.

"Chicken," Jessi said under her breath, but felt a smile tugging at the sides of her mouth. Her step-mom wasn't afraid to tell it like it was, but she wasn't going to stick around to see how it was received.

Jessi sat still for a long time, trying to sort through everything Jari had said. As little as she wanted to hear what Jari had to say, she knew she was right. It rang true in her heart. And truth be told, she felt like the LORD had been saying the same thing for the last five years, whispering to her that He had healing, to come out of hiding. She had simply always been too afraid to respond.

Again, the LORD beckoned to her, reaffirming all that Jari had just spoken. This time, Jessi took a deep breath and responded.

She stood and, after checking to make sure that both girls were still napping, left the hospital room, slipping through the corridors and swinging open the heavy doors of the chapel. It was dim and quiet, and she turned into a middle row of chairs. Going all the way to the wall in hopes of not being seen, she laid down on the chairs and spread her arms. She felt ridiculous, but it was one of the most vulnerable positions she could think of.

"Jesus, come and heal my heart. Make me whole. Teach me to trust." She smiled into the darkness. "I don't want any more gaping, festering wounds."

~~~~~

Jessica woke slowly, becoming aware of her surroundings over several moments. She was still in the hospital. She checked her watch. It was three in the morning. She yawned and rolled over carefully, curling up to Kamryn. The warm heated blanket the nurse had brought not only served to keep Kamryn's body temperature normal, it also helped to warm Jessica up. She had never quite thawed from her morning at the cemetery. Jessi pulled the blanket up farther and turned her attention to her daughter.

The little girl had to sleep on her back, her casts too heavy and awkward to sleep any other way. Jessi knew she was sore all over and tried not to touch her, other than to lay her arm carefully across her tummy. Kamryn smiled in her sleep, a sight that was even sweeter just days past the little girl who could not respond to anything.

Jessica studied her, trying to put to memory every little detail of her sweet daughter – the dip in her nose, the delicate point of her chin, her soft, fluttery blonde hair. Her heart swelled as she again thanked the LORD that she had more than just a memory of her daughter.

Kamryn had been such a good sport. Aching and immobile, she had taken it all in stride and resumed chattering and laughing with her family. She hadn't complained more than once or twice, and even that had only been when something was particularly painful. Jessi brushed a kiss across her cheek, proud of her.

She looked across to the next bed over, and let her eyes settle on her other daughter. She was proud of her, too. She hadn't complained about her broken arm either, and had gladly stepped into the role of mothering her twin sister. She brought her anything and everything she needed. She played and looked at books with her on her bed all day long, brought her drinks of water, and helped her put on the pink lipstick they thought looked so grown up. Now, she lay on her side, snoring just a little, her good arm anchoring her to her father who slept beside her.

Jessica's eyes moved to Joe. He was sleeping facing toward her, his arm around Kelsi. The picture they made looked so natural, just as everything had between him and the girls since he arrived on Saturday night. Her heart swelled with emotion until she couldn't quite contain it. A few tears escaped and slid down into her pillow.

As if a veil suddenly lifted, she realized that the man across from her wasn't someone to hide from or avoid. He was Joe, the boy she had fallen in love with more than half a decade ago.

And the man he had become was even more gentle, more humble, more patient, more kind than the boy had been. She suddenly felt terrible for putting up walls between them, always holding back and keeping someone around to avoid being alone with him.

Whether she hadn't trusted him or herself, she wasn't sure, but as she lay and watched him, she felt all of the emotions she had kept at bay for five and a half long years come tumbling back.

She remembered meeting him at 7-Eleven and how captivated she had been from that very first encounter. She smiled. He was still as captivating as he had ever been. To this day, there was something about him that was different from any other man she had ever met. She was still unable to identify it, but she was certain that she loved it.

She let her gaze move slowly over his face, studying every feature. He was so handsome – more so than any man she had ever seen. His features were masculine, the line of his jaw, strong. His skin was naturally the color of a great tan, and his hair was as dark and smooth as dark chocolate. His shoulders were broad and defined, and the muscles in his arms stretched the fabric of his long-sleeved t-shirt. Jessica found herself wishing she was in Kelsi's place, cuddled close to him, lying encircled in his arms.

She studied his mouth and remembered what it had been like to kiss him. She remembered how it had felt to be his girlfriend in high school, and wondered how it would feel to be his wife now. It's what he wanted, she knew it was, and as she studied him, she realized that she wanted it, too. More than anything. She always had.

He had been so gentle and kind in the last several days, and despite her most valiant efforts, her walls were slowly crumbling. She was finding it harder and harder to resist him. Yet he was being more patient than she ever thought possible, always hanging back, giving her space. It was what she had wanted, but she found it was beginning to have adverse effects. In the last day or two, she found herself being jealous of the attention and affection he lavished on their girls and wished for just some of it to be pointed in her direction.

She watched him sleep, wondering what would happen after Kamryn was released from the hospital. Would he go back to his mom and dad's? Would he stay with her? Was he going to be a permanent part of their lives now? Would they really get married and be a family? Would she really go from being a single mother to a happily married woman? Would there really be someone to help with the laundry, the baths, the bills and the cooking? And someone as wonderful as Joe?

She had adored him before, but now, the emotions that continued to build in her heart seemed deeper. He had been just a boy six years ago, but he had matured. He was somehow kinder, softer – more grace and less law. He was patient and gentle. Pride had gone, and in its place was a humility that was more confident in who his God was and less in who he himself was.

He had led them in prayer every morning and evening since arriving and had pointed her toward the LORD over and over again. He would be a strong spiritual leader. At every turn, in every situation, he had been at her side, offering his quiet strength as they waited for news, good or bad.

He had become her helpmate, dressing one of the girls while she dressed the other, taking Kelsi out to the nearby park to let her run off some energy, helping to reposition Kamryn when she was uncomfortable. He had watched both girls so Jessi could get out of the hospital for awhile and entertained them with silly stories. He asked the doctors important questions and shared the load of decision-making. She appreciated him being there more than he would ever know.

She lovingly traced his face again with her eyes. Her heart pounded so hard she was sure it was audible, as she came to a stunning realization – she was no longer simply in love with the memory of her high school sweetheart, she was very much in love with the living and breathing man in front of her.

Twenty-Three

It was the day before Christmas Eve and Jessi was hoping and praying the doctor would let them go home. They had been in the hospital for a week, and Christmas was on Monday. Jari and Carla had done what they could to make the room look festive, but the girls wanted their own Christmas decorations, their own house, their own beds and their own rooms. And she couldn't say she was any less ready.

She didn't want to leave too soon and put either girl in jeopardy, but Kelsi was completely back to normal, save her broken arm, and Kamryn was off all her machines and medications. She would still need physical therapy and frequent check-ups for some time, but was doing amazingly well. Jessi felt like it was time to go home.

She sent Joe to ask, hoping he could work his magic with the doctor, just as he had when asking to have Kamryn moved into Kelsi's room. When Joe came back, his usual grin in place, she knew he had been successful. She wanted to throw her arms around him and thank him for making a way for them to go home, but instead, she smiled and asked the question she already knew the answer to. "What did he say?"

"We're going home!" he announced jubilantly.

Jessi's heart skipped a beat at Joe's proclamation, whether out of joy at being released from the hospital or the realization that he had called her home his own, she wasn't sure. It was likely a mixture of both. She smiled at him, and watched Kelsi dance her way across the room and fling her good arm around his leg. On the bed, Kamryn was smiling and cheering.

"I'm going to show you my toys and my favorite dolly and how I can move the step stool so I can brush my teeth and...." Kelsi's list of what she would show him as soon as they arrived at their apartment continued.

"And we can have tea parties, and you can watch our Barbie movie with us!" Kamryn added.

Jessi shot Joe an amused smile. "That's quite an honor. Grandpa Bill has never been invited to watch Barbie. Only Mom, Grandma, Jari and I get to."

"And now you!" Kamryn told him.

"Well, that is quite an honor. I thoroughly accept your invitation and would be delighted to watch Barbie with you," Joe told the girls, bowing like a fine gentleman, his voice taking on a British accent. Both girls giggled.

Joe's demeanor changed. "Guess what, girls!"

"What?" they asked expectantly.

"We'll be home for Christmas!" More cheering erupted. "Who wants to watch Rudolph with me? I haven't seen it yet this season." Kelsi was now jumping up and down, her hand in the air.

"I do! I do!"

"Me too!" Kamryn added from her bed.

Joe acted as if he was scanning a crowd above them. "Oh, nobody wants to watch Rudolph? Come on, surely there's somebody who wants to eat popcorn, drink hot chocolate, and watch Rudolph with their dad!" he said, pretending to be sad. The girls were giggling, Kelsi was still jumping, and both were becoming more animated as they chanted, "I do! I do! I do!"

Jessica watched the scene unfold in front of her, and let herself take a moment to enjoy it. Her daughters and Joe were celebrating their homecoming together. She wanted to join in, but there was a lot to do, and she wanted to leave the hospital as soon as possible.

"When can we go?" she asked, breaking into the joyous scene.

"Doc said he would discharge us right away, so as soon as we get everything gathered and fill out the final paperwork, we can go." She sent the father of her children a long, lingering smile.

"You're very good with people, Joseph Colby." He looked taken aback by her direct compliment, and she enjoyed seeing his surprise transform into a slow smile.

"Thank you, Jessica Cordel."

She turned and got busy. She dumped the water out of vases full of flowers and packed the vases in a box Jari had brought specifically for that purpose.

In the first several hours after the accident, the room had filled with flowers – one of the benefits of being part of a beloved senator's family – and they continued to come until they lined nearly every available space. Jessi had already sent several bouquets home with Jari, Carla, Maybelle and Hannah, but still, a couple dozen remained.

"Kelsi, why don't you pick up all of your books and toys and put them in your backpack?"

"Okay, Mommy!" The four-year-old got to work. Jessi sneaked a glance at Joe and saw he was collecting all of their clothes and miscellaneous items. With all three of them working, they would be headed home soon. Jessica let out a soft sigh, realizing how nice it was to have Joe around to help. It wasn't all up to her anymore. That felt good.

Twenty minutes later, Joe offered to get everything loaded in the car while Jessica did the final paperwork. She willingly agreed. As she entered the room after finishing, Joe looked up and held her eyes. "Are you ready to go home?" The intensity in his gaze took her breath away. She nodded and turned away, feeling shy.

Everything had already been taken out, so she boosted Kelsi up onto her hip, seeing that Joe was carefully, gently, scooping up Kamryn. The little girl could do nothing to hang on without the use of either of her hands, but she put her face against Joe's shirt.

The girls chattered like magpies all the way through the hospital. As Jessi buckled Kelsi into her car seat in the vehicle her father and Jari had loaned her until she got a new one, she felt a bad case of nerves come over her.

She had only driven once since the accident, and she hadn't had either of the girls with her then. Now, she felt weak just thinking about getting behind the wheel and taking the broken little girls out on the roads.

"Want me to drive?" Joe asked, finishing with Kamryn's buckle. Jessi didn't look up, hoping she hadn't given away how fearful she felt.

"Sure." She tossed him the keys, which he caught. By the time she had Kelsi settled and had reached across the seat to spread a blanket over Kamryn, Joe was standing at her door, holding it open.

Although she should have expected it, she had forgotten, and she thanked him before getting in. She felt cared for and remembered. Finally, like a light bulb going on, she understood why Joe and his father opened doors for women. It showed a certain amount of respect and consideration. It showed a woman she was treasured and cared for. It was a little gift in a busy world.

Joe got in and started the engine. With him behind the wheel, Jessi felt herself relaxing. He was a good driver. Knowing he wasn't well acquainted with the city, she gave him turn-by-turn directions until he pulled into her designated parking place in front of her apartment building.

"I'm glad to be home," Jessi told him, relaxing in her seat for just a moment. He leveled his gaze on her and it turned tender.

"So am I." He didn't look away for several moments, and neither did she.

"This is *our* home, Silly!" Kamryn told him from the backseat.

"Can I pretend like it's mine for awhile?" Joe questioned, turning to her. She nodded, grinning.

"That reminds me, what are your plans?" Jessica asked, looking down at her hands to ask the question.

"Maybe we should get everybody in and settled, have some dinner, and we can talk about it later?" Joe asked, his voice hopeful. Jessi nodded and got out of the car. "I would have gotten that for you," Joe told her. She didn't respond.

Why didn't he want to talk about his plans? Was he leaving? Did he not want to say so in front of the girls?

Jessica sent a silent plea toward heaven, asking for the strength and grace to deal with whatever was coming. She unbuckled Kelsi and grabbed what she could. She instructed the little girl to carry her backpack, and Joe offered to come back for the rest.

Jessi led the way into the apartment building and summoned the elevator. She unlocked her front door and swung it open wide, standing back so Joe could carry Kamryn inside.

"Ladies first," he told her, his voice as cheerful as ever. She went in and set her stuff down, then shut the door and locked it as he eased Kamryn down onto the couch.

He stood up and let out a low whistle as he looked around. "It's nice in here, Jess." Despite her worry about the upcoming conversation, she smiled.

"Thanks. We like it."

"You always did have great taste," he told her with a wink, waiting for her smile before going on. "Will you give me a tour?" His expression was hopeful.

"It's been awhile since we were here," she said apologetically, hoping she had left her house clean. He waved her comment aside.

"It's not like you have company, Jess, it's just me." She liked that he didn't consider himself company in her home.

She led him through the house, showing him the living room, the dining room, the kitchen, the guest bathroom, the girls' bedroom and bathroom, the master suite, and the guest room. He complemented her decorating and told her several times that he liked the colors she had used. His compliments made her feel happy and confident even several minutes later as she escorted Kelsi into the bathroom for a bath.

After bathing her, taking extra care with her cast, she got her dressed in warm pajamas and settled in her room with crayons. Then she carried Kamryn into the bathroom and washed her with a warm sudsy washcloth before changing her into a matching long nightgown, which nearly hid her pink casts. Satisfied that the hospital germs were off, Jessi stood, ready to go out and start dinner.

She nearly collided with Joe who had been standing in the doorway of the girls' room watching. "Feel better now that they're clean?" he asked.

"Yes," she answered with a guilty smile. He had known what she was thinking.

"Why don't you get cleaned up, too, while I start dinner? I put your bag in your room."

The simple way he extended the kind offer, his hands resting lightly in his pockets, leaning against the door frame, made her want to walk over and thank him with a kiss. She quickly averted her eyes to hide her thoughts while attempting to keep a blush from rising into her cheeks. "Thank you," she told him as she quickly brushed by him. He turned and caught her hand. She glanced up and realized his grin was back.

"What?" she asked, trying to sound casual.

"I was thinking of cooking up some chili. Do you have the makings?"

"I should," she paused and broke into a smile. "That sounds amazing." He released her hand.

"Good."

She quickly retreated to her room and shut the door behind her. She unpacked her bag and took a shower, slipping into a sweater and a pair of jeans. She did her hair and makeup, spending more time on it than she cared to admit, then wandered out to see what Joe and the girls were doing.

As soon as she opened her bedroom door, the smell of cooking food caused her stomach to rumble. She walked out to the living room and found Joe sitting with an arm around each girl, their Barbie movie playing on the television screen. Sensing her nearness, he tipped his head back and smiled up at her.

"I voted Rudolph, but was outnumbered."

"They like to use their numbers to their advantage," she told him sympathetically.

"So I've learned. Do you want to check the cinnamon rolls? They should be done soon." She agreed and headed into the kitchen. She checked on the cinnamon rolls and set the timer for two more minutes. Then she lifted the lid off her big soup pot and stirred the chili.

The smell of the chili combined with the smell of the baking rolls made her mouth water. They had eaten far too much hospital food in the last week, and a home-cooked meal sounded amazing.

She heard Joe stirring in the living room then heard the girls tell him it was okay to leave because Barbie didn't get saved for awhile yet. She directed her attention back to the chili as he walked into the kitchen. She moved past him to get four bowls down from the cupboard. As she did, she felt him lean in close to her and breath deeply.

"You smell good," he told her, easing back a step. She couldn't help it; she froze for several moments before moving away to get spoons. His nearness unnerved her.

"You're more than welcome to use the guest bathroom to take a shower after dinner," she said, recovering. He took the bowls and spoons from her and put them on the table.

"I might just take you up on that. Then I was thinking of starting a fire in your fireplace. Is that okay? I see you have wood."

"Absolutely. I've been wanting to since getting home from Texas, but just haven't done it yet."

"I'm glad you waited for me." She smiled at him.

"Me too."

The timer went off, and she hurried to take the cinnamon rolls out of the oven. She put them on the table, and he carried over the pot of chili. She set bowls of crackers and cheese next to the chili while Joe paused Barbie and carried Kamryn into the dining room, towing Kelsi by her hand.

Jessi dished the food while Joe got the girls settled. When Jessi took her seat, Joe said grace. The girls began to chat happily as soon as he finished, obviously glad to be home. During the meal, Jessi and Joe exchanged several amused glances at things the girls said, and she realized how nice it felt to have him at their dinner table.

After dinner, she cleaned up while the girls finished their movie, and Joe went in to take a shower. When he emerged, she had thoughts of leaning in close and breathing deeply as he had in the kitchen, but decided against it, enjoying his fresh masculine scent from a safe distance instead. Finishing with the dishes, she dried her hands on the dishtowel and went in to turn off the movie and get the girls moving toward bed. Joe fell into step beside her and scooped up Kamryn, tickling her softly to draw several precious giggles.

Once both girls had gone potty and were tucked into their warm beds, Joe sat on Kamryn's bed and Jessica sat on Kelsi's. Both girls snuggled in, glad to be back in their own beds and in their own room.

"Don't forget to plug in our Christmas tree," Kamryn told her, pointing to the white tree with pink lights that stood in the corner of their room.

"I won't," Jessi promised. She leaned over and picked up a book. She held it out to Joe with a smile. "Would you like to read tonight?" He took it and grinned.

"Absolutely."

Jessi laid down with Kelsi and closed her eyes, listening to Joe's voice as he read the bedtime story. When she heard him close the book quietly, she opened her eyes and realized that both girls were asleep, just as she nearly was.

She sat up and stretched, covering a yawn with the back of her hand. She carefully kissed each girl and turned on their Christmas tree as she had promised. Joe put his hand on her back, letting her know he was behind her as she straightened, and the warmth that came from his hand made her shiver. He followed her out of the room after pausing to kiss each girl's forehead, and softly shut the door.

~~~~~

Joe wanted to reach out and gather Jessica into his arms, but instead he grinned. "Our girls are in bed, and we have the whole evening to start a fire and talk." As she had done so often that day, Jessi shifted her eyes to the ground and stepped around him.

"I'll make us some hot chocolate," she offered over her shoulder as she walked down the short hall.

He stood still for a moment, wondering about her odd behavior. She had been so stand-offish for the first several days he had been in D.C., then this morning she seemed a little flirty once or twice. When they got home from the hospital she had seemed mad and now, she was as shy as if he were a stranger. He couldn't make any sense of it and wished his dad was there to help. If only his parents hadn't flown back to Glendale, or if he could go somewhere private and call him. But Jessi was waiting.

He went out to the living room, knelt down at the hearth, and busied himself starting a fire. It had just taken off when Jessi joined him, two mugs of hot chocolate in her hands. She sat down on the couch, and he took the spot beside her. They both just sat there watching the fire for several long minutes, neither of them saying anything or even moving. Joe waited for Jessi to begin the conversation.

"It is really nice to be out of the hospital," she finally said, the relief evident in her tone. He glanced at her and found that she had her head tipped back, her eyes closed and her knees drawn up to her chest. She looked exhausted, and he considered telling her to go to bed. But he had waited too long to get her by herself. He wasn't going to send her away when it finally happened.

"It is," he agreed. "It's quiet, clean, private and comfortable here," he continued. "Did I tell you I like your house?" She grinned.

"Once or twice."

"Well, I do. I think you have a great place."

"Thank you."

He took a drink of his hot chocolate. "Jessi?"

"Hm?" she answered, her eyes still closed. He wondered if she was really that tired, or if she was afraid to face him. "You know the accident wasn't your fault, right?"

She opened her eyes, sitting straighter. He sensed her tension and knew she wasn't sure how to answer. "There was nothing you could have done," he told her, hoping she would believe him. She shook her head.

"I could have swerved."

"You did."

"Well, I should have sped up." He shook his head again.

"Jessica, there is nothing you could have done to avoid it. It was an accident. The other guy made poor decisions. That's all there is to it."

"And our daughters paid the price," she said, her voice rising. Joe nodded.

"Unfortunately, that's true."

Jessica took a deep, shuddering breath. "I wanted you there, but Joe, when you walked in, when my family walked in, I felt so ashamed. I felt...I feel...so guilty. I should have been able to stop it somehow or at the very least, I should have been hurt instead of them." He shook his head.

"No, Jess, don't think that way." His heart hurt at the pain and guilt he heard in her voice.

"I don't know how not to. A mother is supposed to

protect her children. They almost died, Joe!"

This was the girl he wanted to talk to, the conversation he had wanted to have since arriving. Finally, he was hearing what was really going on in her mind. It was what he had thought all along. These were the lies he wanted to rebuff.

"Jessica, they didn't. They are fine. They're sleeping in their beds, warm and safe." Still, she shook her head.

"I almost killed one of my children and walked away without a scratch." He wanted to remind her that she had several bruises and scratches of her own, but didn't waste his breath. "I almost killed your children and you didn't even know them. Don't you understand? I could have just been calling you there to say goodbye, just as you said. Or worse yet, you may not have even made it. Your children could have been dead before you even knew their names."

"But they weren't. Don't spend time dwelling on what could have happened." She turned pain-filled eyes up to him.

"I kept them from you for years."

"You only did it to try to protect me," he argued, sticking up for her.

"Partly. But I also did it to protect myself. It started for the right reasons, but then, even when I wanted to tell you, I felt like it had already gone too far. I was ashamed. And then…then I just started believing I could do things on my own, and that if I didn't let you get close, then I wouldn't get hurt."

Joe wanted to take her in his arms and cover her in kisses for being so honest, for being willing to be vulnerable enough to tell him all she just had. But, he had a confession of his own to make.

"Jessica, I've known about the girls since August, and I hadn't come back. The fault doesn't lie entirely with you." She studied him, her expression as open and honest as it had been before.

"I know. Why didn't you?"

"I was angry and hurt. I felt betrayed and thought you didn't want me in your life. Then, when I was done being angry, I felt guilty that you had been so selfless while I had been so selfish. I thought I should give up what I wanted for what you wanted. But in the last few days I've realized that my desire to match your selflessness was actually more self-ishness and pride on my part." He shrugged his shoulders. "Sometimes, even when I want to do the right thing, it ends up being wrong."

"I understand that completely." And he knew she did.

He squared his shoulders toward her. "Jessica, I'm sorry that I stayed away so long." She took a long moment to reply, as if she were examining her heart.

"I forgive you," she told him, and he believed her. "I'm sorry I kept your children a secret from you." He studied her face, her eyes, and saw she was remorseful – she realized as much as he did what all he had missed.

"I forgive you." He paused. "And about those children," he paused again, embarrassed to go on. Summoning his courage, he plowed ahead. "I'm sorry I took advantage of you and got you pregnant in high school." He couldn't bring himself to look at her. Instead, he studied the patterns his hand made in the suede fabric of the couch as he pushed it back and forth.

It was quiet for a long time. "It wasn't like I was opposed."

"I knew better," he told her, still looking down. His apology was sincere, but he wasn't brave enough to face her while uttering it. Again, it was quiet, and when she spoke, there was no condemnation in her voice.

"I forgive you," she told him, "but what the enemy meant for harm, the LORD turned to good. What happened that night turned out to be the two greatest gifts God could have ever given me."

Joe finally looked up at her, knowing his face was

probably still red. He saw that she too was blushing. "Given *us*," he corrected. She sent him a warm smile.

"Right."

Feeling free and weightless, knowing he had confessed the sin that had already been forgiven by Jesus, and that he had Jessica's forgiveness as well, he took a chance. He picked up her slender hand, weaving his fingers through hers.

"So, you asked me today in the car what my plans are." She nodded, and he could see the hesitancy in her face, as if she was worried about what would come next. Did she really think he would leave? The thought was absurd to him.

"I want to be close to you," he paused. "I *will* be close to you. We need to figure out the details of that in the future, but for now I wonder if I could stay in your spare room in case you need help with the girls during the night – at least for the first night or two, until we know how it's going to go with Kamryn."

Her smile was instant and shot a jolt of warmth through him. Her smile made him feel things no other girl ever could. Her eyes were warm as she squeezed his hand.

"I hoped you would." Her eyes were shining, and he was suddenly aware of how right her hand felt in his. His eyes moved over her face, her eyes, her hair, her simple sweater and jeans.

She was beautiful. Absolutely, stunningly beautiful. She had always been gorgeous, but now the new grace and gentleness she possessed transformed her from simply being an object to admire to an absolute beauty – one to stop and take notice of, not just for her outward looks, but her inward beauty as well.

Suddenly, all the patience he had been graced with during the past week was gone, and all of the emotions that had been so familiar in high school were back. He wished he had the freedom to reach out and kiss her and pull her close. The inches separating them suddenly seemed like miles.

Heeding caution, he faked a cough and then took a long swig of hot chocolate. In the meantime, she stood up from the couch and went to sit directly in front of the fire, facing the flames, seeming to aid in putting distance between them.

He wisely stayed on the couch. He watched her sitting silently before the fire, her back straight, her legs folded underneath her, and her long hair hanging down her back. He was tempted to go run his fingers through her dark tresses, sit down behind her and pull her back to rest against his chest.

She turned suddenly and caught him looking at her. He wanted to look away, but forced himself not to. After five years, he felt shyer and more like a school boy than he had in high school. Still, he took a deep breath and smiled, hoping he looked more confident than he felt. She smiled back.

"Do you still want to watch Rudolph?" she asked, taking him by surprise.

"Sure," he said quickly, thankful for the distraction. She jumped up to find the Christmas classic.

While she got the movie ready to roll, he stood up, stretched, and went to get a glass of water, doing whatever he could to put distance between them for the time being. He needed to get his emotions back under control.

She was even more desirable than he remembered, and even after a week in her presence, he was struggling to keep his thoughts straight now that they were alone. The air between them felt electric and he was being pulled to her as if she possessed a magnetic force that drew him. They had been through so much together over the past week, as well as the past six years, and he wanted to draw her close and enjoy her nearness as they celebrated being out of the hospital together.

He turned his thoughts to the girls, desperately hoping

some of the patience and discipline he had experienced during the week would return. But he only found himself wondering what it would be like if they were a normal family and now that the girls were in bed, he could enjoy the evening with his wife, cuddling on the couch instead of standing in her kitchen gulping down water.

He drank three full glasses, stalling all he could, then went back to the living room. Jessica was waiting with two candy canes. She handed one to him.

"With hot chocolate, Rudolph, and the fire, it wouldn't be right without a candy cane," she said cheerfully. He took it and sat down on the opposite end of the couch, where he watched the movie, reminding himself that he would not do anything that would make her uncomfortable. He knew what he wanted, but he wanted to give her time to come to the same conclusion.

Near the end of the movie, Jessi stood and headed to the kitchen. He was keenly aware of her absence until she returned, but this time, she didn't sit at the far side of the couch. Gripping her cup of hot chocolate, she sat down beside him without a word, and pulled her knees up to make a little table for her drink.

"Joe?"

"Hm?" he asked, pretending to watch the movie.

"I've wondered before what it would be like to have you here for an evening – to make dinner together, eat as a family, put the girls to bed together and then…do this – just hang out."

"Have you?" he asked, not trusting himself to look away from the television.

"Yes."

Finally, he couldn't help himself. He stole a glance. Her eyes were shining again, and her cheeks were slightly flushed. "What do you think about it now?" he asked, quickly turning his attention back to the movie. She took so long to answer, he glanced at her again. As soon as he did, she broke out into a glorious smile.

"I love it." She stood. "I'm going to head to bed. With all the change, the girls are likely to wake up in the middle of the night." He caught her hand, wishing she wouldn't go. But instead of asking her to stay, he steered the conversation in a safe direction.

"If they do, will you please wake me up? I want to help." Joe knew he wasn't a deep sleeper, but mothers had a strange habit of waking up if their child needed something, even if no word was uttered. He didn't want to miss it and wasn't confident he had the same intuition.

"I will." Jessica bent down and, thoroughly surprising him, pressed a soft kiss against his cheek. "Goodnight, Joe." He was so stunned, he couldn't respond.

As she walked down the hall to bed, he realized that maybe the reason he was having such a hard time containing his feelings for her now, was because they were finally reciprocated. He had a feeling she had come to the conclusion he had hoped she would. He had a feeling Jessica Cordel had realized she was still in love with him.

211

Twenty-Four

On the morning of Christmas Eve, Joe woke early and couldn't sleep. He threw his blankets off and got up, leaving the guest room for a drink of water. As he passed through the living room, a photograph caught his eye and he walked to the hearth. He stood and stared at the picture of Jessica and the girls and found himself smiling.

All three of them looked like they were having a blast. They were all simply in black sweaters, jeans and scarves, and leaves were going everywhere. Kamryn was standing with her arms stretched upward, leaves she had thrown having just left her fingertips. Her smile was one of pure, childlike wonder. Kelsi was throwing more leaves into the already leaf-filled air, her mouth open, obviously either squealing or giggling. Jessi was sitting in the middle, laughing as the leaves the girls had thrown rained down on her. It was a breathtaking photo, and Joe wanted a copy.

Coming up with a great idea, he started a pot of coffee and went snooping through Jessica's house until he found what he was after. Then he poured two cups of coffee, added flavored creamer, set everything up on the coffee table and padded down the hall.

He checked in on the girls, but they were both still sleeping, completely and totally zonked out. He wondered if they had gotten up at all during the night, and Jessica simply hadn't woken him up as she said she would. Stepping back out of the room, he carefully shut the door and went several feet farther.

He knocked lightly on Jessi's doorframe. He peeked in just in time to see her sit up in bed looking adorably confused. He knew she was surprised to see him, and she quickly started messing with her hair and wiping the makeup from underneath her eyes. He found it humorous that after sleeping merely a few feet apart in a hospital room for a week, she now worried about her appearance.

He entered without waiting, worried she would send him out until she had time to freshen up. "Good morning!" he told her softly, not wanting to wake the girls. He loved his daughters and treasured every moment with them, but this morning he wanted alone time with their mother.

"Good morning," she told him, smiling sleepily. "You're up early."

He nodded, bending down and scooping her up in his arms. She was stunned, yet she laughed.

"What are you doing?" He didn't answer, but took her out to the living room and set her carefully on the couch. He handed her one of the mugs of coffee, then one of the thick books he had found.

"What's this?" she asked, confused by what he wanted.

"Show me what I've missed the last five years."

Understanding spread across her face, and as she ran a hand over the photo album, she sent him a brilliant smile, one that took his breath away.

"I would love to. Give me just a minute," she told him, setting her coffee down and running from the living room into her large bathroom, shutting the door behind her. He groaned, amused. Women.

Jessi shut the door and quickly ran to her bathroom counter, grabbing her toothbrush and toothpaste. She brushed her teeth with one hand, while trying to straighten her disheveled hair with the other. When she finished, she quickly covered a small spot of acne with concealer. She thought about makeup, but knew the girls would be waking up soon and didn't want to miss the early morning time Joe had planned for them. She wouldn't have wasted any time at all, but she was hoping maybe this morning he would kiss her, and she wanted to be prepared.

She rubbed lotion into her hands and arms, and hurried back out to the living room. Joe was now sitting on the couch, a blanket dragged out and waiting for her, sipping on his steaming brew.

"Feel better?" he asked, amused.

"Yes," she answered with a smile. She sat beside him and let him spread the blanket across her legs. She leaned back against the plush couch and used the coffee table as a rest for her toes. Joe handed her the other cup of coffee, and she took a small drink, letting the flavor wash over her.

"How did you sleep?" he asked, grinning at her. Her heart flopped. His grin was so endearing, especially so early in the morning. His hair stuck up on one side, and he had the faint hint of facial hair. He had never been more handsome.

"Good. The girls didn't wake up at all."

"I wondered," he told her, taking another drink of coffee. "Jessi, you didn't have to do anything to yourself, you know. You're beautiful even if your hair is a mess," he mused after a short silence, grinning at her again. She sat speechless. How did she explain her reasoning? She didn't want to share that she was hoping for a kiss.

He seemed a million times surer of himself this morning than he had last night, while she now felt shy and giddy. She scolded herself as she took a drink of coffee and grabbed the first picture book.

She sent him a pointed look. "This starts when I was pregnant." She flipped through the pages of the book recounting funny stories and telling what was happening in the photographs. She stole a glance at Joe when she turned the page to where she had pasted newspaper clippings about his football season.

He sent her an amazed look. "You kept these?"

"Just because I wasn't with you, didn't mean I didn't

care," she told him with a smile.

"Wow," he breathed.

"I wanted the girls to know about you – what a star their daddy was," Jessi paused. "I watched every game you ever played."

"You did?" She nodded, still smiling.

"It was torture every time you got sacked. I held my breath every time you didn't pop right up. I wanted to talk to you about every play."

His amazement turned into a smug grin. "I turned you into a real football fan, didn't I?" She elbowed him.

"I liked the game before I ever met you." She knew it wasn't true, even as she said it. He did, too. Still, she had to try. He made a face at her.

"Whatever. You didn't know a touchdown from a first down." She took a drink of coffee.

"Next," she said firmly. She turned the page and Joe's teasing stopped as he ran his hand over the page lovingly.

"You were beautiful." She laughed.

"I was nine months pregnant and as big as a house."

"And glowing." He reached over and tweaked her nose. "Not every girl can be nine months pregnant and still that beautiful." She stored his comment away in her heart. She had always wondered what he would say about how she looked pregnant.

She felt his gaze on her, even as she turned to the next page. "In fact, pregnant or not, no other girl is as beautiful as you are. You are the most beautiful woman I have ever seen, Jessica." She laughed.

"You get the cheese of the day award. Look, this is when your daughters were born." He surprised her by reaching over, taking her chin, and turning her toward him.

"I'm serious, Jess," he told her, looking right into her eyes. "With makeup or without it, your hair curled or straight, you are beautiful. The most beautiful girl I've ever seen."

"And you would know. I'm guessing you've seen your fair share of girls," she answered, trying to keep the mood light.

"I have. And many of them wanted me." She burst out laughing, surprised by his conceited comment.

"Well, aren't you modest?" His expression stayed serious.

"Jess, college was crazy. There were so many girls, and so many that wanted to go out with me, but the only one I ever wanted was you. I never dated one of them. I couldn't even consider it," he paused and rubbed his thumb across her jaw.

"I wanted you to know that. When I said all those things about wanting my wife to know she was my one and only, I meant it. And I want you to rest assured that it's just as true today. I'll never be with you and think of someone else, or look at you and see another girl. You are the one I want, the girl I think is most beautiful, most desirable."

Joe's words made her shiver as they soaked in, answering so many questions she had. For four years she watched him on TV, watched his fame and popularity, and wondered who he spent his time with, and if he still thought of her.

"Every day I prayed for you, Jessi, then I'd offer you up to the LORD and ask that His will would be done in your life. And then I prayed He would bring us back together when the time was right. It was a daily discipline, a daily battle to lay you down before Him instead of making things play out the way I wanted them to." He brushed her hair back out of her eyes.

"The LORD said once that He would restore you to me in D.C., and it would be a chance meeting, so every August I came and simply walked around and looked for you, hoping it would be the year He gave you back to me."

"Every year?" she asked, shocked by what he was telling her.

"Yes. Every year. Four years I came and this year, this year was the one."

"That's why you didn't seem surprised when we met on the street."

"I had been looking for you," he told her.

"And why you grinned so much at dinner."

"I was ecstatic that it was finally time." He was grinning again.

"And that's why you couldn't leave it at that," she said, connecting the dots.

"I had to come the next morning. I couldn't just get on a plane and leave."

"And then you saw the girls, and you were angry. Angry at me and...angry at God?"

"He knew. He could have told me. I could have found you sooner."

Jessi tentatively touched his face, pushed the hair back from his forehead. He leaned his head into her hand. "His timing is perfect," she told him softly, growing more mesmerized by the man in front of her by the second.

He was gentle, he was kind, he was handsome, he was faithful, he had sought after her, and he had obeyed the LORD rather than doing what he wanted. This was a man truly desirable, one who stood out among all others.

She felt the mood in the room changing. The comfortable sweetness from the last half hour had given way to the quickening intensity of attraction. Jessi's heart began to race as Joe's gaze dropped to her lips.

"It is perfect," he answered, leaning closer, his eyes still on her mouth. The chemistry between them felt like a physical force.

"Joe?" She waited for him to look back up into her eyes.

"Hm?" he asked, finally glancing up from her lips, his face so close now that she could feel the warmth of his breath on her face.

"I'm glad His timing is now." Unable to resist any longer, Joe covered her lips with his own. With a sweet sigh of relief, she ran her hands along his shoulders and up behind his neck.

He leaned across her to set his coffee mug on the coffee table, and she could feel the strength of his arms, the firmness of his chest as he wrapped his arms around her, pulling her closer. He took it slow as they both remembered their way, but then let it deepen as they found themselves on familiar, if long-forgotten, ground.

He kissed her nose, her cheeks, her eyes, and she let him, enjoying every second of it, her heart racing, her insides full of butterflies. He ran his fingers through her hair, then traced the line of her jaw. He kissed her again.

"I love you," he told her, his voice husky. "I've loved you for six and a half years, and I promise I will love you for the rest of my life." She kissed him again.

"I love you too, Joe Colby."

There was noise behind them. "Mommy, Kamryn has to go potty and needs help," Kelsi said from the hallway, still sounding sleepy.

Jessi groaned. "Oh and real life begins again." The moment had been so long in coming, she hated to see it end.

"I love it," Joe told her, kissing her once more, then jumping up with a grin. "I love every minute of it. You know why?"

"Why?" she asked, unable to stop herself from grinning back at him.

"Because real life includes you and our girls."

"*Our* girls," she echoed, loving the sound of it.

Joe scooped up Kelsi, drawing a giggle, and went to assist Kamryn. Jessi got up, set her coffee down, and laid the photo books aside before going to help.

Ten minutes later, both girls were settled on the couch between Joe and Jessi with mugs of hot cocoa. Jessi opened the photo book again to the page they had left off on, and she and the girls showed Joe the photo documentation of their lives.

They laughed and talked all morning, sitting together in their pajamas, remembering and sharing days past, looking forward to days ahead.

~~~~~

Joe watched as the presents were opened one by one. He was sitting in Bill and Jari Cordel's great room with the twenty-foot Christmas tree towering in front of him. Kamryn was on his lap and Kelsi and Jessica were sitting at his feet. Jessi's family was gathered around. They had just finished dinner and were opening gifts before singing Christmas carols and listening to Bill read the Christmas story. After the festivities were over, their little family of four would get in their loaned vehicle and drive through the night to Glendale, where they would celebrate Christmas Day with the Colbys.

Joe watched as the pile of gifts dwindled, bringing them ever closer to the biggest present in the bunch. Finally, it was the only one left and Tim, wearing a Santa hat, handed it to Jessi. Joe could tell she was surprised the giant present was for her, and he could barely contain his excitement.

Jessi took off the paper, used Joe's pocket knife to cut the tape on the box and pulled a smaller wrapped box from inside. "What?" she asked, laughing, shooting him a sideways glance. He couldn't stop the grin from coming. He glanced at Bill, and realized he was grinning, too.

Jessi took the wrapping off the second box and cut it open, only to pull out another box. Then another and another and another until it was obvious she expected that inside the box would be another box. And it was, except this one was small and velvet.

Joe heard her breath catch, and she shot him a questioning glance. He quickly handed Kamryn to Carla, and went down on one knee before Jessica, taking the box from her hands.

Around the room, Jari, Maybelle, and Carla were gasping, their hands going to their mouths. Joe glanced quickly at Bill for support and found Jessi's dad still grinning, smugly now, excited he had been in on the secret.

Joe turned to Jessica. "I know that we've only been seeing each other for a week." That drew a laugh from his audience and a delighted smile from Jessi. His mission accomplished, he continued. "And only in a romantic way since this morning." Another adorable smile. "But I have loved you since high school, Jessica Cordel, and I don't ever want to live life without you again. I want to love you and serve you and be with you for the rest of our days. Will you marry me?" He opened the velvet box to reveal the stunning ring he had purchased a few years back in an active proclamation of faith.

Expecting that she would say yes didn't make it any less special. When she did, he drew her up with him, and, wrapping his arms around her securely, kissed her softly, those around them forgotten.

"We've been through a lot, Jess, but this moment right now, this make it worth it. I've wanted this since high school. Promise me that whether you move to Michigan, or I change schools and move to D.C., that we can be together from this day forward. You, me, and our daughters." She was all smiles.

"I promise."

Twenty-Five

The night was dark and there were very few people on the road when Joe, Jessi and the girls traveled from D.C. to Glendale late Christmas Eve. On such a special Christmas, they wanted to spend it with both families, no matter how long the drive.

The girls were sleeping in the backseat, Christmas songs were playing softly on the radio, the cab of the car was warm and the clock showed two a.m.

"I almost had an abortion," Jessi said softly. Joe's head snapped around quickly. He was caught off-guard by her change in the easy conversation they had shared for the last several hours.

"What?" he asked stunned.

"I was scared and alone, and in a temporary lapse of reason, I went to an abortion clinic." She saw Joe's face grow pale, despite the fact that his daughters were sleeping in the backseat.

"It was before I became a believer, and all I could think about, Joe, was how much I hurt. I missed you, I missed my mom and my grandparents, I missed Kara and your parents, I missed Tacy, and I missed Glendale. My dad and I weren't getting along, and I was in a lot of emotional pain and turmoil. I thought maybe, if they were to grow up in the same situation, in the same family, feeling the same way, then maybe the babies would be better off never being born."

"Jessi," Joe breathed quietly.

"I know. But my dad told me I wasn't welcome in his home if I had them, and I didn't know where to go, or what to do. I felt overwhelmed and alone, and I wasn't thinking straight."

"What changed your mind?"

"The LORD spoke, and the girls kicked," Jessi said, the memory bringing a smile to her face.

"They kicked?" Jessica nodded.

"It was the first time I felt them. They didn't do it again for several weeks, but I know I felt them kick."

"What did you do?"

"I got back in my car and I left," Jessi paused and gave him a sheepish grin. "Then I bawled my eyes out thinking about what I had almost done."

Joe was quiet, absorbing her words. "I wish I had been around to feel them kicking and moving." Jessi smiled, looking at her beautiful diamond ring.

"You can be for the next one."

"Or the next ten," Joe told her, giving her a mischievous grin. She laughed quietly, not wanting to wake the girls.

"Oh, we're having ten more, are we? Are we going for a dozen?"

"At least. All of them boys. We can name them Joe the second, Joe the third, Joe the fourth, Joe the fifth, Joe the sixth, Joe the seventh," he paused. "That one – Joe the seventh – is going to be a trouble maker. I can feel it already." Jessica laughed and held his hand when he reached for hers.

"How many kids do you actually want?" she asked after they were quiet for several seconds.

"Well...I don't know. We can make our plans, but the LORD will have His way. Let's just leave it up to Him." Her thoughts exactly.

"Sounds like a plan."

Several minutes passed, and Joe turned his head to her, grinning. "Remember how you asked if I was married?" She nodded.

"It was all over the news for a few weeks. Then it was said to simply be a rumor," she answered.

"I told my teammates I was." Her eyes grew wide.

"You did? You're the one that started it?" It was his

turn to nod. "I was so tired of them constantly badgering me to go to different clubs or chase different girls with them. I didn't know how to explain that I was already taken, so I just got fed up one day at practice and told some of the guys I was married. I didn't think anything would come of it, but they blabbed it to everyone." Joe made a face.

"The next weekend, my parents came up for my game, and by then the rumors were flying. Reporters were trying to ask my parents if it was true, if I was married, and if so, why my wife was in hiding. Finally, I had to explain that it was a misunderstanding and then tell my teammates what I had meant." Joe chuckled. "My poor parents were so confused. What I thought would get me off the hook, ended up being a nightmare."

Jessica laughed, her heart warming at the realization that all the fuss had been about her. She had worried for nothing. She had watched the stories and wondered what was going on, who the reporters were referring to, and if Joe was seeing someone else. And all along, it had only ever been meant to explain his devotion to her.

Her chest filled with pride and warmth until she felt as if she might burst. Joe had been sought after by dozens, if not hundreds, of girls. The reports that he was married had crushed multitudes, and here she sat, his engagement ring on her finger, headed to his family's house for Christmas Day. All was right in the world.

The night stretched on without either of them getting tired, despite their crazy week. They talked the entire way to Glendale, sharing things about the last five years, filling each other in on their lives. They stopped once for coffee and a bathroom break before getting on the road again.

They watched the sun come up together, and Jessica felt her heart swell as they drove by so many familiar places as they came into Glendale. She watched the 'Welcome to Glendale' sign as they passed it. Joe pointed out things that had changed and things that were the same.

It was the first time Jessi had been back since she left the summer before her senior year, and she wasn't sure whether to laugh or cry. She had thought of this place, the memories she had here, the people she had learned to love here, so many times.

Joe turned the car down the gravel road that led to his parents' house, and then turned down their lane. Memories flooded Jessi's mind, and Joe reached over and grabbed her hand.

"We're at Grandma and Grandpa's house, girls!" Joe told Kelsi and Kamryn. They erupted into cries of delight. "It might be a little tricky this time because of your casts, but next time we visit, you girls will have a lot of fun here! There are woods to explore, a pool to swim in, Grandma's cookies to eat and a river to fish in. There's a tree house in the back-yard that my dad and I built, and lots of my sisters' Barbie dolls to play with," Joe was telling the girls. "And, of course, lots of cousins!"

Jessica looked back at her bright-eyed daughters, who were clapping their hands, chattering excitedly. She looked at the man she was going to marry, whom she had loved since she was fifteen, explaining all the thrills of his parents' house to their daughters. She looked at the familiar house that felt so comfortable and held so many memories. She watched Joe's family – her family – come out onto the front porch to meet them. Justin, Kara, Kimberly, Greg, Carson, Samuel, Kaitlynn, Jake, Chris and Hannah were all there, waiting to greet them, to hug them and welcome them.

"Jessi," Joe waited until she turned to meet his eyes. He broke into a grin, his green eyes lighting up, and nodded back to the house. His family, all of the people she loved and had missed for the past five years, the people who first introduced her to love, family, and belonging, were holding up a long sign with a simple message written on it.

"Welcome home, Jessica."

A NOTE FROM ANN

Dear Reader,

Writing this book felt like telling the story of a close friend. However cheesy this may be, I still tear up every time I read it. At first, I thought it was because I was such a good writer (Ha!), but then I realized that maybe my emotions, and the emotions of those I asked to read this book as my first audience after it was completed, were so stirred because our hearts were created to long for and delight in reconciliation. We were called to forgive and live in reconciled and restored relationships – with those around us and with our Savior.

Jessica's story of salvation, as well as her family's story of salvation, is not my story; however elements of it are, as well as being reflections of how I see the Savior moving in the lives of people all around me. He is real, and He is moving, working out the details and writing beautiful masterpieces intricately designed to bring people to Him, to the cross. I hope as you read this book, you found yourself encountered by the One who invites us closer over and over and over again. He invites us in, invites us to know Him, love Him, and live in daily relationship with Him, because that's what He longs for with us. That, dear reader, is not fiction, but truth.

When I first started writing this book, I thought my main character was Jessica, and everyone else (save maybe Joe) were supporting characters. However, as the words filled page after page, I found myself zoning in on Jari. She is quiet and somewhat in the background, even though she's a key character in many chapters, but she is the door – the one yielded heart that gave Jesus an 'in' to an entire family. She reminded me that one yielded heart, one person who loves Jesus and commits herself to letting Him work in and through her, can be used to make an eternal difference for many. She's not flashy, she's not the life of the party, and she certainly didn't come into the Kingdom with a squeaky clean record, but she has embraced Jesus' forgiveness, is humble, patient and committed to loving the broken people around her. As her character continued to develop, I found a longing in my own heart to be more like this woman and commit to lying down my own rights, comfort, and will for the sake of Christ's greater purpose.

Additionally, writing this book brought healing to my own heart, and, after finishing the manuscript, the LORD put a desire in my heart, then made a way for my husband and I to go back to my hometown – somewhere I hadn't been since leaving for college. I was given the privilege of introducing my husband to a side of my family I had not seen or even talked to since my parents' divorce.

To be honest, on our way into town I felt nervous and shaky down to the very tips of my toes, but in my heart I knew that pursuing reconciliation in my own life was right, and it was key to being a healthy, happy and whole girl myself. So, we went, and although it was a little awkward at first, the LORD was good, and for the first time in six years, I left town on good terms with that side of my family. That was the most glorious feeling.

Time really does heal a lot of wounds, and even wounds that time alone can't heal, Jesus can. Divorce is often a messy thing for all involved, family wounds can brand the heart as few things can, a broken heart can feel unforgiveable, but there is hope! And whether wrongs were confessed or forgiveness asked for or not, truly choosing to forgive someone feels so sweet, and reconciliation is so worth it! Oftentimes we can't truly, fully move on until we've let go of things from our past, and that often starts with forgiveness.

Whether this book finds you in a position to be like Jari and facilitate reconciliation, forgiveness and salvation, or you need to be the one to come face-to-face with the reality of your behavior or words, get down on your knees and ask for a loved one's forgiveness like Bill, or you're like Joe or Jessica and simply need to choose forgiveness and reconciliation so that you can move forward and live the life you were meant to live, it is worth the effort! I promise!

For those of you who are interested in delving in a bit deeper, you can visit my website for questions meant to facilitate conversations about the undercurrents of this book.

Although I love to write, I write for my readers. With that constantly in mind, I would love to hear from you. I enjoy having people stop by my website, getting emails, hearing from you on facebook and getting to know you, so please, always feel free to drop me a note!

Until next time, may the Savior of the world meet you where you are and reveal more of His heart to you!

Ann

www.anngoering.com
ann@anngoering.com
www.facebook.com/AuthorAnnGoering

GLENDALE SERIES

The Glendale Series wrestles with the age-old dilemmas of love, faith, family, forgiveness and growing up in a fresh story format. With relationships that grip readers' hearts as they reflect raw realities plentiful in our society and an ending that will keep readers on the edge of their seats right up until the end, The Glendale Series is one girl's unforgettable journey to health, wholeness and joy.

MOTHERS OF GLENDALE

The Mothers of Glendale Series tells the personal, emotional, and sometimes painful stories of three special women introduced in The Glendale Series. Glendale mother figures Jari, Carla, and Hannah are each on their own journey, with their paths weaving together with one another to create a beautiful tapestry of faith, hope, and unconditional love. With raw realities that women face every day, covered by the grace of a very big God, Mothers of Glendale takes readers a step further than new love to the weathered and deeply beautiful land of seasoned marriages, motherhood and saying goodbye to a full life, well-lived.

A Special Preview of *Promising Forever,* Book III

"What colors are you thinking?" Jari Cordel asked, her hands clasped, her eyes shining. Jessica laughed. She had just returned from Glendale with Joe and the girls the night before after a wonderful Christmas with the Colby family. Today, the girls were at preschool, and Jari had begged Jessica to meet her for lunch.

Jessica glanced down at the sparkly new engagement ring on her finger and again felt the unexplainable warmth spread through her. Her high school sweetheart, Joe Colby, had asked her to be his bride. Yes, a wedding was definitely in her future, and Jari was obviously eager to begin planning.

"Well, we don't want to wait long, so—"

"Have you set a date?" Jari interrupted. She was on the edge of her seat, the chicken salad in front of her forgotten. Jessi laughed again.

"We're thinking the second weekend in May."

Jari clapped her hands and let out a squeal. "Okay, that doesn't leave much time – less than five months – so we'll have to get to work. Have you decided on flowers or colors? Or a location? What about a guest list?"

"Okay, one question at a time," Jessica instructed, swallowing her bite of chicken sandwich, still smiling. "We thought about having the wedding in Glendale, because we both love it there, and we also thought about having it here in D.C., just for simplicity's sake. We haven't decided for sure yet, either way."

Jari nodded. "That's understandable."

"I want it outside with a profusion of brightly colored flowers. Pinks and purples, oranges, lots of green," Jessi went on.

"Sounds beautiful," Jari agreed, nodding and forking in a bite of fresh spinach.

"We're thinking a small wedding, with just our families and a few close friends in attendance," Jessi finished. At this, Jari stopped chewing, and her face fell. She started to say something but someone at the door caught her eye, and she glanced up, then smiled and waved. "Oh look! Your mom finally got here!"

The wedding conversation halted as Carla Cordel Martens rushed to the table. "So sorry I'm late! I was held up in court and then—! Well, I'm sure you read it all in my text."

"The important thing is that you made it," Jessica told her, standing up to give her mom a hug.

Carla hugged her back. "Good to see you, Baby Girl! How was your Christmas?"

"Wonderful!" Jessi answered.

"I'm sure...Christmas with the Colbys is always something special! How is everyone?" Carla asked fondly. "Oh, is that for me?" she continued, pointing to the shrimp salad they had ordered for her. Jessi nodded. "Perfect. Oh, and you even remembered to have them put the dressing on the side. Good girl." Carla flung her coat over the back of her chair and leaned across the table to quickly embrace Jari. "This was a great idea. Thanks for planning it, Jari."

"I had a feeling you were as eager to see your daughter as I was," Jari answered warmly.

As they all took their seats, Carla caught Jessica's left hand. "I'm still not used to seeing that on your finger."

"Me neither. Sometimes it still surprises me," Jessica admitted, feeling a little sheepish.

"Goodness sakes, it's shiny!" Carla continued.

"And sparkly! The boy did good," Jari added.

Jessica smiled, looking at her ring and thinking of her fiancé. "Yes, he did."

Three months later…

Joe turned the diamond engagement ring over and over in the palm of his hand. It was stunning and exquisite, just like the girl who should be wearing it. He looked at each diamond, the clarity and brilliance of each stone. He looked at the small circular band and realized, with a half-smile, that it wouldn't even fit his pinky.

He sat back into his couch with a sigh. What good was an engagement ring if Jessica was no longer willing to wear it?

When she left it with him and boarded a plane back to Washington, D.C., she not only gave back the gift he had so patiently searched for and picked out, but she had shunned his love and removed herself from his life. Since high school, he had been unable to picture his life without Jessica Cordel. No matter how he pictured it, where he pictured it, when he pictured it, one thing was always the same – he was living it with Jessi.

Well, he was somehow going to have to reprogram his mind now, his view of the future, because it was no longer that he couldn't find her or that it wasn't the timing of the LORD. They had been reunited, and the time had come – now he had to find a way to picture life without her because Jessica Cordel simply did not want to be a part of his future.

As that thought settled in, Joe bent forward over his knees, crushing the ring in his hand, as he rested his forehead against his balled fists. He did the one thing he had been fighting since Jessi left him standing at the airport that afternoon, his dreams shattered, the wedding called off; Joe wept.

AWARD-WINNING AUTHOR ANN GOERING

Ann Goering is a four-time award-winning journalist who has worked as a senior editor/writer of magazines, newspapers and online publications since 2005. A theatrical production she wrote was performed on stage in 2005, and she was asked to co-write a screenplay for a Hollywood film in 2009.

She works for an international Christian ministry that specializes in relationships and evangelism to children, youth and families around the world. Her involvement in that has given her a heart for the broken, hurting and lost and a desire to see individuals and families operate in healthy relationships.

She has her degree in communications and enjoys writing Christian fiction and speaking to groups of women about the love of Jesus. She resides in the Ozark Mountains with her husband, whom she's terribly in love with, their baby girl, Alija, and their fluffy white dog, Sheesha.

40340166R00140

Made in the USA
Lexington, KY
02 April 2015